WEST CHICAGO PUBLIC LIBRARY DISTRICT

3 6653

31

P9-EGL-720

West Chicago Public Library District
118 West Washington
West Chicago, IL 60185-2803
Phone # (630) 231-1552
Fax # (630) 231-1709

The Pawnbroker

ALSO BY DAVID AND AIMÉE THURLO

THE ELLA CLAH MYSTERIES

Blackening Song

Death Walker

Bad Medicine

Enemy Way

Shooting Chant

Red Mesa

Changing Woman

Plant Them Deep

Tracking Bear

Wind Spirit

White Thunder

Mourning Dove

Turquoise Girl

Coyote's Wife

Earthway

Never-Ending-Snake

Black Thunder

Ghost Medicine

THE SISTER AGATHA MYSTERIES

Bad Faith

Thief in Retreat

Prey for a Miracle

False Witness

The Prodigal Nun

Bad Samaritan

The Pawnbroker

DAVID AND AIMÉE THURLO

MINOTAUR BOOKS

NEW YORK

This is a work of fiction. All of the characters, organizations, and events portrayed in this novel are either products of the authors' imaginations or are used fictitiously.

THE PAWNBROKER. Copyright © 2014 by David and Aimée Thurlo. All rights reserved. Printed in the United States of America. For information, address St. Martin's Press, 175 Fifth Avenue, New York, N.Y. 10010.

www.minotaurbooks.com

The Library of Congress Cataloging-in-Publication Data is available upon request

ISBN 978-1-250-02798-6 (hardcover)
ISBN 978-1-250-02799-3 (e-book)

Minotaur books may be purchased for educational, business, or promotional use. For information on bulk purchases, please contact Macmillan Corporate and Premium Sales Department at 1-800-221-7945, extension 5442, or write specialmarkets@macmillan.com.

First Edition: January 2014

10 9 8 7 6 5 4 3 2 1

To David's Uncle Albert,
the first pawnbroker in the family

The Pawnbroker

Chapter One

"If Baza even touches Gina, it'll take the jaws of life to remove my size thirteen boot from his rear end," Charlie Henry muttered. His eyes were constantly in motion, but kept returning to the red Passat. Gina Sinclair, his old high school girlfriend and current attorney, was in that car, parked beside the curb one block down on Commercial Avenue.

Charlie was seated behind the wheel of his Charger, a car that comfortably accommodated his broad shoulders and six-foot-one frame. His much shorter army buddy and business partner Gordon Sweeney, who swore his blond hair was a product of his Irish ancestry, was riding shotgun. They'd had each other's backs for years in the unit, and habits learned in special-ops missions remained sharp despite the fact both had been civilians since last December.

"Easy, Charles, you've said that Gina's a hard-ass lawyer used to moving among the cockroaches. She can take care of herself. All she has to do is hand him the three hundred dollars and we'll finally have the key and combination to that antique Detroit Safe Company safe," Gordo said, his gaze shifting constantly from storefront, to sidewalk, to passing car. "He said that's where he kept the computer backups, and we need those files."

"Yeah, well, I still don't trust the bastard. It took a week to track him down, and then he tried to screw us," Charlie said. "He could still be lying, just to raise the price."

"Hey, if he'd have just kept his mouth shut and taken the fifty bucks in exchange for the combo and key, I wouldn't have had to bounce him off the wall," Gordo said.

"That bounce is gonna cost us $250 more. Was it worth it?"

"Damn straight, if it'll help us straighten out the bookkeeping and inventory. Besides, nobody refers to my best friend as 'a dumb Indian.'"

"In case you haven't noticed, I'm the Navajo here. I should have had the honor of roughing him up."

"And spoil my reputation as a violent street punk? No way," Gordon said, grinning. He looked down at his watch. "Once this is over, you wanna get lunch?"

"Yeah. Wait, there's our guy." Charlie pointed with his lips, Navajo style, toward a tired-looking apartment building. A tall, muscular man in sunglasses, wearing a blue windbreaker and matching baseball cap, had stepped out the front entrance and was standing on the stoop, looking around casually.

He looked in their direction, and Charlie felt a chill go up his spine.

Baza turned away, apparently disinterested.

"Damn, is this ever going to go away? Every time a target looks in my direction, instinct tells me to duck, no matter how good the cover," Charlie said, angry at his reaction.

"Me too. But if you react and they see movement, all it does is create more attention. You'd have never made it through sniper school, bro."

Out of the corner of his eye, Charlie noticed that his pal's hand had gone to the familiar 9 mm Beretta at his waist. He'd been tempted to do the same with his own weapon in the shoulder holster under his left arm. Having been married to the similar M9 for their years of deployment, the Beretta 92 had been their choice for concealed-carry permits here in New Mexico.

Gina climbed out of the shiny new Passat after an older-model red Chevy passed by, waved her hand to catch Baza's attention, then crossed the street. "It's going down," Charlie muttered. "Be careful, girl."

"Hey, dude, we're not in 'stan anymore, and she's an attorney, not an asset," Gordon said. "Obviously the guy's hurting for money and on the run from creditors, or we wouldn't have had such a hard time finding him the first time. If we don't learn how to make a profit with our little pawnshop, before long we'll be the ones hustling for bucks."

"Except we won't be assholes, like Baza."

"No, we'll be much bigger—ass craters, ass canyons?"

Charlie chuckled, then grew quiet and leaned forward slightly as Gina strode confidently up to the lowlife. Gina was slender and only five feet tall, and Baza was built like a linebacker, towering over her. If Charlie hadn't known that Gina was a longtime student of Krav Maga, he'd have never let her make the meet.

"Maybe we should have wired her or at least had her leave her cell phone on," Gordo said, bringing up his Leica binoculars. "I'm glad we bought this little puppy. I can make out Gina's shade of lipstick from fifty yards away. She's a beautiful little thing. Why'd you two ever break up?"

"We weren't right for each other. And speaking of not right, since when do you know about lipstick?"

"Shit. Baza's packing. Check his right waistband." Gordon handed him the binoculars.

Charlie quickly focused on the target and recognized the butt of a small autoloader. Compared to the AKs and RPGs he'd spotted tucked beneath a man's chapan, the equivalent of a coat in Afghanistan, Baza was almost unarmed. "Looks like a thirty-two. He's new at this. It's jammed in so far, he's likely to blow off his junk if he tries for a quick draw."

"Small hands, so his loss will be minimal. You think we should move in a little closer?"

Charlie shrugged, trying to read the man's expression. "Whoever he's looking out for, it can't be Gina, but as long as she's over there, I'm worried. From what we've heard about the guy, he's been ripping off his creditors for months. He's gonna have enemies."

Baza took her hand in an unnecessary handshake, then hung on to it a little too long before letting go. "He's trying to flirt with her. Good luck with that. Come on, numb-nuts, just make the exchange," Charlie mumbled, now watching Baza's eyes, which roamed up and down Gina's frame.

Charlie switched the Leica's magnification from fifteen back to ten, giving himself a larger field of view. He watched Gina reach into her pocket and bring out the "letter" containing the three hundred.

Baza held out his hand, but Gina shook her head, withdrawing the envelope, then holding out her other hand. Baza smiled, maybe even chuckling a bit, then reached into his jacket pocket and brought out a small manila envelope. He handed it to Gina as she gave him the letter, then both took a step back.

Baza stuck the money into his pocket, but she opened the envelope and looked inside.

A blue shape, a vehicle passing in front of the lens, broke up the image. Charlie lowered the optics, noting the vehicle was an old Ford Taurus. The Taurus stopped in the street right behind Gina just as she nodded, the signal she had a combination and key—hopefully the right ones.

"Who the hell is that?" Gordo said.

"Gun!" Charlie yelled, seeing a barrel poked out the driver's side window. He reached for the door handle and his feet touched pavement as his Beretta came up, but by then a volley of shots had been fired from the blue sedan.

"No!" Charlie yelled as Gina and Baza collapsed onto the sidewalk.

Charlie stepped clear of the door, ignored the horn and

skidding tires behind him, and snapped off a round at the driver's side rear window. He was tracking for another shot when the car accelerated and raced past a woman on the sidewalk. He held fire.

The Taurus burned rubber, fishtailing away. Charlie jumped back into the Dodge, jammed his pistol into the holster, and brought the Charger to life. "Keep Gina alive, Gordo," he yelled, still watching the Taurus. "I'm capping this bastard!"

"God's ears!" Gordon responded instantly, jumping out onto the sidewalk. "Go!" he yelled, slamming the door and pounding the rooftop. "I've got Gina."

Charlie whipped out into the street, holding out his left hand to ward off the silver pickup that had screamed to a stop after nearly running him down a few seconds ago.

"Stay back, buddy," Charlie yelled, his heart beating through his chest. He hit the gas and raced down the block, honking his horn to keep the foot traffic out of his way. He passed two people already crouched down by Gina and Barza, one an old black woman with a cell phone at her ear.

Charlie knew that Gordon would be closing in on Gina now—and he had experience dealing with gunshot wounds. No time to think of his best girl now, she was in good hands.

The shooter's car swerved right at the end of the block, taking the corner hard, sideswiping a sedan, leaving a five-foot groove in the driver's door and front end. Two elderly civilians on the sidewalk jumped back, one of them dropping a bag of groceries.

Charlie took the corner without losing speed, shifting

gears by instinct, then accelerated toward the Ford, which was throwing rancid blue smoke into the air as the shooter pushed the old car to the limits. Charlie knew he could outrun and out-corner the Taurus, but this was Albuquerque, not Daytona, and they were headed into the metro area.

Ahead were the six lanes of Second Street. The Taurus slowed as it approached the stop sign. The driver signaled right, then took a left, crossed the median, and cut left again into oncoming traffic, now headed south. Brakes squealed, but the Taurus forced himself in between a pickup and a van from a paint company.

Charlie hadn't been faked out. He approached the stop sign, praying for clearance, then his heart skipped a beat. He slammed on the brakes, finally seeing the oncoming monster, a northbound cab-over semi.

His Dodge tracked true, and the shoulder belt kept him off the windshield, but the car slid a foot into the street before stopping. The truck driver leaned on his horn, whipping by at forty miles an hour, its big tires nearly scraping Charlie's front bumper.

Charlie leaned back, nearly out of breath. Four deployments in Afghanistan mostly doing dirty work for the CIA, earning two commendations, then he gets creamed by a Walmart eighteen-wheeler on an Albuquerque street? Hell no, he wasn't going out like this.

Gritting his teeth, he leaned forward, checked traffic south, then saw an opening. He raced to the median, stopped, then jumped into the southbound inside lane behind a fast-moving SUV loaded with a soccer mom and about five hundred kids.

He whipped left and passed the SUV. The mom, cell phone to her ear, probably never even saw him. Charlie scanned ahead, then spotted a blue vehicle ahead in the same lane, smoking like a chimney. It slowed, turned right onto a side street, and disappeared.

Charlie floored the Charger, the engine in a low, throaty growl as he put it through its paces, passing three slower cars by the time he reached the spot. Braking hard, he slid through the turn and found himself on a dead-end street. Ahead was a line of warehouses and behind the long brick structures were train tracks. He drove slowly, checking out the alley on both sides as he cruised west. All he could see on the two-lane road was a city trash hauler lowering a commercial bin and a couple of big rental delivery vans.

At the stop sign ahead, he had two choices, left or right along the line of warehouses. If he'd been making a run for it, he'd have taken the right, so that's what he did. Easing down the street, he looked at the vehicles parked along the street in front of the warehouses. Most of them were different makes and models of trucks and a few sedans. There was no blue Taurus.

Picking up speed and fighting frustration, he took the next right, then headed back toward Second Street. Reaching the alley, he turned into the narrow passage, wanting to check it from this end. Ahead were several vehicles parked beside the loading dock of a four-story brick warehouse. He'd seen these cars from a few blocks down as he'd passed by. Now there was something new—the blue Taurus, complete with bullet hole and the jagged cubes of a shattered rear window still on the back shelf. It was blocking the alley.

Thinking ambush, Charlie pulled left, putting the Hemi engine between him and the Taurus. He turned off the Dodge, grabbed the keys, then jumped out and circled around to his right, pistol in hand as he flanked the Taurus. Using a black Lexus as cover, he stepped out and looked at the far side of the shooter's car. Nobody—no ambush.

Pistol casually down by his side, he walked toward the loading dock, searching for the shooter or anyone who might be around the cars. His gut told him the shooter was close— maybe inside, maybe taking hostages. He walked up two steps of the loading dock, then stopped, checking the alley from his height advantage. He was exposing himself now, so he'd better keep watch. Gordo wasn't there to cover his six.

Several vehicles down to his right, a car door opened. Charlie jumped off the dock, crouching low and listening, trying to find the right car. Out of the corner of his eye he saw a moving shadow against the building wall, arm raised.

Charlie stepped back and sank to his knees just as a gun fired. A bullet struck the bricks just where his head had been a second ago. The blast reverberated down the alley.

From the angle of the sun and the shadow, he knew approximately where the shooter had been, and the low-gear grind of a car backing up cinched it.

"Gotcha now," Charlie said, running west toward the back

end of a puke-green Silverado. He dove to the ground, rolled, and brought up his pistol.

A homeless man in a bulky jacket, pushing a shopping cart stacked high with junk, inched out into the middle of the alley. Just then a white sedan raced by the bum, inches away. The man cursed loudly, shaking his fist. The car, a Camry or look-alike, took the corner in a hurry and disappeared, headed east toward Second Street.

Charlie jumped up and raced back to the Charger, afraid that he'd never catch up now. He'd give it a try, but it was now time to call in the cavalry—and pray that Gina was still alive.

Charlie reached Second Street within twenty seconds, looked in both directions, but couldn't confirm where the white sedan had gone—north, south, or east. At least three white cars were on the busy street, moving away from his position at the moment. He had no idea which one to follow. He didn't even have an ID on the shooter. Maybe one of the pedestrians across the street back on Commercial had gotten eyes on the shooter.

Nobody was behind him, so he quickly backed up away from the intersection, did a one-eighty, and drove back toward the warehouse. Cruising up the street, he called 911 to report the warehouse incident and his meager description of the second car.

He ended the call and turned up the alley, shaking now from the anger and adrenaline. Charlie kept watch, not wanting to collide with the transient he'd seen with the grocery cart.

Halfway down the alley was an empty lot and off to his left the railroad tracks—a spur line. There was the guy, pulling and tugging the top-heavy shopping cart over the rails, clearly trying to put some distance between himself and the excitement.

Charlie thought about stopping and walking over, but the guy probably hadn't seen the shooter's face anyway and would just run for it. All he'd do was scare him away from the only thing he had left of value, his cart of stuff. For some reason it seemed odd seeing the US equivalent of a refugee, here at home. Odd, and sad.

When Charlie reached the warehouse parking area, several people in blue-collar clothes and two guys in white shirts and ties were milling around the Taurus. Charlie brought the Charger to a stop. He wanted a look at the car as well. Maybe the shooter had left something behind.

Ten minutes later, all he'd found besides broken glass was the hole where his 9 mm slug was lodged deep in the center dashboard. He was forced to spend most of his time explaining to the excited workers at the book depository what had happened. After warning everyone for the third time not to touch anything, Charlie gave up waiting for a patrol car to arrive and handed his business card to the warehouse manager. Then he climbed into the Charger and drove away.

Once down the alley and out onto the street, he reached into his jacket pocket and brought out his cell phone, activating the voice-command mode. The cops needed to follow up on the Taurus and the other car, but he knew most of the activity at the moment was going to be at the location where people had been shot. "Call Gordon," he said, pulling out into traffic and heading south.

Not more than five seconds passed until Gordon answered. "Get that SOB?" he asked, his voice subdued.

"Not yet, but he left a trail. His hours are numbered. How badly was Gina hit?" Charlie responded, pulling into a turning lane, signaling to make a left. He planned to go east, hit the next street over, then work his way toward Commercial and the crime scene.

"She took one round high in her back left side as she turned toward the shooter. The slug missed her heart and major vessels, and lodged behind her breast. Another few inches and she'd be dead, according to the EMTs. They're hopeful. She's in surgery right now. I rode with her and the EMTs to Saint Mark's."

"How'd you pull that off?"

"Lies, threats, money. I'm not saying."

"Whatever. I'm calling APD again. Any officers arrive at the scene before you left?"

"Yeah, about the same time as the EMTs. I left my card with a Patrolman Harris and begged off the details until later. You might wanna stop by there and give them the rest. They know how to contact me. I'll stay here at the hospital. It'll be a while before anyone can see Gina anyway."

"Her roommate's an Albuquerque cop—Sergeant Medina—Nancy. I should tell her what happened."

"Medina's already here at the hospital. She's been talking to the staff, barely keeping it under control. Think I should fill her in?" Gordon asked.

"Definitely. She and Gina are close and we're going to need an insider in the police department on this job, mission, whatever."

"So you're taking this personally?"

"Damn straight. And you?"

"I'm already in, bro. And," Gordon said, voice lowered, "I removed the combination and key from Gina's pocket. Nobody noticed. I didn't see any reason for them gathering dust in an evidence locker. We need the stuff in that safe, and I didn't want to lose them to a civilian. We can return them later if needed."

"We can copy the key, probably. Anything to add?"

"Didn't get a chance to look around. The neighborhood ladies who stopped to help were great, but some of the street people wanted to take a look and I had to keep them back. . . ."

"Gotcha. What about Baza?"

"Two shots to the chest and one in the nose. Messed him up. Dead before he hit the sidewalk. He was the target, Gina just got in the way. I left the three hundred dollars, of course. It explains the meet and Gina being there," Gordon added.

"Stay in touch—about Gina."

"Yeah." Gordon ended the call.

Charlie took a deep breath, then called the police station. He identified himself, then added that he was en route to the original scene and would give his statement regarding both shootings to the detectives at that location.

An hour later, Charlie arrived at Saint Mark's Hospital. He had to turn his Beretta over to a Detective Rager at the Commercial location, but luckily he had a twin spare under the seat. He chose to leave it in the Charger, along with his shoulder harness. The four-inch-blade lockback knife in his pocket would suffice at close range. Hospital security frowned on gun-toting civilians anyway, conceal-carry licensed or not.

He entered the hospital lobby and spotted an APD officer in dark blue. The cop intercepted him before he could reach the main desk. "Excuse me, sir," the tall, slender black officer said. "You Charles Henry?"

"Yes, I am."

"You carrying?" The officer gave him the once-over, his left hand near his own service weapon.

"Not now. I turned my handgun over to Detective Rager at the crime scene on Commercial. I've got a concealed-carry license."

The officer nodded, relaxing visibly. "Detective DuPree is in the ER waiting room. He needs to speak with you regarding the shootings."

"Of course." Charlie looked up along the wall and saw a blue colored arrow and stripe that read "Emergency Room." He turned and walked quickly in that direction. The cop followed, clearly wanting him in the lead anyway, to keep an eye on him.

They turned the hall corner and stopped beside the narrow passenger elevator just as the bell announced its arrival at the ground floor.

The door slid open, revealing a tall blonde in an Albuquerque Police Department sergeant's uniform. She reached out and grabbed his arm, venom in her pale-green eyes. "You almost got Gina killed, you know that?"

Chapter Two

"I know, Nancy." Charlie looked up into the woman's broad, attractive face and saw the tears she refused to let spill welling in her eyes. "Gina's holding her own, right?"

"She's still in surgery. The medical team is working to remove the bullet and reinflate the left lung, but the doctors think she's going to make it. According to the EMTs, your friend Gordon kept her alive," Nancy said, easing her hold on his arm.

As soon as Charlie realized that she was grieving, not angry, he gave her hand a squeeze. "It was my fault, Nancy. I had no idea she was walking into a hit. This is on me," he said, meaning every word.

"I heard some of the details from Gordon and Detective DuPree." She stood up to full height, about two inches shorter than Charlie, and glanced over at the patrol officer inside the elevator. "Push B, okay?"

Several seconds later, the elevator door opened again. The waiting room outside the basement-level ER was busy at the moment, with a young Hispanic couple and two children—obviously theirs—sitting anxiously, holding hands and staring at the door leading into the emergency room itself. One of the kids, a boy probably three or four, looked up for a second, then went back to the wooden car he was rolling along the arm of his chair.

A familiar-looking TV reporter in a brown sports jacket was standing in a corner with his camerawoman. Their eyes were on Charlie, perhaps hoping for handcuffs. To their left, judging from the badge and sidearm at his belt, was the plainclothes detective.

The camerawoman, wearing jeans and a sweatshirt, lifted up her camera and swung it around to Charlie.

"Not now," the detective ordered, stepping forward. He was a six-foot-plus heavyset man in his early thirties wearing a tired-looking checkered sports jacket, blue slacks, and scuffed suede shoes.

The woman lowered the camera and the reporter took a step back.

"Detective DuPree?" Charlie said to the big guy, then glanced over at Gordo, who at five-foot-five looked like a buzz-cut hobbit standing beside the detective. Not that Gordo couldn't have taken the guy.

Gordon nodded and rolled his eyes, a sign that revealed his impression of DuPree.

Not good, Charlie thought immediately.

"You the vigilante who was spraying bullets down Commercial Avenue?"

"One bullet constitutes a spray? Detective, I have a valid concealed-carry permit, extensive firearms training, and three combat tours under my belt. At the time of the incident I failed to observe any civilians in my line of fire. I directed my one defensive shot into the rear window of the blue Ford Taurus. Inside that vehicle was the person shooting at Diego Baza and attorney Gina Sinclair. I had to take action in order to suppress the hostile's activity. I placed my shot on target and stopped firing immediately once a civilian came in line with the shooter's moving vehicle."

Charlie was pissed and stuck to the facts, but he wasn't in any chain of command now, so he wasn't about to add "sir" to the end of his report.

DuPree didn't say a word, so Charlie continued. "Your people check out that Taurus for bloodstains?"

DuPree frowned. "A mobile crime lab team is processing the vehicle now, Henry."

"What about the white sedan the perp took later, over by the railroad tracks? Any like that reported stolen recently?" Gordon jumped in.

"The vehicle didn't belong to anyone at the warehouse. We don't have anything on it yet other than Mr. Henry's description. The street person with the shopping cart was tracked down, but he was no help. Instead of duck and cover, Henry, you should have at least gotten a partial on the plate," DuPree snapped back.

Charlie ignored the implication and continued to press. "So why was Baza gunned down like that? Drugs, gangs, jealous boyfriend, a crooked deal? Any theories?"

"You know Baza was the intended target, right?" Gordon added.

Charlie noticed that the black cop was trying not to smile. He knew what they were doing. Even Nancy was shaking her head.

"I'm asking the questions here," DuPree announced loudly, his face getting red and his voice a little too high-pitched to take seriously.

"Of course," Charlie said, looking over at Gordon, who nodded vigorously, a gleam in his eye. They'd had this routine down for years.

The reporter, meanwhile, shook his head in disgust.

Five minutes later, DuPree had regained control, at least in his own mind, and completed his list of questions. As he left with the patrol officer, the press followed close behind.

Charlie, Nancy, and Gordon formed a tight huddle in the corner. "All we have is the description of a white or Hispanic guy wearing sunglasses, a red T-shirt, and a black ball cap. Not even a hair color or length or a gun description, except that it had an obvious barrel, probably a revolver," Charlie said.

"DuPree seems clueless. If he stays on the case, we're screwed," Gordon said.

"Agreed," Charlie added. "What have *you* heard about DuPree?" he asked Nancy. She'd calmed down and had now set her jaw, clearly determined to take action.

"He's the master of the obvious, with a series of easy robbery cases under his belt. As far as I know, this is his first homicide taking lead. He made detective with good test scores, but word is he loses it easily and has a hard time handling his authority."

"A pompous know-it-all who orders his subordinates around?" Charlie said.

"Pretty much. Unfortunately he has connections—his uncle is high up in the sheriff's department and his dad was a decorated APD officer for thirty years. DuPree got this case because his name was next on the rotation. I'm a little worried this investigation is already on the wrong track. He's got people checking into Gina's client list, thinking it's somebody she or her law firm stiffed. She recently defended some people working for one of the cartels who were laundering money through a horse-racing operation. My guess is that's where DuPree is looking."

"He does know why Gina was there, meeting with Baza, doesn't he?" Charlie asked, looking at Gordon.

"I told him the same thing I told the officer at the scene. Gina was there to pay Baza three hundred dollars in exchange for business information concerning his old pawnshop, the business we just bought from the bank. DuPree didn't even ask what the information was about. I think it went in one ear and out the other, bro," Gordon said. "I'd even memorized the safe combination, in case I had to hand over the paper and the key. But he didn't follow up on that."

"The main thing here is catching the shooter," Nancy said.

"For Gina," Charlie added.

"You know we're going to be looking for the shooter on our own," Gordon said to Nancy. "You going to help us out?"

"Officially, no. Unofficially, you bet your ass I am," Nancy said. "What did you observe about the shooter?"

"Zip, except he kept his cool, played it smart, and had a script. My guess he was using a revolver—no brass at either scene, so he'd thought this out ahead of time. He's either a pro or a smart amateur."

"You've got a plan?"

Charlie nodded. "Baza is the key, so anything we can get on him helps. This drive-by was carefully arranged, including the backup car by the warehouse loading dock. My guess is that any prints found won't belong to the shooter. Hear anything on that?"

"Crime-scene team is working the blue Taurus. Nothing yet except for the bullet lodged in the dash," Nancy said. "Yours?"

"Yeah. I missed the bastard."

"Too bad," Nancy said. "But if anything else turns up, I'll pass it along."

"Good. We need to find out, ASAP, who wanted Baza dead and why. We know Gina had nothing to do with this, which puts us a step ahead of DuPree already," Charlie said. "But sooner or later we're bound to cross paths with him."

"Let me get in the way when that happens. I go on shift in an hour," Nancy said, "but before I do, I'll see what I can get on Baza—where he lived, where he was working—basically anything Detective Rager may know. He'd have passed what he had on to DuPree, but frankly I'm not counting on the big guy clearing this case on his own."

"Maybe he'll give you some tidbits. There's that professional courtesy among cops, isn't there?" Charlie asked Nancy.

"Sure, but Gina's my roommate so he'll see my connection as a conflict of interest. Still, I can feed him some of what you get, helping him out. He'll want to close the case. What we need to do is make sure he catches the real perp."

"No problem. DuPree can get Cop of the Year for all I care as long as we get the bastard who shot Gina," Charlie said.

"God's ears," Gordon said, echoing Charlie's thoughts.

"So what's this pawnshop business all about?" Nancy asked.

"After spending several months trying to get our shit together after our enlistments ended, we decided to team up again, so we bought the business. We're used to structure, so it sounded doable to us," Gordon explained.

"The previous owner was Diego Baza, right? Gina mentioned his name and that he'd defaulted on his mortgage and lost the business," Nancy replied.

"Exactly. And Baza had a host of other bills, including gas, electric, and insurance. He let his last employee go just before the bank stepped in. After that, he dropped out of sight, ducking the lawyers," Gordon said.

"It's possible we now own part of the motive for Baza's murder," Charlie added. "We still have no idea why Baza suddenly let the pawnshop go to crap. The place was making money, according to the books. At least the books we can find."

"We got the place for way below market," Gordon said. "The bank was eager, but Baza's records are a major fuckup we're still trying to straighten out. He was forcing us to pay for access to an old safe where he claimed he kept backups on the business."

"What's the name of the pawnshop anyway?" Nancy asked.

"Baza named it the Three Balls Pawnshop. You know—the historic pawnshop symbol," Charlie added with a shrug.

"Disgusting name," Nancy said. "Gina told me you two bought a business. Considering you're just out of the army, I was thinking it was probably a bar or a gun shop."

"Hey, that's a thought. A gun shop/tavern. On tap or double tap," Gordon suggested.

Nancy and Charlie groaned and shook their heads almost in unison.

"Bad day for gallows humor," Charlie said. "The day's fading, how about we get to it?" He reached out to shake Nancy's hand. She gave him a hug instead, something he'd missed out on since leaving the service. He'd had a lot of friends among the women soldiers in his battalion, and women tended to hug a lot.

"Call me when you get anything new on Gina's condition," Charlie said, stepping back. "And Baza's address. Got my number?"

Nancy nodded. "Yours and Gordon's. How about the pawnshop's?"

Gordon rattled it off, and Nancy tapped it into her cell phone. They left by different doors. Nancy had parked in a police slot, and Charlie had left his Charger in another lot on the opposite side of the building.

"So what's the story on Nancy?" Gordon asked as they cruised down Second Street a few minutes later. "She's got the build and looks to be a model. What's she doing wearing a cop uniform?"

"All I know is what Gina's told me. Nancy's father and mother were both career air force, and Nancy grew up moving around her whole life. Military brat."

"You'd think she'd want to fly, then. Go to the academy."

"Naw, her folks were APs, air police. Nancy got a degree in law enforcement, and ended up in the Albuquerque Police Department. She and Gina met at the courthouse, actually, and have been together for about three years, I think."

"Not just roommates?"

"Nothing gets past you, Gordo."

"Well, too bad for me. She comes across as a good cop, so I'll look forward to working with her. Now let's find something to eat."

Twenty-five minutes later, Charlie parked the Dodge in a space along the curb in front of the Three Balls Pawnshop. It was a solid, fifties-era flat-roofed brick structure with a not-so-subtle black-on-white sign centered above the entrance. The traditional symbol for a pawnbroker's shop, three golden spheres suspended from a metal bar, hung above the door.

The windows had been bricked over years ago, and the door was made of reinforced steel with updated locks set in a steel frame.

Charlie reached under the seat and retrieved his backup Beretta, still in the shoulder holster, as Gordon climbed out the passenger side holding the bags with their stuffed sopapillas.

"Think we should change the name of the place?" Gordon asked, looking up. "When Baza bought the shop it was Valley Pawn, remember?"

"Yeah, I'm guessing he thought it sounded too generic. A lot of the businesses in this neighborhood had 'valley' in their name." Charlie looked up and down the sidewalk. Nobody was within sight, and no cars were approaching, so he removed the semiauto and stuck it in his belt, safety on, and held the shoulder setup in his left hand. This wasn't a war zone, but he still felt naked without it, especially after this morning.

Climbing out, Charlie locked the car and stepped up onto the sidewalk. "How much would a name change cost anyway, not including the sign? Would we have to update the business licence and crap like that?"

Gordon had his key in the first of two door locks. "Yeah, maybe we should put that money into conducting business right now. Being closed cost us a day's income."

"Copy that. Once we nail Gina's shooter, we've got to turn a profit if we're going to make this place work for us."

Gordon opened the second lock, pocketed the key, and turned the knob. "Maybe an electronic lock here?" he suggested, opening the door.

"Something to consider down the line. Go ahead," Charlie said, holding the door. Gordon slipped in, set the food down on top of a used microwave oven on the counter, then reached up to the wall panel and entered the alarm code.

Charlie used his own key to lock the door on the inside, looked to make made sure the closed sign was still in place, then punched in a higher setting on the central air, which activated the furnace.

"Cold and as dry as Kabul in September," Gordon said, picking up the food and heading down the aisle toward the back office.

A shadow to the right, at the end of one of the display rows, moved slightly.

"Right on, Ike," Charlie said, trying to avoid any change in tone as he slipped the Beretta out of his waistband, looking toward the shadow.

They'd learned, years ago, to read each other's minds. Gordon set down the bag, reaching for his own weapon after recognizing their old code words. Ike meant insurgent to them, and right indicated the direction.

"How many sopapillas you want?" Gordon replied, watching in the direction Charlie was indicating, unholstering his own Beretta.

"One, I think."

Gordon covered Charlie as he inched forward, weapon

down by his side, safety off. A quick glance had told him nothing seemed disturbed, so if the intruder was a burglar, he'd either taken something small, had just showed up, or was there for another reason.

Charlie reached the end of the aisle. The guy was somewhere close. Then he remembered the mirrors and looked up on the wall. He saw the guy just as he lunged. The blow knocked him to the floor, flat on his back as the guy moved a big screwdriver toward his throat with a gloved hand.

Chapter Three

Charlie clocked the guy on the side of his head with the Beretta, using his other hand to grab the arm that held the tool.

The attacker grunted, struggling for Charlie's gun hand while trying to break the grip on his wrist. Charlie slammed him in the head again with the pistol, using the momentum to roll up and over, pinning the guy to the floor. Astride him now, he stuck the barrel of his Beretta into the man's ear.

A shoe came down, Gordon's, pinning the attacker's makeshift weapon to the floor. His fingers pinched, and maybe broken now despite the gloves, the slender attacker yelled, "I give! Don't shoot!"

Charlie kept the barrel pressed into his ear, looking him over carefully. The guy was wearing tight-fitting black leather gloves and had on expensive athletic shoes, jeans, and a dark green knit shirt. He was maybe thirty and had no obvious regional accent, as far as they could tell so far. He had pale blue eyes and styled yellow hair just a little too long to be current military, with a broad, Slavic-looking face and good teeth. If Charlie had ever seen the guy before, he didn't remember.

"You've got five seconds to tell me your name and what the hell you're doing in here," Charlie said, cocking the hammer for effect, but taking his finger off the trigger. The towheaded guy was bleeding above the ear and would be showing a bruise, but nobody else had to die today. Not yet, anyway.

"Yeah, okay. I'm Eddie, Eddie Henderson. I think my fingers are broken. Could you move your foot?" he added, looking up at Gordon. His voice was surprisingly calm, despite his predicament.

Gordon kicked away the screwdriver, picked it up, then put his foot back down on the man's forearm. The guy groaned, but remained still.

"That better?" Gordon said.

"I won't shoot you; it'll make too much noise," Charlie said, "but unless you want to be carved up with box cutters and carried out of here in an old trunk, I need to know everything, Eddie."

"Okay," Eddie said hurriedly, clearly a little more anxious than before. "I've been watching the shop . . . for a few days now. When you both left this morning and didn't come back, I decided to wait until dark and then come inside. The guy who used to own this place, Baza, loaned me some cash for a couple of things I pawned. The stuff belonged to my grandfather and

I planned to retrieve them within a few months. But then the place shut down and the bank put it up for sale. Who knew what was going to happen to my grandfather's stuff? Since I don't have enough money at the moment and I can't find the pawn tickets, I decided to . . . steal them back," he added, his voice fading away.

"Okay, so far so good. I'm going to move the pistol away for a moment. When I do, I want you to roll over, facedown, and keep your hands away from your body. Do it slowly, because if you move too fast, I'm going to shoot you in the back of your knee," Charlie said, glancing up at Gordon, who grinned. He'd made the same threat several times in the past, in more than one language, and only had to act on it once.

Slowly, Eddie, if that was really his name, rolled over, yelping as his injured hand touched the floor. He was shaking now, barely keeping it under control.

Charlie rose to his knees, lowered the hammer on his 9 mm then thumbed on the safety and handed it to Gordon, who'd already holstered his own weapon.

Eddie was now covered as Charlie reached into the man's back pocket and hauled out an expensive brown leather wallet.

Charlie first noted that the guy had at least three hundred dollars in fresh fifties and twenties, then found a New Mexico driver's license. It looked genuine for Edward J. Henderson, age twenty-eight, six feet tall, and weighing one sixty-two. The address was local, on Albuquerque's west side, and

the photo a reasonable match. There were no credit or insurance cards, however.

"How'd you get in the building, Edward?"

There was a long sigh, then he spoke, almost casually now.
"Through the roof. I pried open a skylight with the screwdriver
and snaked through, coming down through the air duct. Over
there by the restroom."

Charlie motioned for the screwdriver, and Gordon handed
it to him, handle first. "I'm having my friend check it out. If
he's not back in one minute, I'm returning your screwdriver—
through your neck."

Gordon brought out his own Beretta, walked away, looked
around the back, then checked the rear entrance. His next
stop was the storeroom, with all the pawn—merchandise—
still serving as collateral. He was back in thirty seconds.

"Nobody else here except for us owners and the burglar.
The storeroom is still locked, so it looks like skinny Eddie's
telling at least some of the truth. The ceiling tile is askew,
the duct is bent up, and the skylight is loose. I also noticed
pry marks and some threads up there, yanked from his shirt
where he got caught on a screw," he announced, pointing to
a tear on Eddie's left sleeve.

Charlie stood, then handed the screwdriver back to
Gordon.

Gordon fingered the blade of the big screwdriver. "Want
me to mess him up?"

Charlie knew his pal wasn't bluffing. Gordon Sweeney
had grown up in one of Denver's poorest neighborhoods, an

Irish white boy among mostly black and Chicano kids. The guy had learned survival the hard way—one fight at a time.

They'd met early in their first deployment, trained together, and hunted their enemies for years, and now trusted each other more than any two brothers. Gordo had told him once that if he hadn't been a soldier, he'd be dead or in prison right now. They were an odd team: a tall, reservation Navajo from a small town and a rough, streetwise city punk who'd already seen it all. They weren't at all alike, but after all these years they were close.

Their silence had the desired effect on Eddie, who was either frightened to death now or the best actor Charlie had ever seen.

"No cops. No cops. I'll tell you everything. I didn't steal anything, and I'll pay to have the skylight fixed," Eddie pleaded, his eyes wide, his voice rising in pitch.

"Now that we've got your attention, Eddie, tell me why you broke in, what you took, and where you put it," Charlie said.

"I'm looking for a watch that my grandfather had for years, a Rolex. And there are two rings—one's a man's gold band, the other is diamond and gold. They were my grandfather's. I pawned them for a thousand dollars. The watch is still with the other watches, I guess, and the ring is wherever you keep the rings. You guys showed up before I had a chance to get them. I started by looking around in the office for the receipts, because I needed to make sure I got the right watch. I'd recognize the ring—at least the diamond one."

"You were also going to destroy the receipts, right? Because once we found the watch and ring were gone, we'd find your name and address and hunt you down," Gordon said.

"But I haven't found them yet," Eddie replied. "Where are they, anyway? The papers in that back office are a mess."

Charlie ignored the question. "Why are the ring and watch worth risking jail time—or getting shot breaking in?"

Eddie managed to look pathetic. "My grandmother doesn't know I took them, and I'm trying to get them back before she finds out. You gotta help me."

"So you've been stealing from Nana for how long?" Charlie asked. Not getting an answer, he turned to Gordon. "Keep an eye on the evil grandchild while I make a call to a friend of a friend."

Gordon nodded, bringing out his pistol again.

Charlie stepped into the back office, noting the open file cabinets and desk drawers where Eddie had apparently been nosing around. Most were empty, including a folder on top labeled "Employee Records" that they already discarded. The business records for the past few years had been dumped out of their folders and into cardboard boxes haphazardly, with no order whatsoever. Baza had apparently been responsible for creating this chaos. He'd also erased the computer accounting files and much of the software, which was why they'd wanted to get at what was inside that safe.

They were still playing catch-up on the physical inventory, but also paying a computer guy, Rick, to try and restore the lost computer files, one by one. So far, they'd been totally dependent on claim slips, quickly alphabetized by last names, to satisfy clients paying the fees to extend their loans or trying to retrieve their property. Clearly, Eddie had been looking for something. Wondering if anything was missing or had been compromised, he found Nancy's number and touched the call icon on his phone.

Five minutes later, Charlie walked back into the front room, where Gordon was watching the burglar. "Just a few more questions, Eddie. If I end up happy, you might earn your freedom and be allowed to leave. Otherwise, I'm going to turn your ass over to APD for breaking and entering, possession of a burglary tool, and assault. I might even frame you by stuffing some watches and jewelry in your pockets."

"Give me a break, man, I've never even been arrested. I'm not a criminal," Eddie sputtered frantically.

"Or maybe you've just never been caught. Either way, that all changed today, Eddie. Quit with the excuses, I need your cooperation. Your future's in the balance now."

"Fine. Ask your damn questions."

"Where are you parked? Describe your car."

"I have an '03 gold Mustang, and it's parked in the laundry parking lot one block south of here."

"You have a job—other than stealing?"

"I operate a forklift at GA Foods—the warehouse on Buckner Avenue, graveyard shift. That's from midnight to eight."

"We know graveyards," Gordon said. "Who's your supervisor?"

He thought about it a few seconds before answering. "Tim Gallegos."

"We'll be checking this out, you know," Charlie said, nodding to Gordon. "Next question. What do you know about Diego Baza?"

"When I was trying to get in contact with him, I asked around at the laundry and the gas station up on the corner. Baza supposedly owned this shop for several years, then all of a sudden he got foreclosed and was locked out. He had a couple of employees, and they lost their jobs. Nobody around here has seen him or those employees since."

"What did you hear about the employees?"

"There was a woman, part-time bookkeeper. She worked here for a couple of years. Attractive, kinda high-class, according to the men I spoke to. She left, laid off maybe, sometime before the shop shut down."

"Catch her name?" Gordon asked.

"Ruth something," Eddie said. "Maybe she's come around looking for work since you bought the place?"

Charlie shook his head.

"Can I turn over now?"

"Not yet," Charlie said. "What about the other employee?"

"Some retired guy named Salazar. After Three Balls closed down he moved to live near his kids. Colorado, I think, maybe Denver. He keeps in touch with the lady who runs the laundry."

"Sounds like you've been doing your homework on this place," Gordon said. "Lived in the city long?"

"Northeast Heights, then moved to Pennsylvania my junior year of high school. I moved back to New Mexico two years ago but couldn't find a cheap place, so I lived with my grandmother for a while. I just want to get my grandpa's stuff back. I've been planning today for almost a month," Eddie said. "Now can I move?" He turned his head and looked up at Charlie. The bloody spot on his head had caked up already.

"One more thing. Actually two. You're gonna leave me two hundred dollars to have the vent fixed. And, secondly, I want you to ask around again and find out everything you can for me about Baza. You've got until Saturday. Then call us here at the shop and spill what you get."

"But what if I don't get anything you don't already know?"

"If you don't get something, you'd better leave Albuquerque before I find you, Eddie. We're letting you go, but now you work for us."

"Shit. That's not right."

"911 okay with you?" Gordon said, bringing out his cell phone.

"Okay, okay, I'll get what I can," Eddie said.

"Then we have a deal. Stand up, then empty out your pockets onto the counter," Charlie ordered, wanting to make sure the rings hadn't been removed already.

Eddie brought out a neatly folded handkerchief, a car key ring for a Mustang, and another key ring with two door keys.

"That it?" Gordon asked.

"Hang on," Eddie said, grumbling. He pulled out a cheap

pair of needle-nose pliers and an unopened pack of spearmint gum. "That's it."

"Turn your pockets inside out, bro," Charlie ordered.

"Yeah, okay." Eddie complied. "What's next, a strip search?" he added sarcastically.

"And have to look at your skinny ass? Hell no," Gordon said. "Where's your cell phone?"

"Left it in my car. I didn't want it to fall out of my pocket while I was climbing through the roof."

"Makes sense. Okay," Charlie announced. "You can keep everything except for the pliers. But if we see your face around here again, you'd better have enough money to reclaim that ring and watch—that is, if Baza didn't take them when he left. Otherwise, after Saturday, we're done," Charlie said.

"How about my wallet?" Eddie asked.

Charlie tossed it over. "I already took out two hundred for the damage."

"Damn," Eddie said, checking inside the billfold before gingerly sticking it in his pocket. He walked stiffly to the front entrance, then paused while Charlie unlocked it. Five seconds later, he was out on the sidewalk, walking away almost at a jog.

Charlie watched Eddie go down the block, then stepped back inside. "Think we should have turned him in?"

"Probably. He's dangerous. You know he might have stabbed you with that screwdriver," Gordon asked.

"Yeah, I'm out of practice—or slowing down."

"It's always more dangerous taking them prisoner. You have to get up close and personal."

"But we're not in a war zone. Here, you've got to prove they're the enemy first," Charlie said. "Even then, you'll likely end up in court."

"I'd rather err on the side of, say, staying alive."

Charlie looked around the big room. "Speaking of staying alive, where did we put those sopapillas?"

Chapter Four

Ten minutes later they sat in the business office of the pawn-shop, polishing off the last of their fast food with day-old coffee, reheated in the microwave.

Charlie's cell phone began to vibrate. He picked it up and looked at the display. It was Nancy. He put the phone on speaker so Gordon could hear.

"I've got the background you wanted on Edward J. Henderson," she said. "Tell me again why you wanted this?"

Charlie was looking for discrepancies in Eddie's story but didn't want the cops to intervene until they'd learned all they could from him.

"We talked to him in the store recently, and then his name came up here at the pawnshop regarding some possible missing items. I wanted to see if he had a record," Charlie said, leaving out the details.

"I couldn't find a thing in the files except what's on his

valid New Mexico driver's license, which lists an address cor-
responding to the Premier Apartments, west of the river.
There's no NM vehicle registered to him, no military or
criminal record, and no busts or warrants. I couldn't find him
in other state databases, so he can't have lived in the state for
very long, unless he's been ducking his taxes. He's never been
fingerprinted either, if we're talking about the same Eddie
Henderson," Nancy said.

She continued. "His social matches up with a Pennsylvania Edward Jerome Henderson of the right age, and he still
has an unexpired driver's license from that state. What set
you off about this guy, anyway? You think he might have had
a beef with Baza?"

"Maybe, which is why we wanted anything you had. We
have an address and a work location, so we're gonna keep an
eye on him."

He looked over at Gordon, who nodded.

"If you learn anything else that might link Henderson with
Baza in a way that suggests they had a problem, let me know
and I'll pass it along to DuPree," she said. "Meanwhile, I'll see
if I can get anything on Henderson from some of the other
databases I can access."

"Sounds like a plan. Do you have an update on how Gina's
doing?"

"Her vitals are coming around and both lungs are func-
tioning. She's in recovery now."

"Call me if you can when she wakes up."

"Of course."

"Anything from the crime scene team you can share?"

"Not yet, but the bullet that struck Gina was removed and has been turned over to our lab. I heard it was a thirty-eight hollow point, but they should be able to confirm that in a few hours," she said.

"Anything on Baza?"

"Nothing new. The Office of the Medical Investigator isn't in such a hurry with the dead," she said. "Gotta go. If you learn anything new, call."

"Sure. Bye."

"At least it sounds like good news on Gina," Gordon said, sipping the last of his coffee from his Lobo mug. "A thirty-eight revolver—a good choice for an amateur hit. Cheap and easy to obtain in this country, simple to use, and deadly enough without overpenetration. If you can't do the job on one target with six rounds up close, hire it out."

"Sounds about right. Witnesses described a revolver." Charlie stood. "Now let's see if we can find what Eddie was looking for. I don't remember any Rolex, though."

"Neither do I. Everything he said might have been on-the-spot bullshit. There's no way he would have gotten a thousand bucks on a pawn, even with a high-end watch and a couple of rings. I may be new at this, but even I know that a realistic loan wouldn't top more than two hundred maybe, even with the rings. Now if he'd have sold them outright . . . ," Gordon said.

"Then he would have had to buy his collateral back for a lot more, especially if he let the loan date expire or missed a payment. Pawn interest is a killer. Either way, there should be a record of the transaction around here somewhere." Charlie stepped around the counter and used a key to open one of the drawers where they kept the ring displays after-hours.

"If not, then Eddie was lying. He sure gathered a lot of intelligence on Baza and this place, more than necessary for a burglary," Gordon said, opening a drawer containing current paper invoices on pawned goods.

"Yeah, and I'm getting some bad vibes on Eddie's background. If he went to school here, there should have been a record, even if he was homeschooled. We're new at this investigation crap, but we should have at least yanked off his gloves and gotten some prints. And checked out his car," Charlie lamented, looking through the rings for something like Eddie had described.

"Too late now. It still leads back to the original question, what *was* he doing here? If he'd wanted to rob the place, why not go straight to the jewelry and electronics, or the guns? Why bother searching in file cabinets?" Gordon said. "He hasn't gone through anything here, at least that I can tell."

Charlie locked the ring drawer and came out from behind the counter. "He may have been trying to find keys to the displays, or something in one of the folders. We need to know for sure. You think he's going to stick around his old address and call on Saturday? If he does, that'll at least tell us something. You notice how his mood kept changing, from terrified to dead calm, then attitude? He's either mostly telling us the truth, or trying to play us, making up a story as he goes along."

Charlie walked over to the office door next and looked

inside at the stacks of folders, now scattered randomly across the joined desks.

"He's playing with the wrong guys, then. Hey, now that you're in the office, you wanna start on the transaction records? I'll take a quick look through the watches in the drawers and under the glass."

"First, Gordo, why don't you try that combination on the Detroit safe?" Charlie suggested, coming back out front.

Getting the combination to Baza's safe was the reason Gina had met with Baza, and that had almost gotten her killed. Charlie was still trying to deal with the baggage of combat—of torture and death—but this was the first time he'd gotten a friend shot. This wasn't supposed to happen—not on his watch, anyway.

"Damn, I forgot all about that."

"It's written down, right?"

"Yeah, I meant forgetting about the safe—not the combination. If there's anything inside besides stale air, I'll let you know in just a few minutes," Gordon said, stepping out of the small office.

Charlie decided to follow and see for himself.

Gordon crouched down in front of the waist-high, five-hundred-pound-plus, black Detroit Safe Company safe. A piece of blue plastic label tape that read "Computer Backups" was stuck on the frame just above the center of the door. He twisted to the first number Baza had given Gina, then turned the center wheel and stopped at the next number. He continued the process two more times.

"I think I heard a click," Gordon said, turning his head and nodding to Charlie. "Got your fingers crossed?"

"Just open the damned thing."

Gordon reached to his left and turned the big steel lever. The heavy door moved easily, all the way open. The interior was stacked with labeled manila folders bulging with papers. On top of the stack were several plastic containers with old floppy disks and CDs, along with business software for long-obsolete operating systems.

"Crap. Windows 95? This stuff is ancient. These are records from the owner before last," Gordon said, rummaging through the boxes. "Baza ripped us off."

"Yeah, well, karma evened things out for him today, I guess. Check out that locked compartment," Charlie suggested.

Gordon brought out the key and unlocked the interior door. On a shelf were four flash drives sitting atop two familiar-looking magazines.

"Finally! Treasure!" Gordon yelled, setting the flash drives on top of the safe and bringing out the *Playboys*. "March and April, 1967. Hell, these are older than me."

"I was hoping for gold coins and maybe emeralds, but we can put these jewels in our collectors section. They're in mint condition. I bet they'll sell within the week."

"Don't you think we need to check them out first, page by page? Maybe there are secret documents inside," Gordo said.

"Carefully folded, in the center?"

"Right," Gordon said, placing them atop the safe, beside the flash drives.

"Now let's see what's stored in the memories of those things. Maybe we'll finally get lucky," Charlie said.

Five minutes later, Gordon looked up from the laptop he'd used to read the flash drive files. "We're still missing the last six months of Three Balls, and the file labeled 'Personnel' is empty, probably deleted. So all we have is inventory and business current to May. Not a total loss, I guess, but there's still that big hole in the records we need to plug."

"At least we can remove these old folders and sell the safe. It'll be good to get this beast out of the display area. Roger, at the Old Desert Inn, left me his card. He wants to put it on display in their lobby. If we give him the combination and key his offer goes up to five hundred instead of one fifty. We'll call him first thing mañana," Charlie said, carefully pulling off the plastic "Computer Backups" label.

Gordon moved the *Playboy* magazines over to the counter, then locked up the inside compartment and closed the safe. "Until tomorrow. Guess we need to get back to finding whatever Eddie was after."

"Look out for anything: big transactions, documents, deeds, anything that might have given Baza's killer his or her motive."

Charlie glanced at the cover of the March *Playboy* as he passed by. There was a blonde with bunny ears twirling her black bow tie. She had a white collar, and though you couldn't see much, it was obvious she was topless. In those days innuendo was king. Now you could see that much booty in a grocery aisle. Progress.

●　　●　　●

A few minutes after seven that evening, Charlie walked into the Saint Mark's Hospital lobby. Nancy had called to give him Gina's room number. Nancy was still at work, supervising several patrol officers.

Gina would probably welcome a friendly face once Detective DuPree was done interviewing her. Looking at the wall signs and trying to locate which hall Gina was in, Charlie saw DuPree and the same patrolman he'd been with earlier. DuPree was talking to a nurse about security, and Charlie passed by without a word, though the officer looked in his direction for a second.

A uniformed security guard was at a nurses station at the end of the hall, so Charlie walked over and identified himself.

The tall, middle-aged man, maybe ex-military from his stride, walked to Gina's door, making it clear he was sticking close by, and waved him in.

Charlie walked in quietly, moving over to the high off-the-floor hospital bed. Gina's eyes were closed. She had an oxygen tube inserted in her nose and an IV was feeding her fluids through a vein in her left arm.

He watched her for several minutes, whispered an old Navajo prayer, then placed a tiny piece of turquoise in the palm of her left hand—a blessing. He'd carried a similar stone in his pocket for most of his deployments—a token given to him by his grandfather, a *hataalii*. The old man—he'd always seemed old to Charlie—was a medicine man.

Charlie was no traditionalist, but the medicine had

worked. He'd never been wounded or injured in any measurable way. Only those he'd fought against had suffered. That was the way of a great warrior, his Navajo friends and relatives had said.

His culture also taught that there needed to be balance. That meant that sooner or later, it would be his turn to pay the price. Maybe that time was now. He prayed that Gina wouldn't be the one who paid for the blood on his hands.

Gina had been his only real girlfriend back in high school. He'd loved her then, but one evening she'd discovered that friendship was all she could offer him. At first, it had destroyed him, but he eventually got over it and they'd become best friends. Now she was more like a sister, even more so than Arlene, his biological sibling. Even after all these years, his friendship with Gina remained strong.

He backed away, looking at the medical gear and smelling the disinfectant. Except for the quiet and the near-sterile environment, he was almost back in Afghanistan. He remembered the dirty, streaked, and pained faces of all the soldiers he'd seen on the ground or upon litters, bleeding, screaming out, or gurgling as the life spirit streamed right out of them.

But there was much more to remember. How many times had he carried wounded insurgents or village leaders and placed them in Blackhawks or Humvees to be evacuated and interrogated? They were involuntary assets, sources of information, and once they were out of his and Gordon's hands, no longer his concern.

He and his intelligence team had been trained to seek

out and take prisoners based upon whatever information they could provide. Usually their captives, ranging from boys to old men, had been roughed up or injured by the time they were turned over to the civilian spooks. Charlie never knew what happened after that, but he had a good imagination. He'd heard stories, and he didn't want to know the rest.

Shaking himself from his reverie, not wanting his mind to wander back to those memories, he looked down at his watch. He had to get back and help Gordon block off that hole in the roof, at least 'til morning.

"Hey, Charles, what did you put in my hand? We engaged or something?" Gina said, her voice a drugged whisper, but quite clear in the silence of the room.

"How you doing, best girl?" he said, stepping up beside the bed. "I didn't mean to wake you."

"Just resting my eyes. If you hadn't put that rock in my hand I never would have known you were here. How'd you learn to move so quietly? Oh, right, the army."

"The noisy don't come back, not unless they served in an artillery unit," he joked. "That pebble in your hand is a piece of turquoise. It's part of an old Navajo blessing my grandfather taught me. Keep it close."

"I will. Have you spoken to Nancy yet?"

"Yeah, twice. She was here earlier while you were still under, but she had to leave for her shift. She'll be back after midnight. You scared the hell out of her—and me too. Were you able to give anything useful to that detective? He was on his way out when I got here."

"No, I can't remember much. Baza and I exchanged the money and the envelope, I checked to make sure the key was in there, then heard the vehicle stop right behind me. Some guy said, 'hey Baza,' then the shooting started. It was so loud. Something struck me in the back and I blacked out. Now, I've got a lump on my head and hurt like hell everywhere else."

"Can you think of anyone who might want you dead? Any enemies?"

"Except for a bee I killed the other day when it flew into my Passat at the stop sign, no. Baza was clearly the target. The guy who shot us called out his name, not mine."

"That's what we're thinking—well, Gordon, Nancy, and I. DuPree has other ideas. At least he did a few hours ago."

"Yeah, he asked me all kinds of crap about my clients, my cases, even my boyfriend. Guess he doesn't know about Nancy yet. When I told him the killer called out Baza by name, I think it just confused him. Is it me, or is DuPree a little—underqualified?"

"Don't worry, the A team's got your back. The guy who shot you is going down."

"You've never been subtle, Charlie, and I'm not sure if that's an asset or a curse. You and Gordon, right? You gonna run that pawnshop and still take down the shooter?"

"We've got help from the inside."

"Nancy? I hope this doesn't get her into trouble."

"She'd go to the wall for you. We all would."

"Don't let anything happen to Nancy, okay? Or Gordon,

or you either." She paused for a moment. "You and I were so close back in high school. I can't lose my best friend now."

"Yeah, you either. Get some sleep, heal, and stay safe. And thanks for getting that combination and key for us, even if it was the hard way."

"So it *was* the real deal. Did you find any of the computer backups or papers you were looking for?"

"Not everything. There are records from before Baza took over, then all but the last six months of his files—minus the employee folder, for some reason. But there was some reading material. I'll let Gordo tell you all about it. Once you're out of here, the four of us can grill some steaks and catch up on everything. Okay?" He reached out and gently closed her delicate fingers around the turquoise.

"Good night, Charlie. And no guilt, or brooding. What happened today wasn't your fault. It was the guy with the gun."

"All right. Okay, good night, Gina," Charlie said softly. He turned and was walking toward the door just as a nurse came in. The nurse nodded, then said something softly to Gina he didn't catch.

Charlie was silent as he walked down the hall and across the lobby, passing people coming in with flowers, or talking quietly in groups.

Then he started shaking, for no reason at all. Embarrassed, he sped up, looking around to see if anyone else had noticed. It used to happen all the time when deployed "in country," but it was always after a mission, never during. PTSD was a bitch, but it hadn't stopped him yet. Still, he had to get out of the hospital.

Once he was outside, able to smell the cool November night air, he stopped shaking and looked up at the stars. To the east was Orion, the Hunter, low in the clear desert sky. It had to be a sign.

"I don't brood," he said aloud to himself. "I feel guilty for a while, maybe, then I get even."

Charlie was back at the pawnshop by 8:30, parking in one of the alley spaces, then letting himself in through the heavy, metal back door. The lights were off except in the office. Gordon was inside, listening and half watching a football game on the small TV as he searched through stacks of folders.

"So she never got a look at the shooter?" Gordon asked, continuing the brief conversation they'd had on the phone during Charlie's drive back. "Think she'd recognize a voice?"

"Don't know, we've got to round up a suspect first. Ready to work on blocking off the skylight until we can call Travis?" Charlie asked, referring to the handyman who'd helped them with repairs when they'd taken over the business.

"Already taken care of. I wired it shut from the inside, then left a surprise for anyone dumb enough to climb on the roof and cut the wires."

"Surprise? Not something that'll blow a hole in the roof?"

"No, I ran out of Claymores. I left something that'll go chomp, not boom."

"That 1920s-era coyote trap?"

"It's not just an Old West collector's item anymore. Uh, but remind me to put it on safe and take it down before Travis goes up on the roof," Gordon said.

Charlie sat down in the swivel chair behind his desk. "Any luck searching through that paperwork?"

"Couldn't find anything that suggests a motive. These folders are a mess. There are years of transactions here. We've got them arranged by last name, of course, but they're still mixed together regardless of date and type of merchandise. Baza sure wanted to drive the next owner crazy. Interesting thing, though. You know how we figured he sold all of the guns from that gun case and storage cabinet just before he was evicted?"

"Yeah. Let me guess, you can't find any record whatsoever for any gun transactions?" Charlie said.

"None, except for those we've done since reopening, and that includes the records we found in the safe. You think maybe he was fencing stolen guns, then reselling them?"

"Maybe. Until Rick brings back those trashed computer files we won't know what Baza had, or sold. Not unless it's on one of the paper copies we still have, or out in inventory." Charlie waved his hand toward the stacks of transaction forms, still in folders, piled upon his and Gordon's desks.

"He's required to keep records on every transaction, and if he didn't, that's one more reason we need a lot more background on the asshole," Gordon said. "His recent behavior sounds more and more like a guy about to go on the run. We've seen most of his legal business records, utility bills, and the like. If he kept all the money intended for those instead of paying his creditors, he abandoned his business with a decent amount of cash."

"Anyone taking several months to amass money like that must have had some idea where to hide. Mexico? Central America?" Charlie suggested.

"Maybe he did some research. How about if we add Web searches to Rick's data-recovery efforts? What were his plans, where was he thinking of going? Maybe he had friends or relatives he was going to meet up with. A girlfriend?"

"Good idea, Gordo. Once we get an address on Baza's last residence, maybe we can find where he shopped, where he hung out, who his neighbors were, and who he met."

"And who's going to deal with the body and funeral services? We need to know about his family, too. Let's call it a night, and meet back here at 0700 and get started," Gordon suggested.

Charlie, who was staying in one of his cousin's rental homes in Albuquerque's lower northeast heights, nodded. "Keep one eye open, bro, on the streets and around your apartment. I have serious doubts about our burglar. He's up to something, and just because he doesn't have a record doesn't mean he's clean. He just hasn't got caught lately."

"Stay alert. It's been a day," Gordon said, checking the pistol in the belt holster just beneath his jacket.

"I'm gonna go. Lock up good, bro. And don't forget the alarm," Charlie said, heading for the back door.

"Yes, Mother," Gordon said, reaching for his keys.

Charlie exited out the back door, locking it behind him, then took a close, careful look around the alley and the Dodge before he unlocked the car door. He thought about checking underneath—being used to car bombs from his army days—then shrugged it off. Paranoia was a hard habit to drop.

Eddie didn't seem the car-bomb type, and was dumb enough to bring a screwdriver to a gunfight, so he started the engine without a pause and a prayer.

The Charger started with the low rumble only Detroit could provide, so he let it run a minute, glad it hadn't been shot up like that Taurus. He was surprised to discover where his round had gone, but, then again, he was a little out of practice.

More tired than he should be, now that the adrenaline rush and the shakes were gone. Charlie headed west to Second, then turned north.

As he crossed over the railroad tracks, heading east, he passed a big white step van with the familiar "24-Hour Plumber" sign parked just off the road. The driver, wearing a white cap, had a handheld radio to his ear.

Better you than me, Charlie thought as he passed by. If the guy was lucky, it was a water leak, not a backed-up sewer line. The guy pulled out right behind him, then accelerated, keeping pace and making the same green light as Charlie.

Charlie looked at the dash clock. He'd be in bed in a half hour—a quick shower was all he needed, and he was so used to bathing in five minutes he could almost do it in his sleep.

He and the plumber were the only vehicles on the road as they passed under the freeway, again making the light, but just barely. The plumber was keeping a respectable distance and not blinding him with high beams. The guy certainly didn't seem to be in much of a hurry.

Charlie touched the radio button, set for a local station that played mellow jazz this time of night. He'd grown up with country music, but lately had found it too depressing.

So, Gina thought he was a brooder. She'd always claimed he was too serious. Charlie grinned at the thought as he made the slow curve at the top of the hill, the Charger creeping along at the posted thirty-five mph. Ahead was a bridge over the large flood channel.

The plumber's truck behind him accelerated, pulling out into the passing lane. "In a hurry *now?*" Charlie said, glancing over as the truck breezed past.

"Hey, too close, bro," Charlie yelled, looking over at the van's rear wheels, just to his left and less than three feet away. He touched the brakes just as the truck suddenly cut him off.

Chapter Five

The truck must have cut his speed. The Dodge struck the truck's rear end with a sickening thud, then bounced to the right. Charlie clung to the steering wheel as he slammed hard on the brakes, fighting the momentum as he tracked toward the narrow sidewalk and bridge railing.

His right tire bounced off the curb, throwing him up into the ceiling and yanking his feet off the floor as the Charger jumped onto the sidewalk. Only the shoulder belt kept him from losing it completely.

All he had to hang on to was the steering wheel. He straightened it out, scraped the steel side railing with the passenger side panels, then eased back down onto the street. Just as he found the brake and gas pedal, the flat left front tire grabbed the pavement, throwing him into a crabbing sideways slide. The tires were screeching so loud that his teeth hurt. He'd roll the car if he didn't act fast.

Charlie forced the wheel left again and pressed down on the clutch, gearing down to first. Something in the front right popped, and he slid to a stop. The smell of burning rubber was almost overwhelming now. He shifted into neutral and turned off the engine, not wanting to pump any more gas or throw sparks into the mess.

He shook for a moment, mostly out of anger, knowing that his car wasn't going anywhere on its own now. Down the road, all he saw were the taillights of the plumber's truck. The guy who'd nearly run him into the dry canal was no plumber.

Charlie set the emergency brake, checked the rearview mirror, then opened the door and stepped out. Grabbing his cell phone, he glanced down at the crumpled front end of his car and the shredded tire. The engine was probably okay, but his insurance man was going to have a heart attack. The guy who had tried to kill him just now, however—and, even worse, trashed his ride—was going to die a much slower death.

"Call Gordon," he said to the phone, his voice clear and calm now that he'd made the promise.

"We're going to need to hire someone, at least part-time, Charles," Gordon said, Lobo coffee mug in his hand as he looked toward the big clock on the shop wall of movie posters. "We've run into a hassle and that's going to take lot more of our attention. In a half hour we open for business, and we can't just shut down like yesterday."

"What about one of the former employees that Baza supposedly let go? They'd know the place and the routine, and we can start them with a decent wage and a percentage of anything they sell. There was a woman, Ruth, that Eddie mentioned, and the older guy, Salazar? The initials JS are on most of the transaction forms that don't have Baza's so I guess that would be Mr. Salazar. I don't recall any other employee signing off, though—no R, for sure," Charlie said. "Curiously enough, all the employee records are gone or deleted. I wonder why Baza would do that?"

"You got me. Maybe we need to dig back earlier, or just haven't found any with her initials yet. Or maybe Baza gave Ruth other things to do."

"Well, until my rental gets here, I can't run any errands anyway, so let's check for either one of those names in the papers Baza left scattered around. I'll give Rick a call and see if he's managed to recover any employee or personnel folders from those backup drives."

"How about talking to the owner of the laundry on the corner when they open up? If Eddie wasn't lying about that too, someone there might be able to give us a heads-up," Gordo suggested. "A last name for Ruth? Salazar's first name and new address?"

"Good idea. I can prime the pump by taking in that wool Navajo rug on the wall over there. You never want to wash one, I know that, but some of them can be dry cleaned. The laundry can test the dyes."

"You know more about that than me," Gordon said. "On another matter, do you think that whoever killed Baza and shot Gina just might be the same person who tried to take you out last night?"

"That's what my gut says, which suggests he'll probably strike again because I managed to screw up his plans. We need to be ready. Our best strategy has always been to take the offensive—get to him first," Charlie said.

Charlie walked back over to the coffeemaker to top off his mug. "We need to track down Eddie Henderson and maybe lean on him some more and see where that leads. He admitted having an interest in Baza and the woman employee, Ruth. Otherwise, why ask if she'd been coming around?"

"Yeah, and Eddie admitted knowing our routine, something he may live to regret now. That plumber's truck was waiting in just the right spot because the driver knew the route you usually took home," Gordon said. "Put Eddie at the top of the list. Hell, he may have even followed us to the Baza meet yesterday and done the shooting. You suppose we should ask Nancy to request an ATL on Eddie's vehicle and maybe have someone drive by his home and workplace?"

"Doesn't hurt to bring it up. I'll try her cell. Since she works the evening shift, she's probably getting out of bed right now, and will be heading for the hospital after that," Charlie said. "But maybe she can make some calls on the way."

"Meanwhile I'll get hold of Travis and check where we're at on his work schedule. Until we get that entry point neutralized there's at least one person who already knows how to get in," Gordon said.

Charlie put the cell phone back in his pocket as he climbed into the loaner car his insurance agent had arranged. The

Charger was going to be in the body shop for several days, but at least it wasn't totaled, and the insurance would cover all but a thousand for repairs. He had the money, but it would be tight for a while. They were barely making enough now to pay the bills—forget about profit. Gordo said not to worry, they could always set an accidental fire and get their money back.

He hadn't had any luck learning Ruth's last name, but Melissa, at the laundry, had been able to help with the other employee, Jake Salazar. Right now Gordon was trying to contact Baza's former clerk to see if he was available for a part-time position. It turned out that the sixty-four-year-old man had moved back into the area and was looking for work.

Melissa also remembered Eddie, who'd talked her head off maybe six months ago, then came back with more questions just last Friday. Both times, most of his questions had centered around Baza—and Ruth—which had creeped Melissa out a little. The laundress admitted that Ruth had been pretty and charming, but very private. She had no idea where Ruth lived, either.

Charlie had just spoken to Nancy, who'd been in contact with Detective DuPree. The lead investigator had already run into a significant snag—he hadn't been able to get a location for Baza's residence. There were no utility records for the man—phone, gas, electrical, cell phone, or anything else since he'd defaulted and walked away from Three Balls four months ago. His driver's license still listed his old address.

Baza had a cell phone on him when he died, but it was a disposable one with no real hope of backtracking.

Charlie and Gordo had been able to find Baza for their first meeting via an e-mail account they'd discovered in some paperwork at the shop. Gina had set up the second meeting, also using that account, and got him to agree to terms.

DuPree was having the police department's computer people try and track down a physical address via that account, but were having no luck at all.

Fifteen minutes later, Charlie parked along Commercial Avenue, less than a hundred yards from where the shooting had taken place yesterday. He'd driven by a few minutes ago and noted that the blood had been washed off the sidewalk in front of the apartment building Baza had emerged from, though he hadn't lived there. A witness had come forward and reported seeing Baza coming in the back entrance, and that had been confirmed by the building manager, according to DuPree, via Nancy.

Charlie climbed out of the rental car, a three-year-old compact white Chevy with a four-cylinder engine that supposedly got twice the milage of his Dodge. Saving money right now was important, but so was staying alive. If he ever had to outrun anyone now, except on foot, he was seriously screwed.

It was barely nine A.M. and most day workers were already on the job, so the sidewalks were only occupied by the very young and a parent or two, the very old, and the unemployed. It wasn't a barrio here, but definitely low-rent, a tired commercial zone along the main streets backed by fifty-year-old apartment buildings and old homes from more prosperous days.

Charlie decided to circle the neighborhood on foot, getting a feel for the community and trying to decide how and where Baza had entered the area. If he'd lived close by, the cops hadn't found his place, and no vehicles linked to him had been located, according to Nancy.

Just how far did you walk, and where did you park? Charlie asked himself, walking east on the sidewalk, trying not to look confrontational, nodding to anyone who looked over as he passed.

It was a mixed-race neighborhood, true of most of Albuquerque outside the extreme Northeast Heights, so nobody was concerned that he was Navajo. If they'd known he was carrying a handgun, maybe he would have earned a second look. But maybe not. Lots of New Mexicans were strapped these days, and people who lived in this part of the city probably wouldn't have been that surprised.

As he walked east, the apartments and older homes looked tired, and some were boarded up. The lucky ones had been converted to small offices for lawyers, bail bondsmen, or secondhand shops, judging from the signs.

After walking about a half mile, he heard the ringing of loud bells and a train whistle. He looked up, heard the rumbling, then the sound of metal on metal—the Rail Runner commuter train was coming to a stop. There was a station close by, he suddenly realized, and it was very possible Baza had boarded somewhere up or down the line and gotten off here.

All the stations were new; the Rail Runner system had only been in use for a few years. It'd started up when he was halfway around the world, fighting insurgents and the Taliban.

The stations he'd already seen as part of this commuter service were small, usually no more than a narrow building beside the tracks with benches under a long porch and a place to buy tickets.

Charlie hadn't ridden the train yet, so he'd have to get a schedule. Baza could have come down the line from as far north as Santa Fe, or as south as Belen, but he doubted that. The man had grown up in Albuquerque and probably lived somewhere in the metro area.

The train had already left by the time he arrived. He quickly spotted one of the ticket agents, a dark-haired woman wearing the standard blue pants and yellow vest over a white blouse. She had a ID on her belt and a large black ticket scanner in her hand.

"Excuse me, ma'am," Charlie said to the woman.

"You just missed it," she said automatically. "Next departure from here isn't until 4:26 this afternoon. You can pick up a schedule at the counter." The woman motioned toward the narrow structure at the opposite side of the platform.

It was time to make up something—the truth would only raise eyebrows and maybe attract security. "Thanks, ma'am, but actually I'm a counselor at a group home off Rio Grande, and I'm looking for one of our patients, Paul, who loves trains. We think he may be taking rides up and down the line recently, then sneaking back into the facility. He's been giving the staff the slip, and we don't want him to get lost or confused. He's in the early stages of Alzheimer's, so some days he's perfectly normal. May I show you a recent photograph of Paul? Perhaps you or one of the other ticket agents have seen him. He's a big fellow, about my height."

"Certainly, but shouldn't you put out an alert for this man?" the woman asked, frowning.

"Oh, he's back at the group home right now, playing cards in our rec room. We just want to make sure we know what's been going on so it doesn't happen again," Charlie said, handing her Baza's photo. "Take your time."

The woman stared at it a moment, then took off her sunglasses and looked again. "He looks familiar, but he's not one my regulars. If it's the same guy I'm thinking of, he boarded the northbound 508 either yesterday or the day before. That's an 8:42 morning departure. So your man's been sneaking out that early?"

Charlie nodded. He was making this up as he went along anyway. "He knows all our work schedules and apparently has been slipping out during shift changes."

"Now, I could be wrong. You might want to check with Marie over at the counter," the woman said. "But you should keep a better eye on this patient. He could end up anywhere from Santa Fe to Belen if he has the money for a ticket."

"That's why I'm here. Thanks so much for your help." He shook her hand. "Marie, you said?"

The ticket agent nodded. "Good luck. . . ."

"Jack. I'm Jack Natani. Thanks again."

Charlie walked over to the counter, careful not to glance up and be captured full-on by one of the surveillance cameras. He'd thought about posing as a cop, but that could come back and bite him on the ass.

Marie didn't recall seeing Baza, suggesting he might have purchased his ticket online, which made sense. Charlie thanked her, then took a quick look toward the parking lot, wondering if Baza's car was there somewhere. This time of day the lot was three-quarters full. There were a lot of Albuquerque residents working in Santa Fe, mainly state workers, who took the train round trip every weekday.

Not knowing what car to look for anyway, he turned and retraced his route west.

On his way back to his car he called Gordon, who picked up within fifteen seconds.

"Can I call you back in a few?" Gordon said immediately. "Got a customer."

"Take your time," Charlie responded. It would take five minutes to walk back to the rental anyway.

Gordon called back just as Charlie was climbing into the car. "Yo," Charlie said. "We making money today?"

"Yep," Gordon said. "I also managed to get hold of Jake Salazar, and he's coming in this afternoon to talk about working here again. He's back in the city, bored with retirement, and sounds eager. I'm hoping maybe he can also help sort out all the paperwork. Any leads on Baza?"

"He was clearly trying to keep us from finding out where he was staying. He might have taken the train from another station close to his residence and gotten off at the stop near here. He didn't take a taxi or bus, and nobody around here, according to the cops, seemed to know who he was and where he came from. So I went farther north and spoke to a station employee who may have seen him the day before the meet with Gina."

"Planning ahead, checking out the timing. Makes sense if you're planning a meet in another neighborhood. So you think he may live within walking distance of one of the northern stations?"

"Exactly. I'm driving up the line and planning on showing his photo to the ticket agents at each station, maybe even as far north as Bernalillo. If he boarded twice at any station, that might identify his residential area. And if I get a hit, count on me checking out any apartments within walking distance."

"That could take hours. Do you think we should bring in APD?"

"Nancy, maybe, if we need the manpower. DuPree, I'm not so sure. If I get a solid hit on Baza's apartment, however, I really don't have much choice. But Nancy would be my first call."

"Yeah, you don't want to get caught breaking into the *wrong* apartment. That would be hard to explain," Gordon said.

"Any news on Gina?" Charlie asked, changing the subject.

"Not a word, so I guess it's all good. Keep in touch, bro," Gordon added, then ended the call.

Charlie started up the Chevy's anemic engine, then eased out into traffic. He was tempted to call again about the Charger, but that might just piss off the mechanics and body shop people. He'd wait until tomorrow.

Chapter Six

"That man, Paul, came on foot, walking in from the west, both days." The ticket agent nodded, still looking at the photo.

"Paul wanders away from the group home once or twice a month," Charlie lied. "It's off the road over by Rio Grande," he added, pointing vaguely west. "Usually we find Paul over on the riverbank watching the ducks and geese, but recently he discovered trains. We've got people checking the other stations, and hopefully somebody will get a lead. He's healthy, and once he gets hungry enough, he'll probably find someone to call us to come and get him. Paul's actually pretty bright. I appreciate your help, and I'll work my way down the route to see if anyone else spotted him. I hope he didn't go all the way south to Belen," Charlie added.

He walked off the platform and headed toward the parking lot as he brought out his phone and called Gordon.

"Yo, what's going on?" Gordo said.

"Got a hit at the Los Ranchos station off of El Pueblo in the north valley. Baza walked here from the west, according to the employee I spoke to. So I'm going to canvass the area and check out an apartment complex off Second Street. Anything new on your end?" Charlie said.

"Several pawns, three with jewelry and one with a laptop. Sold a watch. Going crazy sorting out all those transaction receipts. At least Baza didn't screw around with the pawn tags attached to storeroom inventory."

"The bank would have come after him on that, maybe brought in the law. I think he was planning on dropping out of sight permanently. Any news on the deleted files?" Charlie asked.

"Rick is trying to find which one had the personnel records, but I'm hoping Mr. Salazar will be able to help us out, tracking down that Ruth woman. Oh, and the skylight is fixed. We can lock it from the inside now. There's a steel grid in place that'll keep anything fatter than a snake from wiggling through."

"Good enough. Keep at it, bro. I'm going to be busy for a while," Charlie said, ending the call as he reached the Chevy.

The apartments he planned to check out were in a complex with three main buildings on El Pueblo Street's north side. He drove into a curved driveway, parking in a visitor slot in front of the doors with the big "Office" sign. As he climbed out of the car, Charlie tried to think of a new excuse for waving the photo around. He couldn't use the mentally challenged group home scenario here—what would "Paul" be doing renting an apartment?

Seeing a woman in her early fifties behind the front desk, which contained photos of herself and what looked like a daughter and grandchildren, he came across what he hoped was the perfect angle.

"Excuse me, Mrs. . . ."

"Todd," the woman said, standing out and extending her hand. "Madeline Todd. How can I help you, Mr.? . . ."

"Charles Henry," he said, shaking her hand, something many Navajos were reluctant to do with a stranger. "I'm working for the Valley Associates law firm, representing Gina Sinclair, attorney-at-law."

He brought out Gina's card and placed it on the desk in front of her. "Madeline, I'm trying to locate an ex-husband who owes a substantial amount of child support. I'm here to serve a court order.

"Our client needs that money to help pay for her child's corrective surgery," he added, hoping to seal the deal.

"That's terrible. How could a man hold out on his own child? I wish I could help you, but we're not allowed to give out the names or apartment numbers of our tenants without some kind of court order or an obvious emergency," the lady said, sounding apologetic. "Are you sure he lives here?"

Charlie had known he might need a plan B, and already had it ready. "Yes, but the problem is that he's apparently using a fake identity, so if I told you his name that wouldn't help anyway. But I do have a photo. If he's *not* a resident, all you will have to do, Mrs. Todd, is shake your head no. Any conclusion I'd reach after that would be strictly on my own," Charlie said, then paused for a few seconds. "Will you help me do the right thing, Madeline? If not for me, for his daughter?"

The woman sat there for several seconds, then she glanced around. They were the only ones in the office. "Let me take a look at this lowlife SOB."

Charlie placed Baza's photo in front of Mrs. Todd, watching her eyes. The pupils shrunk immediately, a sure sign to him what the answer was.

She looked at it for a mere five seconds, then slid the photo back to him. "Bastard," she muttered, then sat back in her chair and pointed to apartment 108 on the building diagram beneath the glass on her desk.

"There won't be any trouble, will there?" she asked. "Our tenants want to feel safe and know that their privacy is being respected."

"I guarantee that this man will not be creating any problems for you or the residents," Charlie said, putting the photo back into his pocket. "Also rest assured that your name will never come up in my workplace. Good morning," he added, walking to the door.

Should I enter apartment 108 before or after I call Nancy? he thought as he walked back to his rental car. Rejecting the first alternative almost as quickly as it occurred to him, he also knew he'd need some kind of probable cause.

Instead of using the voice command this time, he entered

Gordon's cell number while walking down the sidewalk past the apartment entrances. Each was set back behind a tiny, open porch, some containing planters, flower boxes, or a small round table and a couple of metal chairs. He also noted that each door had a tag on it that listed a first initial and name.

Gordon didn't answer right away, and Charlie was already approaching 108 when he heard Gordon's voice.

"Chuck, you find Baza's place?"

"Think so. And if this is Baza's place, he's going under the name D. Tyler."

"Wish I was there. Gonna call Nancy? She'll be off duty now," Gordon reminded him.

"Longer I wait, the more time the shooter has to cover his tracks," Charlie replied, turning to the left and walking over to a bench beneath the shade of a locust tree. "I'll make the call."

"Copy. Just watch your back. Someone knew when and where Baza was meeting Gina yesterday, and we have no idea where the shooter got the intel."

"So he might have followed Baza from here," Charlie said, looking around, seeing only a young woman with an infant entering a second-story apartment across the lawn. "But if he was going to kill him, why not here instead of when he met up with Gina?"

"Maybe he wanted to know what Baza was up to first? Without more information, it's hard to say."

"And easy to speculate. I'll keep my eyes open. Gonna call Nancy now," Charlie said, ending the conversation.

Nancy arrived a bit later, in uniform, and together they went to the apartment complex office. Charlie remained by the door as Nancy showed the Baza photo to Mrs. Todd, who confirmed with a nod that he was the man was renting apartment 108. Charlie didn't hear the rest of the conversation, but from the one glance Madeline shot his way, it was clear she wouldn't be talking to him again anytime this century.

"What in the hell did you tell her?" Nancy asked as soon as they stepped back outside. "You see that look? She's going to hate you for life."

"I told her the truth, that Gina was my attorney, and we were looking for the man in the photo, who was faking his identity."

"And?"

"I said he was a lowlife hiding out from his obligations. Still true."

"Get to the smoke and mirrors or I won't let you through the door," Nancy said, holding up the passkey Mrs. Todd had given her. They were halfway down the sidewalk, approaching apartment 100.

"I said he was not making his child-support payments and that his daughter needed the money for her medical care. Okay, I played on her sympathy after seeing she was probably a grandmother from the photos on her desk. All I wanted to do was find out if he was staying here. Come on, you've never massaged the truth with a witness or suspect to get the answer you need?"

"Did you say you were a cop?"

"No. But I gave her my real name and showed Gina's business card. True and true. Now, what's the procedure checking out the dead guy's apartment?"

"One step at a time. I just hope to hell that Baza *was* living here. Everyone has a doppelganger somewhere, a look-alike," Nancy said, stopping in front of apartment 108.

"Like you and Scarlett Johansson?"

"Think that's going to get you anywhere?" Nancy said, putting on a pair of latex gloves she pulled from her back pocket.

She sighed loudly, then handed him a pair. "Put these on. This doesn't mean I actually want you to touch anything. Permission first, got it? I'm going to have to call Detective DuPree in a few minutes, so our time here has got to be productive. And make sure when he shows up you're standing in the door and those gloves are out of sight. What he doesn't know can't cost me my rank—or worse."

"Gotcha, Scarlett," Charlie said, grinning.

"We don't know if anyone is inside, so stand back," she said. "Police, open up," Nancy called out, key in the lock as she drew out her weapon. She waited ten seconds, then turned the key and opened the door, standing by the jamb.

A warm, gentle breeze greeted them, but the only sound was from the heating system. There were no lights on. Nancy held up her hand, signaling him to wait, then advanced into the living room. The place was furnished with a generic fabric-covered sofa, two chairs, and a simple end table and lamp. A short hall was to the left, and across the room a breakfast bar extended out from the kitchen area. It held a small LCD television and a foam Starbucks coffee cup.

Her eyes shifting from hallway to dining area, Nancy kept her pistol up and ready as she crossed the room just far enough to see behind the bar.

Shaking her head, she moved down the hall. Ten seconds later, she spoke. "Clear! Come inside and lock the door behind you. Don't touch the inside knob, you might smear any prints.

"You can look around," Nancy added after a moment, "but don't let me *see* you taking any photos with your cell phone of stuff in the closet, drawers, or anywhere else. I'll be checking out the kitchen area," she said, walking out of sight.

"One more thing," she said, coming back into the living room. "You know that everything in here has to be in the exact position it was when we came in. We can't afford to have anything challenged in court later on, and I'm not going to lie to save your butt, so don't take anything. I'm calling Detective DuPree now, so watch your time."

"Understood." Charlie had been on many intelligence- and prisoner-gathering missions while deployed and he knew how to sift through rooms and homes with efficiency, searching for useful information. The advantage he had here was that anything he read was likely to be in English, not Pashto or Dari, so it would go a hell of a lot faster.

Although Nancy had the freedom to work beside other cops—assuming DuPree allowed it—as a civilian, his time was limited to the detective's generosity. After DuPree found

out that he'd located Baza's residence ahead of APD, he'd either be secretly grateful, outwardly pissed, or both. Either way,
there would be no reason to let a civilian participate in evidence collection.

Charlie had his phone's camera ready as he walked down
the hall. Nancy had already turned on the lights, so he didn't
have to use the flash.

Atop the dresser was a tooled-leather belt, two expensive-
looking watches, a flashlight, a box of tissues, travel brochures,
an iPhone and iPad plugged into chargers, and a leather portfolio filled with papers he was dying to examine and photograph. What intrigued him most, however, was a silver-framed
snapshot of an attractive brown-haired woman. It was a bit
grainy, probably blown up from a smaller image and cropped
to create a portrait. The woman was standing on the front
step of a building, an apartment probably. He could make out
a wall of mailboxes in the background.

Charlie took a photograph of the woman, then quickly
opened the drawers, searching inside. He saw two pistols, one
a Glock and the other a sand W revolver, plus three boxes of
ammunition. One of the boxes, for a .32 caliber handgun,
was missing eight rounds—a clip full, probably. A .32 was
found on Baza's body, Charlie recalled—unfired.

There were also boxes containing rings, silver jewelry,
and a variety of newer cell phones and other electronic devices. These were part of Baza's stash—taken for later sale
when he bailed on Three Balls. There was probably cash
hidden around as well, but he could leave that to the cops.

What he wanted was an obvious motive for Baza's murder. Clearly, Baza was trying to remain as invisible as possible. The man had made at least one enemy angry enough to kill him. Why?

He didn't find much clothing in the drawers or the closet. All but a few possessions were packed away in two expensive-looking suitcases under the bed and in the closet. Baza could have loaded up everything he had and be out of the place in ten minutes or less. That thought reminded him of the travel brochures on the dresser, and one look at those told him that Baza had printed out price quotes to Costa Rica for two adults and a child. No tickets, however, but the dates were for next month. Who was he planning on traveling with? Could it be the woman in the photo and a child? Baza, according to Nancy's information, had never been married, though through the years, off and on, he'd lived with one woman or another.

"I found a laptop under the refrigerator," Nancy yelled. "What about you?"

Charlie started looking though the leather portfolio, finding a passport and other papers in Baza's real name, nothing fake. There was also a list of a half-dozen banks, and a full-page printout of sets of numbers. They were probably real and fake account numbers, and anyone finding them would need hours to put the right combinations together. It was amateur stuff, but pretty secure in the short run.

Remembering Nancy's question, he told her what he'd found as he took photos. Then he checked his watch, put the portfolio just where he'd discovered it, and walked over to the window.

"I think DuPree's arrived. There's a generic sedan and a squad car. I'll remove the gloves and step outside so he won't throw a tantrum."

"Give me your cell phone to hang on to. DuPree has a suspicious mind. He might ask to see yours," Nancy suggested, walking over to join him.

"No prob. I've already uploaded everything I have to a computer at the shop." He held up the phone and pressed the delete button. "Every photo is going away, right now."

"Glad you're on my side. And Gina's," she added, opening the apartment door. "Better get out on the porch. He's on his way over, and judging from his stride, he's . . . pissed."

Chapter Seven

Detective DuPree was surprisingly nonhostile, thanking Charlie for his efforts, but he was clearly not happy about being the last one invited to the scene. Nancy had taken off, wanting to visit Gina at the hospital before her next shift. Charlie had stayed behind, standing in the open doorway as the detective wandered from room to room, examining everything without comment.

After about five minutes, the bulky-but-fit detective returned to the living room and accepted a can of Mountain Dew from the uniformed officer who'd accompanied him to the scene. Sipping the cold drink, DuPree made a call to the station, summoning a mobile crime lab while the officer began to photograph the interior of the apartment.

"You still here, Henry?" DuPree said, looking over finally.

"Yes, sir. I was wondering if you'd found Baza's vehicle yet? If it wasn't at the shooting scene because he took the Rail Runner . . ."

"Then it should be here, yeah. Officer Chavez, go see if the apartment management has a record of Baza's vehicle. That's usually entered in their rental paperwork. The name he used, is . . ."

"Doug Tyler," Chavez added, nodding. "Got it, Detective."

Chavez left, nodding to Charlie as he went outside.

"Now you gonna tell me you've already found Baza's vehicle, smart-ass?" DuPree said.

"No, I'm no detective. Just a client who asked for a favor from his lawyer friend and got her shot. I have some intelligence-gathering training and skills I put to use. Anything I can do to help you catch the shooter, I'm there."

"I read your file, Henry. War hero, commendations, special ops in Iraq, then Afghanistan. Same with Sweeney, your business partner. Just don't go mercenary on me—we're stateside now."

"I prefer to work within the system, Detective, and I don't give a shit about Baza. But Gina Sinclair is my friend. If you shut me out, I'll go my own way and maybe get there first. I can help you out, unofficially, or leave you in the dark. Your call."

DuPree was about to explode, judging from the color shift on his face. Then his expression cooled. "Thanks for your help, Mr. Henry, but we've got it from here. Once I make an arrest, I'll personally call and let you know. Go back to your pawnshop and trust in the system."

Charlie knew he'd been kissed off, but at least it had been polite. He didn't give a crap about words, it was deeds that counted, so it was clear he'd want to stay out of DuPree's sight wherever possible. He and Gordon were still pretty much on their own, and the only thing he had to worry about was keeping Nancy out of trouble with the department.

"Okay, I'm going. By the way, if I were Baza—who was ostensibly living under the radar—I wouldn't have driven the car listed on that rental contract. I'd have something else, parked out of sight of that office window, that I could get to in a hurry. Just a thought." He walked out, closing the door before DuPree could reply.

He didn't plan on going far. He'd left his binoculars in the rental car so he could watch the place and see what, if anything, the cops found. Chances were, Baza's vehicle would be a low-profile, older-model car with a big trunk to hide stuff from view.

Charlie drove out of the complex, found a Burger King a block down and bought a carton of milk, a Double Whopper, and fries. He drove back, parking along the street south of the complex, where he had a good stakeout view of apartment 108 while he ate lunch.

Within a few minutes, Patrol Officer Chavez walked to his patrol unit, then started cruising through the complex, looking at the vehicles, stopping once to check out a white Ford Focus. For a few minutes he was out of Charlie's sight, circling around the other side of a building, but he quickly returned, parking next to apartment 108. Detective DuPree came out, motioned to the big black-and-white mobile crime lab vehicle entering the parking area, and then spoke to Chavez briefly.

Clearly, the vehicle, perhaps a white Focus, wasn't on the grounds of the complex. It was a small car, impractical for Baza. Charlie suspected it didn't exist except on paper.

The patrol officer walked back toward the office.

Charlie suspected that the officers were now going to have to rule out the parked vehicles, checking against an office list. It might take hours, with most of the residents at work. If they didn't find Baza's vehicle soon, the search would take on a new level of complexity.

Charlie finished his fries and watched the crime techs as they hauled out the suitcases and a few cardboard storage boxes, which likely contained the guns, papers, and electronics. Those with memory cards would be examined for names, addresses, and messages.

Bored, Charlie glanced around the neighborhood, wondering if Baza had parked elsewhere, but close by. Immediately he spotted a gold Mustang pulled up beside a van parked at the curb. From his angle, Charlie couldn't see the driver, but the guy was talking to the person behind the wheel of the van. *Eddie!* Charlie thought immediately. He looked for the Mustang's plate and saw a registration sticker taped to the rear windshield, and one of those parking stickers. This one had a big P in the center, maybe the Premier Apartments? That's where Eddie lived, supposedly.

The Mustang pulled away before Charlie could read the letters and numbers on the windshield. He reached down to turn on the ignition, planning to follow. Then he realized that the guy in the van was watching the police with binoculars—

like him. Flipping a mental coin, Charlie decided to stay put. Better to find out what this guy was after right now. Besides, if it was Eddie, and he realized he was being followed, the Mustang would leave the rental Chevy in the dust.

The vehicle was about fifty meters ahead, parked on the same side of the street as he was. Charlie's heart started beating just a little faster as he wrote down the license plate sequence of letters and numbers. *Who was this person, and why was he watching Baza's place? Was he working for Eddie?*

The guy in the van could also be Baza's killer, unless Eddie had done the job himself. But why stake out the place now and not yesterday, or last night? If they knew Baza lived there, why wait until after the cops had found it?

The only answer Charlie could think of at the moment was that Eddie and the guy in the van *hadn't* known where Baza lived. They'd followed DuPree—hoping he'd find Baza's apartment for them.

If the crime scene techs or DuPree uncovered what Eddie or the guy in the van were after, though, it would be out of the bad guys' reach pretty soon. The question was puzzling, and Charlie wasn't used to all these options. In his special-ops unit, his job had been simple. Find someone who might have useful information—hopefully an insurgent, then haul him in for interrogation. And, stay alive while doing that.

"Call Nancy," he spoke to his phone.

"What's going on, Charlie?" was the first thing she said. "You still at Baza's place?"

"I'm watching the officers clean out the apartment and

search for Baza's vehicle. Guess what? I just discovered I'm not the only one interested. I think I just saw Eddie Henderson, at least based on the gold Mustang and a parking sticker. And he just had a conversation with someone in a van who's watching Baza's apartment with binoculars."

"You sure it was Eddie Henderson in the 'stang?"

"The vehicle and parking sticker fit, but I didn't get a look at the driver or read the registration sticker on his rear window before he took off. Sorry."

"Okay, then what about the guy in the van? Who else besides us wants to find out where Baza lives and what he was up to? Eddie? His killer?"

"I was wondering the same thing. I can't make out any details on the person in the van; he or she is wearing a hoodie. I also can't confirm there's only one individual—the headrest hides the passenger side from my position. The van is a dirty blue Chevy with a bad paint job, not sure of the exact model. It's got side windows, though, and they're tinted. Again, I can't confirm if the guy is alone. The tag is yellow, New Mexico, ALT-753."

"Hang on, and I'll go to my cruiser and run it on my MDT—mobile data terminal. I'm in the kitchen right now. Call you back in a few."

"Copy," Charlie answered, setting the phone on his thigh and holding the binoculars with both hands again. The angle right now didn't give him more than the back of the driver's head, but it also kept him from being easily seen. He was in a deep shadow beneath the thick branches of a mulberry tree just beyond the sidewalk.

A minute later, he felt the phone vibrate. It was Nancy.

"Unless the vehicle is a white Toyota Corolla, the tag is stolen," Nancy said. "Which gives me a reason to speak to the driver and search the vehicle. Stay out of sight and keep watch. Let me know if anyone leaves the vehicle or it drives off. I'll be there with backup in ten minutes. And don't approach the van, Charlie. This guy could be the shooter."

"That's why I stuck around. But if the van leaves, I'm following."

"That would be your decision, of course. Just don't provoke a confrontation, and stay in your car. By the way, what car are you in now? Not something flashy, I hope."

Charlie described the Chevy, which could go unnoticed in a two-car garage, then ended the call. He hoped DuPree and the crime-scene people wouldn't leave before Nancy and her backup arrived. Otherwise, he might end up having to tail the van.

The minutes passed slowly, but the guy in the van kept watch on the police activity, only putting down his binoculars from time to time to look around for anyone who might be watching him. So far, he hadn't given Charlie's car a second glance.

Tenants who were coming home from work were also curious about the police, and several were standing around the big black-and-white van, watching. Officer Chavez stood outside the apartment, keeping the onlookers at a distance. So far, it didn't appear that Baza's car had been found, and no officers were checking vehicles at the moment. Perhaps DuPree was no longer convinced it was in the area.

Nancy called again. "I'm a block away. I have backup in another unit, and we will approach the van from east and west simultaneously. Stay in your car and out of the line of fire—just in case."

"I will," Charlie lied. "Be careful."

Up the street, a red-and-blue-on-white patrol car came around the corner in the oncoming lane. In his rearview mirror, Charlie saw a second patrol cruiser closing in, Nancy at the wheel.

The second Nancy passed, Charlie slipped out the passenger side of the Chevy and up onto the sidewalk. A line of mulberry trees were to his right along the well-manicured grass of a residential yard. If there was trouble, these trunks were his closest cover.

The two cops coordinated their movements, and as the units reached the van, they swerved and screeched to a halt, pinning the van to the curb.

Charlie sprinted toward the rear of the van, Beretta in hand, realizing there was a blind spot the officers couldn't cover. Immediately he heard gunshots, but he kept his eyes on the curb side of the van. Less than twenty meters away now, he swerved onto the grass and stopped behind a tree trunk, his pistol up and ready.

More shots erupted, and he noticed Nancy inching around the rear end of her cruiser, handgun out. She glanced toward the rear of the van, where there were doors, and saw him. She nodded, held up two fingers, then turn her head back to the van.

"Give up, you two, or you're going down!" she yelled, confirming the count. "You're surrounded and outgunned, with more officers on the way. Set your weapons down and put your hands out the window so we can see them."

A few seconds went by, then a voice came from the van. "We give up. Don't shoot!"

It was a trick. Immediately someone fired two more shots. At the same time, the passenger door opened and a man jumped out, firing a pump shotgun blind over the van's hood toward the cop in front. The van driver wearing the hoodie followed, holding a pistol, and he crouched, looking toward the back of the van, waiting for Nancy to come around from behind.

Instead, he saw Charlie. He paused for a second, then took aim. The hesitation was fatal. Charlie fired twice at the center body mass, and the man fell forward onto the sidewalk.

"Fuck you!" the guy with the shotgun screamed, swinging his weapon around and pulling the trigger. Charlie knew to fire and move, however, and was already diving to the grass as buckshot ripped away tree bark from where he'd been two seconds earlier.

"Get up, Weed!" the man with the shotgun shouted to the downed man, pumping another round into the chamber. He crouched down now, the door to his back. He fired another load of buckshot at Charlie, the BBs going high over his head. Charlie held fire, trying to get a sight line on the guy's leg. He wanted to take the guy alive, just as he'd done in Iraq and Afghanistan.

By then, Nancy had reached the back of the van. She took a quick look, ducking back just as the remaining perp swung around the shotgun barrel, blowing away the van's taillight and shredding a handful of sheet metal.

When the guy raised up to blast away at Nancy, Charlie squeezed off a shot, striking him in the thigh. The guy flinched, but hung on to his weapon and didn't go down. Maybe he was high on something.

The guy screamed like a banshee, raised up, and fired at Charlie, missing by a mile.

Nancy reached around and fired two shots into the man just as he was feeding another round into the chamber. The shooter sagged back this time, bumping his head on the door. The shotgun clanked to the sidewalk and the guy slumped over, head on his chest.

"Edwards, you hit?" Nancy yelled, coming around the back end of the van, her weapon aimed at the downed shooters.

"No, ma'am. Window glass cut me up. I'm okay," the second officer called from the other side.

Charlie stood and walked forward quickly, his pistol aimed at the rear doors of the van. "Anyone else inside?" he yelled.

Nancy turned, then stepped over the body of the pistol-wielding perp and took a quick glance into the rear of the van via the passenger door. "Clear!"

Charlie placed his weapon back into the holster and continued toward the van, his eyes on the downed men and the growing pools of blood on the sidewalk.

Shouts came from across the street, and he could see officers from DuPree's scene running in their direction. "More backup!" Charlie said to Nancy, who was staring at the bodies. From her expression, this was probably her first shooting—and future nightmare.

"Huh? Oh, yeah." She stepped around the van. "We're clear here," she yelled. "Bring over the van and call 911. We have a wounded officer and two shooters down."

Charlie remained on the lawn as he approached the scene. He now had the angle to see Nancy's patrol-officer backup, a short, slender kid who couldn't have weighed more than 140 pounds. He was leaning against the hood of his car, a handkerchief soaking up blood from his right forehead and cheek. Shattered glass cubes from the driver's-side door of his unit revealed the source of the cuts. At least the officer had stood behind the door and kept his head down. Another few inches to the right and the shotgun pellets would have done a lot more damage to the officer's face.

Nancy got a radio call just then and turned away, so Charlie walked around to see what he could do for Officer Edwards.

"I'm Charlie Henry, Officer Edwards. Sergeant Medina is a friend of mine. How you doing? Any glass splatter get in your eyes?"

"Don't think so, my glasses protected me. Just blood and sweat bugging me right now. What does it look like to you? Think I can wipe it away before it gets on my uniform?"

"Bad idea, you don't want to scratch yourself with glass.

Best bet is to leave it alone and let the EMTs irrigate everything with water and saline when they get here."

Charlie recognized a loud voice yelling his name and turned to greet Detective DuPree. Charlie knew he'd be unarmed again before he left the scene, but hopefully this time he wouldn't have to spend the rest of the day at the police station.

Chapter Eight

"So, other than the firefight, how was your day?" Gordon said, greeting Charlie when he let himself in through the back door of the pawnshop. It was already six in the evening.

Charlie just shook his head. "If you bought us dinner, we can catch up."

"How about a bucket of chicken and some potato salad? The chicken's probably a little cold, but the salad tastes better that way anyway. We can eat in the office," Gordon added, motioning with his hand toward the interior of the shop. They were closed for the evening and had the place to themselves.

"Sounds good. So you hired Jake Salazar? Of course that means we'll both be taking a cut in pay."

"Yeah, but it looks like we should probably be working together on running down Gina's attacker anyway. Last two times you were out alone you cut it pretty close." They walked into the office and Gordon reached into the small refrigerator, and brought out the container of potato salad. "Wanna grab the beers?"

Charlie took the bottles, and they sat down at their respective desks, which were pushed together facing each other.

"Yeah. Speaking of Gina, how's she doing?" Charlie said, reaching for the church key he always kept in his desk drawer.

"Nancy called and said Gina was already complaining about the food. That's a good sign," Gordon said, handing Charlie a paper plate and a sealed package of a napkin and plastic fork. The bucket was in the middle of the two desks.

"Sure is. She's one tough little woman," Charlie said.

"You and Gina went to high school together up in Shiprock, right?"

"Yeah. Her dad and mom were teachers, and the three of them drove in from off the Rez every morning." Charlie thought about it for a while. Gina had been the only Anglo cheerleader at SHS and very popular. They had some classes together, and finally he'd gotten the courage to ask her out. Surprisingly, Gina'd said yes. They went around together for months, then at their senior homecoming dance, they broke up. It had been awkward for months after that, but finally, by senior prom, they went together—as friends. He hadn't seen her since, until earlier this year when he'd attended the funeral of her father. They rediscovered their friendship, and up until now, they'd spoken at least once or twice a week.

"Reminiscing, bro?" Gordo asked.

"High school seems like decades ago."

"It was, actually. But both you and Gina made it out just fine. Must have been that small-town air."

Charlie knew that Gordon had grown up in an area in Denver that, by all accounts, had been an urban hell for the guy—and not just because Gordo had a crappy family. Charlie felt almost guilty at times talking about his boyhood days. Gordon, in contrast, played things close to his chest and never let his demons out for anyone to see.

Gordo took a long swallow of beer. "Coming on back to reality, catch me up to speed on today. Besides the Eddie cameo, what about the guys in the van? Was one of them the shooter? Are we done?"

Charlie shrugged. "I have my doubts. According to what Nancy was able to tell me—we spoke on the phone after I left the station—both of them had legitimate alibis for the time of Gina's shooting. They both work, worked, at a tire store in the south valley. Their boss said they were on site from 7:30 AM till 4:00 PM, and had lunch at the shop."

"How solid is that?"

Charlie shrugged. "DuPree is going to get surveillance feed for the shop owner. The video is time stamped. We know how long they'd have to be gone—plus travel time."

"No chance to question them, I guess. Both of them bought it, right?"

"Yeah, I saw the dead check. I was hoping to take the passenger alive, but he was either high or he just freaked out. He was spraying shotgun pellets everywhere. I can't fault Nancy for taking him down. As for the other guy—it was him or me."

"Gotcha. Any idea how they fit in to all this, and to Baza? They were watching his place, right?"

"Yeah, and I think maybe it was our not-friend Eddie who put them up to it," Charlie said. "Unfortunately, I didn't get a visual to verify the ID. Nancy's had officers stop by the Premier Apartments, but no Eddie so far. She's not completely convinced he's involved, either. She says there are probably a hundred or more gold Mustangs around the metro area."

"But *you* think it was Eddie?" Gordon said, looking up from his pizza.

"I do. There was that parking sticker—along with the fact that this was Baza-connected. Or maybe she's right and I'm jumping to conclusions. The Mustang had one of those taped-on dealer registration things on the back window, and Eddie's car should have had a plate by now."

"Not if he was trying to cover his tracks since the other day. Anything else on the dead guys?" Gordon asked.

"Yeah. Both had east-side ZanoPak gang ties and Z tats on their knuckles. That stands for Manzano Park, Nancy said, which is in the center of their turf. They had records— arrests for burglary, assault, and a bunch of related charges. My guess is they were working for the shooter, trying, like us, to find out where Baza had been staying."

"So, how'd they find the place? You think they followed you or Detective DuPree to the apartment?"

"If they'd followed me to the apartments they would have picked up on my white Chevy. I'm guessing it was DuPree they tailed."

"What about that plumber's van last night? Any news on who and what that was all about? Eddie again?"

Charlie shrugged. "I called the officer who left me his card, and he said the plumbing company had reported the van stolen from in front of their shop—but that they didn't notice and report it missing until this morning. It's still out there somewhere, apparently."

"So we'll have to wait on Nancy and APD for any connecting leads on the dead guys from the van? Or Eddie Henderson?"

"Yeah," Charlie replied, dishing himself out a big glob of potato salad. "The gang unit is going to touch base with Detective DuPree to see if there's any way they can connect Baza or Eddie to gang activity," he added.

"My understanding is that gangs are pretty territorial, at least for small, local gangs. What are these guys doing messing with someone like Baza, what, ten miles from their 'hood?"

Charlie reached into his pocket and brought out a piece of paper with two names on it. "Who knows? Let's see if either of these guys ever did business with Three Balls. And speaking of business, what about Mr. Salazar?"

"It's just Jake. He's a bit of a surprise. I had him pictured as some mellow old grandpa who sat around watching TV or raising vegetables in the garden, but Jake is in his early sixties, fit and healthy. He could probably take you in the ring."

"Boxing?"

"Naw, he was a professional wrestler twenty years ago, and he still works out and runs five miles a week—or so he says. His ears look like they've been twisted around two or three times, and his nose has been broken more than once. Even better news, he knows the shop like the back of his hand and says he can straighten out the paperwork in a week. We can leave him here alone anytime, nobody is going to give him any crap."

"Can we trust him?"

"He gave me Father Mondragon as a reference. Father Dragon, they call him, lives at the rectory of the Catholic church in Alameda. He's the head priest, or whatever you call it. I called him up after Jake left and the priest said he'd back Jake a hundred percent."

"So when is—Jake—coming in?"

"Tomorrow at 7:30. He also told me he prefers to have lunch delivered, eating here in the store like we do, then taking off an hour early. According to him, the shop used to get a lot of local clients who stopped in during their own lunches. That meshes with what we've also noticed. If we decide to add more part-time help, Jake has a nephew who knows computers and business software and is going to night school."

"What did Jake think of Baza?"

"I didn't press him on that, thinking if he got the job he'd open up and we'd get more out of him in time," Gordon said, reaching for another chicken leg.

"Yeah, but . . ."

"I showed Jake that photo you sent over today, and Jake ID'd the woman as Ruth Adams, his coworker here. Jake said that Baza had a crush on her. Said she played it cool, not really pushing him away, just behaving professionally, like anyone should toward their boss. Friendly, cooperative, respectful, but careful to not get personal. She never flirted back—just smiled, Jake said."

"Hmmm. In control, or being careful. Private, Melissa at the laundry said. Anything else about the woman?"

"Jake said she was quiet, and had a kid, he thought, a young boy. She only spoke about the boy once or twice, when she had to miss work or come in late. Ruth wasn't married, or at least she didn't wear a wedding ring. That's all I got," Gordon said.

"She was definitely on Baza's mind—hers was the only photo I saw over at his place. We need to track her down."

"Being rejected by someone you care about might make you fall apart and stop caring about your life—or your business," Gordon suggested.

"Naw, I'm guessing he never lost her. He kissed off the business to raise some quick cash, and clearly had plans to leave the country soon. He wasn't going alone, either, based upon his ticket searches for two adults and a child. We should pass this by Nancy and see if she can use APD resources to help us find Ruth Adams—and maybe her child."

Charlie brought out his cell phone, checked for the photos, then shook his head. "I forgot I sent them all here. Remind me to make a printout of her photo before we leave tonight."

"We'll print several. But tomorrow, I'm sticking close to you. What's the plan?"

"First let's see if Jake Salazar ever saw Eddie Henderson or heard of him. Then we'll hunt Eddie down and see how he reacts. I don't recall him having any gang tats, but this time, keep that in mind. We know that he lied his way out of here last night, and there's that gold Mustang I saw today."

"I like Jake already," Charlie said, looking over at his pal and partner. Gordon was driving—it was his pickup.

"He's going to be real asset. Already checking the shop records for Eddie and those two gangsters."

Gordon nodded, then reached over and called up the address he'd entered for Eddie Henderson on his GPS. "What do you know about the West Mesa?"

"Well, most of the east side close to the mountains is called the Heights, and the Valley is in the middle. What's left but Westside?"

"Okay, clearly you don't know squat about Albuquerque."

"We've only lived here for five months. Actually, I remember reading something in the paper not long ago about an outbreak of burglaries in some West Mesa neighborhoods. So, if Eddie still lives there, and he's a burglar . . ."

"Well, it'll take us fifteen, twenty minutes, so crank up your Droid and kick back to some tunes."

"Better than that, I'll call Jake and see how things are going this morning at Three Balls," Charlie said.

Two minutes later, Charlie put away the phone. "Jake says he's already had a dozen people stop in, five for pawn, two to pay on their loans, and three who bought jewelry or electronics. And Roger sent over a crew from the Old Desert Inn and they picked up the safe. Five hundred cash, though Jake says they tried to talk him down to $450. Sounds like we have a winner with our new old guy."

"Well, that's good to know, since I'm still getting a feel for pawn pricing and I'm always having to check the price guides and bring out the pocket calculator. Jake has experience, and I noticed this morning how carefully he looks over a pawn for quality before making an offer. I guess I'm not picky enough."

"Hey, we've spent nearly the last decade in villages where anything that works at all is priceless. That's over and done with, bro," Charlie said. One thing he knew for sure, unlike some old Vietnam vets, he'd never go back to where he'd served.

Ten minutes later, as they approached the street where Henderson's apartment was supposed to be, Charlie checked for his pistol. He patted his pocket, then remembered this new weapon—new to him at least—had no spare magazine, though at least it had been sold with a well-fitted holster. It was a Beretta 84 .380, smaller caliber than he was comfortable with, but at least it was light and carried fourteen rounds—one in the chamber. Nancy said he should get his first 9 mm back in a few days, though the one from yesterday, which had taken down his attacker, might be in evidence for months.

"Check out the boyz standing around the black Acura on your right, Charles," Gordon said, slowing down.

The whomp/boom of earthshaking speakers announced

the presence of rap fans. Thankfully, unless you were close, the litany of obscenities and trash talk was impossible to follow due to the bass. Charlie didn't mind rap, though—it was his second-most-favorite music. Well, everything else tied for first.

"Beats a mortar attack," Gordon said.

"These aren't teenagers, bro," Charlie noticed, nodding to those watching them pass. "And I see a lot of tats and clothes I associate with gangs."

"Shouldn't stereotype, remember? Or is it profile?"

"You're right. Just keep in mind they probably have weapons within arm's reach. We're outnumbered and my body armor is at the laundry."

The GPS lady spoke. "You have reached your destination."

Gordon stopped the truck in the street, then nodded toward the bronze sign above the main entrance of the apartment building. "Premier Apartments. Here we are."

"Don't see any gold Mustangs," Charlie said, looking around the lot, "but the vehicles here have the same parking sticker I saw on the car I thought belonged to Eddie."

Gordon nodded. "The one with the driver talking to the gangsters in the van? Well, maybe Eddie's at work."

"Yeah. Or he moved on. According to Nancy, the officers who came by spoke to the manager, a new employee who couldn't recall Eddie or find him on the list of residents. Let me check anyway, and see if we can at least get a lead," Charlie said. "Pull into the lot."

As Charlie got out of the pickup, he noticed six young men strolling toward them with their badass walks. "Wanna come back later?" he asked Gordon, who was checking out the approaching gangbangers in the side mirrors.

Gordon reached under the seat and brought out the two-foot-long sawed-off baseball bat he kept within reach, then thumped it against the palm of his hand. "Naw, go on in and check. We're good, and I'm still batting a thousand."

They got out of the truck together.

Charlie ignored the crushed beer can that whizzed past his head as he walked away from the pickup. There was a thud, two grunts, then a curse. Hopefully, the punks weren't going to get hurt too badly.

Here in the US, Gordon might end up in jail for what was likely to happen. He was small, so men of all ages usually thought they could take him. Unfortunately for them, Gordon wasn't only the better fighter, he thrived on the exercise.

Charlie walked to the lobby door, entered a small foyer smelling of cigarette smoke and Pine-Sol. There were mailboxes along the wall to his left, and on the right, a large, pastel watercolor of the Sandia Mountains. Ahead, also on the right, was a door labeled "Manager." There was a small window in the center and as he approached, Charlie saw a red-haired woman sitting at a desk inside. He knocked lightly as he stepped into the office.

"Hi there, I'm Ruby, the assistant manager. How may I help you, sir?" The woman, in her early twenties with a generous bust in a V-necked green sweater, placed her cell phone on the desk and stood to face him. Her voice was low and sexy, and she was attractive enough, even with too much makeup and scary fire-engine-red hair. The diamond in the nose, though, was a turnoff, at least to a guy who wasn't into face jewelry. Not that it was going to be an issue. He hadn't had much luck with women lately anyway.

"Hello, Ruby. I'm Charlie, and I'm looking for a guy I met a couple of months ago at Sliders—that bar on North Fourth. Eddie, Eddie Henderson, I think, was his last name. Blond hair, longer than mine, broad face, but slender. Had blue eyes. He was thinking about having the interior of his gold Mustang redone, and I was supposed to call him, but I lost his number. I was passing by, then remembered him saying something about living at the Premier Apartments. Could you tell me what apartment is his? Or maybe I could just leave a note in his mailbox with my number."

Charlie brought out his business card, but kept his thumb over the Three Balls name.

Ruby didn't seem to notice. "Sounds like our Eddie. Unfortunately he's moved on. Came into some money and left about four months ago. No forwarding address. He did some business with some of the guys around here—I never asked what—so maybe one of them knows how to reach him. I remember he said something about wanting to find a place with better WiFi."

"Guys? Like the crew with matching tats hanging outside?"

"Hey, don't disrespect my friends. Word gets around and you're gonna get a beat down."

"Sorry, don't want to get on the bad side of a gang. What kind of business did you say they have with Eddie?"

"I didn't say, and I don't want to know. Are we done here, Charlie?" Ruby said, crossing her arms over her chest, which had the opposite effect of intimidation, if that was her goal.

Still, it was clearly time to leave. "Well, thanks for your time, anyway. Gotta go. Bye."

She'd already turned her attention back to her cell phone by the time he reached the door.

Charlie walked out to the parking lot. Gordon was leaning against the side of his pickup, cracking open roasted piñon nuts with his teeth, spitting out the hulls. The parking lot was empty.

"Where's our fan club?"

"They remembered a previous appointment." Gordon pointed with his chin toward a splatter of blood on the pavement. It was now starting to cake in the noonday sun. "Watch your step."

"The assistant manager was there, and, unlike her boss, she remembers Eddie. Four months ago he moved out, no forwarding address. Lady said he'd come into some money and was looking for place with better WiFi."

Gordon blinked. "Four months? That's after Baza started to let his business go to hell, but before the bank closed him down."

"So it's possible Eddie *had* come into the shop and interacted with Baza. Also, the assistant manager said Eddie had dealing with the gang members out here."

"Dealings? Like drugs, break-ins, car thefts, guns?"

"She said she not only didn't know—she didn't want to know."

"That's interesting. Maybe Eddie was selling guns for Baza—to the gangs. That would explain why there were no guns in the shop when we took over. And what if Baza screwed him on a deal?" Gordon offered. "Guess that *was* Eddie yesterday, talking to the shooters in that van."

"Looks like. But there's gotta be more to it than just getting even. We've got to find Eddie. If he really came into money, you think he still operates a forklift at GA Foods? Maybe I should give them a call before we go over. The warehouse is close to Central Avenue, a half hour from here this time of day," Charlie added.

"Do it. I'm hungry for a combo dish at El Pinto and a cold Dos Equis. If I recall, it's on the way."

"'On the way' if you make a ten-mile diversion north."

"Work with me, Chuck."

They'd gone a mile, still winding through the eighties-era housing developments full of culs-de-sac and dead ends, when Charlie put away his phone. "Edward Henderson never worked there, and there's no Tim Gallegos. But Eddie got enough attention to be remembered, including his description, which fits our guy. Eddie came by the warehouse a few months ago asking about one of their two women employees, a lady named Ruth. He got real upset when they wouldn't let him speak to her. They had to call a security guard to walk him off the property."

"That it?" Gordon asked.

"There's more. Eddie came back later at the change of shift and confronted two women in the parking lot. According to the guy I just spoke to, Eddie was pissed that neither of them were the Ruth he was looking for. He split when the women started yelling for the security guard."

"Is that all?"

"That night, one of the vehicles in the employee parking lot got its windshield smashed."

"The security guard who'd manhandled Eddie?" Gordon said.

"Exactly, but the outside cameras weren't able to ID the vandal. Wonder if he was looking for the same Ruth who worked for Baza?"

"Yeah, who else? Too much of a coincidence," Gordon replied. "Her name keeps coming up. I wonder how Ruth figures into all this?" he added.

"When we finally get a look at these personnel files, maybe we can get an address on her, or at least a lead. Let's check into this—after lunch. For now, punch in the address of El Pinto on the GPS and get us out of this suburban maze."

Another minute went by, then Charlie spoke again. "What happened to your sense of direction, Gordo? You can't miss the mountains. That's east. We need to go that way, bro." He pointed toward the Sandia Mountains.

Gordon grinned. "I've been dicking around, hoping those two cars following us will finally catch up."

Charlie glanced into the side mirror and saw the cars

that had been outside Eddie's former crib. "Find a dead-end street. I'm pissed off anyway. Gina's in the hospital, my Charger's on life support, and I had to shoot a guy I don't even know. I could use a good hand-to-face workout to take off the edge."

"I was hoping you'd say that. But please don't let them goad you into a firefight, Charles. We're running low on guns back at the shop. And let's not get arrested, okay? We could lose our pawnbroker's license."

Gordon drove around the neighborhood, pretending to be lost, until he found a dead-end street. He turned down the narrow road, almost an alley, that led to a drainage canal on the flood-prone West Mesa. He stopped about fifty feet from two posts blocking the road, which tapered down steeply into a concrete-lined drainage channel.

Both late-model import sedans, one the black Acura they'd seen before, the other a gold Subaru, closed in, blocking their exit. The bump-bump of heavy bass from their massive speakers shook the ground.

Gordon looked over at Charlie. "They've got us trapped, the poor bastards."

The rap tunes suddenly went silent.

Charlie and Gordon climbed out of the pickup at the same time and walked back toward the tailgate just as four, five, then a total of seven young men in their late teens to early twenties piled out of the two vehicles.

"Mommy!" a girl probably no more than five yelled from her plastic playhouse on the lawn of a nearby house. She stood there, pointing toward the cars for about five seconds. A heavy-set young woman opened a patio door, ran out and took her daughter inside, never taking a cell phone away from her ear. Charlie knew she'd be calling the cops next.

"No guns, knives, or shit like that," Charlie yelled to the advancing gangbangers, stopping at the tailgate and pulling out his pistol, setting it in the bed of the truck. "No innocent civilians get hurt today. Just you and your crew."

"Fuck that. And what is this civilian crap, Indian? You ain't no cops, and if you're military, no wonder we've been fighting a war for ten years. You gotta be major stoopid, fucking with Eddie then wanting to throw blows with my crew. Your friend got lucky before, but now you're gonna pay, both of you."

The young man with bleached-blond hair wasn't much taller than Gordon. He turned his back on them and said something to the others.

At least a dozen pistols, knives, and toys of violence were placed on the hoods of their cars.

"Looks like Baza and Eddie sold them all kinds of fire-power. Cocky bunch, laying all that aside to try and take us on up close. Look who's stoopid," Gordon said to Charlie. "At least now you get to hand out some payback to these guys bad-mouthing Indians," Gordon said, placing his own pistol on the truck bed.

"And you're part of the tribe, Gordo." He turned to the seven guys standing there, fists clenched. "Last man standing," he said, loud enough for them all to hear. "Then we're out of here before the law arrives."

"Whatever, asshole. Bring it on."

Charlie walked just a few steps ahead of Gordon as they approached, knowing his partner would be the first target. One of the gangsters in front of the pack had a nasty welt on his forehead, and he hadn't taken his eyes off Gordon since stepping out of his car.

"They'll go for you first, en masse, not Chuck Norris 'take turns' style."

Gordon nodded. "I'll probably get at least four. We going back-to-back with a sweep?"

"Just like last time," Charlie said, noting the group, each one with a black-dog tat on their right forearm, was closing in and spreading out. "Custer's Last Stand," he added in a whisper.

"Except we're the Indians," Gordon said, chuckling.

Charlie watched their eyes, anticipating a signal from their leader. Gordon would be doing the same.

They were about ten feet away when the bleached-blond leader, who'd been watching Gordon, looked at Charlie, then lunged, arm cocked, ready to punch. Charlie, having assumed a fighting stance, kicked up and across with his right foot. His heavy boot struck home, thumping the guy in the side of his knee. The man yelled, stumbling into the path of another attacker. Charlie, who was turning left, now had his right side to a third assailant, whose roundhouse caught air. Charlie countered with a right counterpunch aimed downward. He struck the onrushing man in the groin, which doubled him over.

Gordo had caught the closest attacker, who'd brushed past Charlie, with a rear, straight kick. He'd launched his left foot, turning right as he made contact with the gut of the attacker. His arms were up, blocking a jab from another guy who'd been forced to shift left to avoid the kick.

Gordon, also a student of Krav Maga, caught Charlie's reject in the face with a horizontal elbow strike. Blood flew from his attacker's mouth as he went down. Five attackers remained, but Charlie quickly sent another one onto his back with a shuffle front-leg kick to the chest.

That put Charlie out of position, and one of the remaining fighters came at Gordon's back. Gordon turned to look, at the same time spinning around, using his weight and power to catch the guy with the bottom of his closed fist, a backhand hammer blow.

The attacker partially blocked the strike with his forearm, but the power of the hit must have cracked a bone. The man twisted away, his arm frozen in place as he howled in pain.

Three gang members were left now. Instinctively, they backed off, side by side in a defensive position.

The guy on the left, almost as small as Gordon, reached into his back pocket and pulled out a switchblade, clicking it open. He waved it back and forth, clearly terrified. His friends sidestepped, giving him plenty of room.

"Take a step and I'm going to cut you both," he said, licking his lips. His voice was shaky.

Two of the guys on the ground, still grimacing in pain,

started to get up. Charlie brought out his own four-inch lock-back, flipping open the blade with a sweep of his wrist. "Stay down, boys, and I won't get any of your pal's blood on your slacks."

Gordon did a little loosening-up hop on his toes, then stretched out his arms, pretending to yawn. "I'll take away Shorty's knife," he said, then grinned. "Left mine in the truck."

The blond guy with the bad knee, the leader, struggled to stand, holding his damaged joint. "Enough. You guys know we mean business now. We can respect each other."

In the distance, Charlie could hear the sound of more than one siren. "So, where's Eddie? He owes us a call. We'll keep coming back 'til we connect with him."

"If you're looking for guns, forget it. I hear his source dried up. But he's hiring right now, and he pays well, so I'll tell him you're looking for him. Just leave us out of it. We're done with you." The man nodded to his crew, who began to hobble toward their cars.

Charlie wished he had more time to push for answers, but the sirens were getting louder. Involving the police wouldn't help right now and the gangsters would clam up anyway.

"He knows how to reach us," Charlie said. "Better clear out while you still can."

The guy nodded, then turned and limped away. "Get a move on, assholes," he yelled at the others, who were still collecting their weapons.

"Grab our stuff while I watch our backs," Charlie said.

"Don't trust these gentlemen?"

"Something like that. All they've done is make me even more interested in tracking down Eddie Henderson. I'm wondering just how much we screwed up letting him go. He's connected to Baza, who was probably supplying guns to at least one gang. That fits the 'source drying up' comment. Hell, we might have the answer. Baza stiffed Eddie—so Eddie took him out."

"Or these guys did it for him," Gordon added.

Chapter Nine

They pulled over to the side of the street three blocks later, giving plenty of room for the two police cruisers to race by, emergency lights and sirens going full blast.

"Suppose the lady who called in got the plate on my truck?" Gordon said, easing back out onto the street, then driving away just over the speed limit.

"Probably too worried about the gangbangers to give us a second glance," Charlie said. "One thing for sure, those hoods aren't going to rat us out."

"Yeah, it would make them look bad. Now, can we get lunch?" Gordon said, grinning.

"Yeah, El Pinto. On the way I'm going to call Nancy. Her shift doesn't start for a few hours, but maybe I can get more info on Eddie Henderson. He clearly has some gang connections."

"You going to tell her everything this time?"

"I might leave out the last ten minutes, but yeah, she needs to know what she's trying to dig into," Charlie said. "I'm also going to give her Ruth Adams's name, so she can link it to the photo we found in Baza's apartment."

They were almost to the restaurant, in the north valley neighborhood called Alameda, when Charlie finally ended the call. "That went well," he said.

"Yeah? How many times did she call you a dumb shit? I lost track after four."

"She knew she was on speaker, so one of those had to have been for you. Okay, so she thinks we should have handed Eddie over to APD first thing, I get that. But she saw the light when I said we'd hoped to get more from him by giving him a break."

"Yeah, and once she hears about that backstreet action with the gangsters in Eddie's old neighborhood, she'll know you're holding back. If we want her trust, maybe we should play straight with her."

"Yeah, but Nancy is a straight arrow—doesn't even go barhopping—and for a police sergeant, that's like . . . abnormal. If we report every one of our crimes she'll lose faith in our goodness."

"I see your point. I also see why she thinks we're dumb shits," Gordon said, making a right turn into the El Pinto parking lot.

"Enough deep philosophy for now. I hear a New Mexican combo plate calling," Charlie said, placing his pistol and extra magazine into the glove compartment, then taking Gordon's weapon from him and storing it too. "Hope we weren't followed," he added.

"I was watching. Unless the boys in the 'hood have a copter, they can't know where we are right now."

"How about Eddie? No sign of a gold Mustang?"

"I would have noticed when we crossed the bridge. Now let's eat," Gordon said, climbing out of the pickup. "At least Nancy can pass along the Ruth Adams ID to Detective Du-Pree. I'm guessing he hasn't picked up on that yet."

"I told Jake to call me if he hears from DuPree, or if any cops stop by."

As they walked up the flagstone path, Gordon pointed toward the outdoor patio to the east.

"Yeah. We can keep a better eye on the parking lot from there," Charlie said, reading his mind.

Jake was a handshaker, a good practice for a businessman. When Charlie walked in after lunch, his newest—make that his only employee—was sealing a loan with a new customer. Gordon had come in through the back and was headed for the storeroom. His plan was to read tags on pawn items and make new customer lists.

In particular, they were looking for names that might connect with recent events, including those two young men from the van who'd elected to fight to the death over god knows what.

Charlie stood back, listening and learning as Jake completed his transaction. He and Gordon had been counseled on good pawnbroker practices, and the most important one was to keep all transactions private. Many of their clients, especially those forced to hock personal items, were depressed already. It was bad business to advertise their situation across the room.

The client, a well-dressed woman in her fifties wearing sunglasses and a big hat, avoided eye contact on her hurried exit. Hoping to see if his guess was correct and she was selling jewelry, perhaps a ring, he walked over to Jake, who was behind the counter.

"Every time I see you, it's with a client. You're worth every dollar, Jake," he said.

"Of course I am, Mr. Henry. And you might want to remember that when it comes to Christmas-bonus time." He grinned widely, then crossed his arms across his barrel chest.

"It's Charlie. Mr. Henry is my dad. Since when does this shop give bonuses?" Charlie replied, also grinning.

"Since now?"

"Well, first of all, we have to get into the black by Christmas," Charlie replied. "By the way, was your last customer pawning some jewelry, a watch or ring? She was kinda antsy."

"Yeah, it's a man's watch—she said it belonged to her late husband. I'm putting it on the list today in case it's on somebody's hot sheet. The merchandise retails at around fifteen hundred bucks. We settled on a hundred now and a thirty-day loan. I offered her $350 to take it off her hands, and she turned it down."

"Doesn't that suggest it's not hot?"

"Yeah. A thief would have taken the $350 in a heartbeat. But I want it on record in case it's disputed estate property, maybe left to a surviving son, not the widow. She may not have wanted to barter."

"Hadn't thought of that. Good call, Jake."

"Okay, Charlie. What's really on your mind?" Jake asked. "Does it have anything to do with what's been going on? Gordon warned me about some gang problem. I know you were involved in that shooting where two punks were killed."

"I wanted to ask you to dig deeper into your old boss's behavior, habits, anything you know. All of this seems to be connected to him, even yesterday's shooting, and until we put it together we'll never get to the bottom of this."

"You and Gordon might be targets too, I'm thinking?"

"Just might be, and because you work here, some of that could rub off on you. Gordon already told you about the break-in by Eddie Henderson. There could be more problems, and you need to know."

"I'm former Marine. We know how to deal with problems. Thanks for being square with me, but I'm okay with this."

Charlie nodded.

"So what do you know about Baza? Was he dishonest with customers, vendors, people he did business with? Did you ever see him sell guns without the proper paperwork?"

"Not guns, not anything at all, for that matter—at least while I was working here. It was just like I told Gordon the other day. He did all the proper paperwork, paid Ruth and me on time, salary plus a commission on sales over two hundred, and he never shorted us on hours. He kept me on until the first notice came in about a missed lease payment. Then he said he no longer needed me, gave me two weeks pay, and said goodbye."

"Ruth was gone by then?"

"Several months before. One day she just didn't show up, and he said she wasn't working here anymore. I asked what happened, and he said that was Ruth's business."

"You have any idea what happened?"

"Up to that point, he'd been treating her quite well. He was happy, she seemed happy, and he flirted a lot."

"He hit on her?"

"No, just smiles, compliments, lots of conversation, looks, stuff like that. Never put his hand on her. I think maybe he was falling for her."

"She flirt back?"

Jake thought about it a moment. "She didn't encourage, or discourage, I guess. But she was reserved. Ruth was . . . mysterious, like she was keeping a big secret. She never talked about herself, her family, anything like that."

"Did you ever learn anything about her family, an ex-husband, brother, sister?"

"She had a son, she had to come in late a couple of times, and left early once or twice because of some problem with her kid. No ring, no husband talk, nothing about family. We respected that, Mr. Baza and I. Well, at least I did, I didn't eavesdrop on their conversations. I mind my own business."

"I respect that too, and I wouldn't be asking you this except that I think Ruth Adams may not have stepped out of Baza's life after she left his employment."

"What makes you think so?"

"I saw his apartment after he died and her photo was the only one there."

"Nice-looking lady," Jake said. "Classy. We got along well."

"You know where she lives?"

Jake shrugged. "I drove her home once when she had to take off early. Kid was throwing up, I recall."

"So he wasn't in school?"

"Too young. I got the idea he was four or so, still too young for kindergarten."

"You remember the address?" Charlie enlarged the photo to show more details of the building facade behind Ruth.

"Part of a small apartment building, maybe four to eight units. Think I could find it again. It's a couple of miles south-east of here."

"Okay. How about you driving by there when you leave for the day? Gordon or I will follow and see if we can track her down."

"I can do that."

Jake stood there, clearly something on his mind.

"What is it? More about Baza?"

"Yeah, it just occurred to me that this Ruth thing, for him, was kind of out of character."

"What do you mean?"

"He never hit on the customers, but before her, he was always out trolling for women. He preferred rich divorcées or widows. He even tried to hook me up on a double date or two. He'd meet them at one of the private golf courses, or a charity event, or wine tastings. Baza had a way with women, getting them to like him, and he used that to get them in the sack. The woman he was with before Ruth came along gave him a big white car, a Cadillac or a Lincoln Town Car."

"White?"

"How'd you know?"

"Cops can't seem to find it at the moment."

"So, Jake, what you're saying is that Baza was a gold digger?"

"Looking for cougars, my son-in-law would say. Use them and lose them. Baza joked about it until he saw it annoyed me."

"But when Ruth came along?"

"A complete turnaround, at least that's the way it came across. If she'd had a lot of money, I'd have thought it was the mother of all scams. But if she had money, it sure didn't show. She walked to work—didn't have a car."

A bell rang as the front door opened, and they both looked over as Nancy walked into the shop, wearing her dark blue APD uniform.

"All of a sudden I'm hoping to get arrested, but I guess this attractive officer must be here to see you," Jake said, then winked. "I'll get busy with the paperwork."

"Talk to you later," Charlie said. He turned and walked over to meet Nancy, having noted her somber expression immediately. "Gina?"

Nancy nodded. "She had a setback this morning when a

blood clot was discovered in her left lung. They had to insert a catheter into her vein but they got it out. She's back in the ICU for observation."

"When can we see her?"

"Probably sometime tomorrow after eight AM. I left word to call me in case there's any more complications, and if you want, I'll let you know."

"Please do."

"I lit a candle in the chapel, Charlie." She turned and looked him right in the eyes. "She's going to make it, I know it."

"Of course she is," Charlie said, trying to look positive. Nancy clearly needed the boost. In the service, he'd seen so many wounded or dying GIs, Marines, civilians, insurgents, that he'd developed a tendency to put the injured aside—at least emotionally—unless they were from his unit. His buddies, whether overseas or not, were family, however. Gina had been family long before that, and if she died, he didn't know how he'd handle it.

Nancy cleared her throat before speaking, and crossed her arms across her chest. "Officers got a call this morning about a short-lived melee that took place over in a Westside residential area. Neighbors say a big Indian and a little Anglo did a *Rush Hour* beat down on a local gang."

"Hmmm. I'm a *Lethal Weapon* fan, myself, fighting for the common good. Did anyone happen to get a license number on those thugs?"

"Hmmm back at you. No, just a vague description of a big

pickup. But guess what I managed to put together? This particular gang hangs out at Eddie Henderson's former address—the Premier Apartments. Coincidence, huh?"

"Of course. And on a related subject, has the department had any luck finding Eddie's new crib?"

"I wish. But I'm working on it, and now so is Detective DuPree. I told him about Eddie's visit here, though I sanitized his method of entry and the sequence of events. Skinny Eddie, as you described him, seems to have dropped out of sight. And we can't locate any Ruth Adams that fits the photo. Sorry for all the bad news."

"Well, I've got some good news in the Ruth Adams department, maybe," Charlie said. "I may have a lead, courtesy of our new employee, Jake Salazar, who worked here before, for several years. He may have an idea where Ruth lives, or at least used to live. When we close tonight, he's going to try to point out the place for me."

"I'll be on shift by then. Give me a call on my cell if you actually find this woman," Nancy replied.

"And here's another bit of news, for what it's worth. According to Jake, Baza was a womanizer, always looking for women with money who could show him a good time."

"Let me guess. Cougars who could buy him fancy clothes, take him to Vegas, shower him with gifts? The more I hear about the guy, the more enemies he might have made, me included." Nancy shook her head in disgust.

"Suppose one of these women he dumped along the way was pissed enough to have him put down?"

Nancy shrugged. "Could be. Unless he was involved with a gang and they decided to take him out for whatever reason, it looks more like a hate or revenge killing. He was shot down on the street by someone who was waiting for the opportunity."

"I agree. But how did the shooter know he was going to be there? The only people who know about that meeting were Gordon and me, Gina, and Baza."

"Gina mentioned it to me too, but that's as far as it went on our side. Baza was hiding out, of course, but maybe he told someone, a person he trusted. . . ." Nancy's voice trailed off.

"Like Ruth Adams? We've really got to track her down," Charlie said. "Another thing. A few months ago Eddie tried to contact a Ruth he thought was working at the GA warehouse. It was the wrong Ruth, apparently, but he left his mark after they ran him off, according to the people I spoke to over the phone."

"That's the same place Henderson said he worked?" Nancy asked.

"Yeah. The guy is good at blending truth with his lies. Adds details that make it seem legit," Charlie said.

"Sounds like someone I know," Nancy said, frowning.

Charlie shrugged.

"Well, see what you can do about following up on her residence, then give me a call. Whatever you do, don't let her give you the slip," Nancy said. "Stay in touch. And if you find her, remember that Detective DuPree also has to know."

"If I do, I'll let you tell DuPree. I don't think he likes me."

Nancy walked to the door, and Charlie noticed that Jake was admiring her backside too. Suddenly she stopped and turned.

"Sorry, I'm preoccupied," she said, unaware she was being checked out. "I just remembered something I thought you needed to know. It has to do with yesterday's incident," she said, glancing over at Jake, who was suddenly busy with paperwork again.

Charlie walked toward her, glancing around to make sure no customers had come into the shop while they were talking.

"Okay."

"The shotgun used by the passenger isn't in any records—it's a common model and thirty-plus years old. However, the handgun is last year's model, and was registered and sold to a local citizen at a local gunshop."

"But the citizen wasn't the gangbanger shot yesterday," Charlie guessed.

"No, but the original owner, who has no criminal record or gang affiliation, claims to have sold the handgun to a pawnshop to raise cash toward a fishing boat."

"Interesting. Let me make a wild guess—this pawnshop."

"Yeah, the guy still has the receipt. He sold it to Diego Baza months ago. That sale was never reported to APD, and the weapon was not registered to Baza or this shop. Those are disclosure violations that could have resulted in a fine or the pulling of the business licence and shutting the shop down."

"So, did Baza deal the pistol under the radar to that gang

member?" Charlie wondered. "According to what we heard today, Eddie was the go-between on at least some gun deals."

Nancy shrugged. "That's a question I think DuPree will be asking you before long. Better get your shit together, just in case."

"Jake's trying to straighten out the paperwork that Baza left behind. Baza deleted everything from his computers, at least for the last few months he was here, but if we get the software and files back, hopefully we can print out everything, and maybe even restore the original network."

"Yeah, Gina told me what you guys were going through here, one of the reasons she took on . . ."

". . . the job that got her shot, I know. But now we have one more nasty thing Baza was probably up to from behind these doors—selling weapons. Instead of answers, all we're getting is more questions."

"Well, I gotta go for sure this time," Nancy said, checking her watch. "Find Ruth Adams. Maybe she has some answers."

"What did they say about the Charger?" Gordon asked, taking his eye off Jake's big SUV, which was ahead of them in traffic, as Charlie put down his phone.

"It's going to be another week before they can replace the damaged components and finish up the bodywork. At least that's the story I'm getting." Charlie looked ahead, making sure he could still see Jake as he drove east.

"Maybe I should put the fear of Gordon . . . Hey, we've got company."

"Besides Jake in front?" Charlie glanced in the side mirror of Gordon's pickup. "The minivan two cars back?"

"No, the silver Mazda behind it. I remember seeing it parked down the street when we left the shop."

Charlie thought a second, looking ahead again at Jake's blue Excursion. "I don't want to lead anyone to this Ruth woman. Let me call Jake before he points out the apartment or something."

Fortunately, they had to stop at a red light, and Charlie got the man on his cell phone immediately. "Jake, this is Charlie. Somebody is following us, and I don't want to pass by Ruth's place. Turn away and go home, and we'll try to find out who our tail is. I'll tell you how this works out in the morning."

"Suppose it's a police detective?" Jake asked.

"Guess we'll find out. You watch your back."

"Count on it. Be careful, boss," Jake said, then the light changed and he ended the call.

"Get that?" Charlie said, watching as Jake took a right turn.

"Yeah. I'll go straight, then take the next left. Hope it doesn't go by her place."

"Think you can get on his tail?"

"Does a bear shit in the woods?"

"Not a polar bear in winter. But, okay. Just don't get us pulled over. Traffic is heavy this time of day, so Smokey will be on the prowl."

"Smokey the Bear? We back in the forest?"

"Smart-ass. 'Smokey' is seventies slang for a cop—John

Law, The Man, pigs, 5-O, like that. Don't you know any American television history?"

"Hey, I went to public school, watched *Beavis and Butthead,* and played video games. I'm lucky I can think at all."

"Says the man with a degree in sociology from CSU. Why couldn't you have gutted it out and earned an MBA before you enlisted?"

"If I'd become a suit, I would have never enlisted, and never met you, and never been shot at by more than one guy at a time, and . . . hey, you went to public school too," Gordon said, taking a quick left at the next light, barely missing an oncoming UPS truck. "Hang on!"

Gordon cut into the alley, circled quickly, then came up several cars behind the silver Mazda, which was still waiting at the light, turn signal on.

"How long you think he'll keep looking for us?" Gordon said.

"If he really wants to find us again, he'll circle, hoping we haven't gone far."

"If he's not working alone? Then we're still being followed, right?" Gordon said.

"Yeah, and if it's Gina's shooter, watch out for a drive-by."

"I know drive-bys. I grew up in Denver, bro, remember?"

"Yeah, and I grew up where beer was illegal. Didn't stop me. Just keep sharp."

"Okay, but what if all this is a coincidence and this guy wasn't following us?" Gordo asked.

After the light the street became four lanes, and Gordon

kept to the outside, trying to stay in the guy's blind side as they checked the car out. The Mazda was low to the ground, and up in the pickup they couldn't see the driver's face, just a shiny blue jacket and orange ball cap. But they could read the license plate number.

"I'm calling Nancy on this plate," Charlie said. He left a quick voice mail, then hung up. Two minutes later his phone rang.

"The plate is registered to a Javier Espinosa, and the vehicle is supposed to be a 1998 green Nova," Nancy said.

"Okay, it's on a silver Mazda right now. We'll hang back and keep it in sight as long as we can. We're heading north on Fourth Street, passing El Pueblo."

"Copy. Let me know what you learn, but no shooting, please," Nancy said.

"I hear you," Charlie said, then ended the call and looked over at Gordo.

"If he takes the next left, he's heading across the river. Maybe going home. On the west side," Gordon said.

"What the hell is going on? Gangs, guns, Baza, and Eddie Henderson," Charlie said, trying to make sense of it. In the army, they were always told what to do. Here, there were too many questions and too many choices to make. Or maybe he'd gotten lazy not really having to think for himself. That had to stop.

"But where does Ruth Adams fit into this? Is this one of Eddie's people looking for her? And why?" Gordon asked, watching the Mazda moving through traffic.

For this, Charlie at least had some possibilities. "Maybe she knows where Baza hid the money, guns, diamond ring, Rolex, drugs, counterfeit twenties, cookies, or the Maltese Falcon."

"You watched too much TV growing up, bro. And that's the Millennium Falcon. Whoa, here we go!"

Chapter Ten

The Mazda suddenly cut right across two lanes, barely missing a FedEx step van. It raced onto the grounds of a big Westside mall.

Gordon hit the brakes, made the corner with squealing tires, then raced up to a service road that circled the mall parking lots.

"Right," Charlie said, and Gordon took the turn.

"Where?"

"Ahead—north. I'll watch my side, you watch yours. All I know is that the left side was clear."

"Got him! He's in the Macy's parking lot," Gordon said. He had to stop, letting an oncoming car pass, then went left, driving down a parking lot lane toward the Mazda, which had pulled into a slot about fifty feet from the entrance of the big department store.

"Block him off," Charlie said, checking his handgun with a touch.

Charlie jumped out and raced over to the passenger side, looking in, his hand on the butt of his pistol. "Empty. Look around, he can't be far."

"There, blue jacket and orange cap, going inside," Gordon said, pointing toward the glass foyer at the store entrance seventy-five feet away. "He's about my size."

"Disable the Mazda, then park where you can keep watch," Charlie said.

Charlie jogged toward the entrance, reaching the heavy plate-glass doors just as two slender teenage girls came out. They were both on their cell phones and oblivious to the world.

They stood there a second, looked up and finally saw him, then giggled and scooted out of the way. "Sorry," one of them mumbled, then they both started laughing.

Charlie hurried through the foyer and opened the inside door. He looked around and saw the Mazda driver at the top of the escalator, stepping off and disappearing. Charlie was too late to get a look at the face, but the guy was wearing black slacks, not jeans, and black athletic shoes with orange laces.

He took the escalator like a stairway, two steps at a time, then stopped at the top. Scanning from right to left, he looked into a women's clothing department, then straight ahead. An orange Broncos cap was visible for just a second, then dropped out of sight.

Charlie hurried across the floor, dodging candy displays and a low counter with sweaters and tops. He was on the second level of the store and the mall, and the person he was following had taken the stairs down to the first floor. Below, he knew, shops lined both sides of an open walkway that was interrupted by kiosks and displays.

He reached the stairs and went down slowly, in scout mode, waiting for the opponent to expose himself.

Five minutes went by, and Charlie, now at the bottom, still hadn't seen any man with the right combination of size, shoes, cap, and jacket. Then, out of the corner of his eye, he caught a flash of orange. Stepping back, he watched as a guy wearing the right clothing, minus the cap, stepped out of a poster shop carrying a cardboard tube and something orange in his other hand.

The dark-skinned guy, either Indian or Hispanic from this distance, walked casually west, then subtly dropped the cap in a trash bin.

Charlie stepped out, his back to the guy, and watched the man's reflection in Macy's glass storefront. The guy took several more steps, turned and looked back, then continued west.

Charlie kept the subject in sight until the guy stepped into a cell-phone dealer's shop. Then he moved toward the phone shop, positioning himself so he could watch the entrance reflected in the sports-shoe store window.

Mazda guy came to the entrance to the phone shop and stood there, watching. Then he walked past Charlie, sticking to one side of the mall and looking into the windows. He also had a cell phone to his ear.

Charlie brought out his own cell phone, pretended to be texting, and took a photo of the guy as he crossed in front of him and went into Sears. If he waited in the mall walkway, he'd lose sight of the guy who could just exit to the outside unnoticed.

Just as Charlie decided to go in, his phone vibrated. He looked down at the text message. "Cmng frm wst on fut."

"Damn," Charlie said aloud, and stepped back behind a pillar. If Gordon was still in the truck he could have gone around to the outside Sears entrance and they could have squeezed the guy.

Charlie took another look toward Sears, trying to decide, when he caught a break. The guy stepped back out into the mall. Charlie stood there, pretending to text, hoping the guy wouldn't come by and spot him. Listening, he heard footsteps heading west again, in a hurry.

Peeking up, he could see the guy almost running toward the mall's big north side entrance. He'd been made.

"Call Gordon," Charlie said into his phone, picking up his pace, trying to screen himself with people, pillars, and kiosks as he moved.

"Yeah," Gordon said.

"I've been made. He's entering the food court, heading northwest. Where are you?"

"Coming your way past the Victoria's Secret. I see you."

There he was, about a hundred feet away, entering the food court from the west.

"He's by the Starbucks," Charlie said, watching blue jacket maneuvering around a cluster of bistro tables.

The guy stopped, turned, and looked right at Gordon, who was only fifty feet away. "Fire!" he yelled at the top of his lungs, then sprinted toward the main entrance.

Everyone froze for a second. "False alarm!" Charlie shouted, racing to cut off the guy before he got outside. "April Fool," Gordon added, then laughed at the top of his lungs.

"Assholes," somebody else shouted, followed by a mixture of laughter and curses. It was November.

Mazda guy saw Charlie closing in from the right. He swerved, leaped the counter of a lost and found, bounced off a wall, then threw open an emergency fire exit fleeing outside as the alarm went off.

Charlie followed four seconds later, with Gordon at his heels. Charlie reached the wide sidewalk and stopped at the curb. Their guy was running into the parking lot toward a white Ford sedan full of people.

Gordon raced past him in pursuit.

"No!" Charlie yelled, seeing at least two pistols at the open car windows.

Gordon dove to the pavement and rolled, and Charlie chose the closest concrete planter to duck for cover. Bullets started flying, but they were high, fortunately, showering him with clipped debris from the potted plant.

Tires squealed, and he raised up to look, seeing only a mud-smeared plate on an otherwise spotless car. "Gordo!" he yelled.

"Yeah? I'm fine. Pissed, but fine."

Charlie stood, watching as Gordon rose to his feet, dusting himself off.

"There they are!" a woman yelled from his right. Charlie turned and saw several shoppers and a mall security officer looking at him and Gordon.

Charlie held his hands up where they could be seen, then began to walk slowly toward the man in the gray uniform, who was armed with a Taser. "We didn't yell 'fire.' We were helping the police run down a suspect." It was a stretch, but not by much.

"Call APD Dispatch, and have them contact Detective DuPree," Gordon added, following Charlie's lead.

"We just got shot at by someone in a car," Charlie added. "Was anyone inside hit?" It was unlikely, but it shifted focus. He stopped twenty feet away, not wanting to alarm the guard any more than necessary. If the fifty-five-year-old couch potato saw their weapons, he might have a heart attack or, worse, Taser one of them.

"All this because someone was following you? Bullshit. This isn't Afghanistan, boys," DuPree argued, standing next to his unmarked cruiser beside the crime-scene van.

"So why are we still taking fire?" Gordon shot back.

"From some guy in a Mazda wearing a Broncos cap?"

"Actually, it was his limo service that opened up on us. If you lift some prints and trace from the Mazda, you might get DNA and a hit. I'm betting this guy has been arrested."

"If not already, then soon enough." Gordon said.

"Enough, you two," DuPree said, his voice reaching soprano—the pitch, not the TV mobster. "I've already forwarded your photo. We've got units looking for this white Ford, recovering slugs, and processing one Mazda, recently stolen, according to the woman owner. Either of you know about the flat tire on the Mazda?"

"I didn't see anything," Charlie said.

"And you, smart-ass?" DuPree asked Gordon.

"You heard Charlie," he deflected.

"Have you been able to get an address, phone number, social, or anything else on Ruth Adams?" Charlie asked the detective.

"No more since you last asked."

"Nothing plus nothing is still nothing," Gordon said.

DuPree shot him daggers. "If we don't have anything local, we're going to run the photo through some national databases that have image-recognition systems. We might get a hit."

"What about Baza? Guns from his time at the shop are showing up in the hands of someone staking out his apartment," Charlie prodded.

"Gun. And if you morons had your shit together, we might have some pawnshop records to track recent gun sales."

"Baza was the one who screwed up the records, and now we're seeing why. We've heard, but can't prove, that he supplied guns to gangbangers," Charlie added. "We also heard that Eddie Henderson was doing the selling for Baza through his gang contacts. Sergeant Medina informed you that Eddie was talking to the gang members in that van just before she came on the scene, didn't she?"

Gordon jumped in before DuPree could respond. "Yeah, and the guy from the Mazda and his well-armed pals all fit in with what's going on. Are they all from the same gang?"

This time Detective DuPree looked puzzled instead of angry. "I'm checking with the gang unit on all this, including any Eddie Henderson involvement. They haven't gotten back to me yet."

"Well, the night is young. Keep in touch, Detective. Right now, we've got a wounded friend to check up on."

"Gina is looking better, huh?" Gordon asked as they walked out the front entrance of Saint Mark's Hospital.

"Her face is a little thinner, but, yeah, her eyes were bright and her attitude is improving. If she can avoid an infection it won't be long before her voice comes back full strength."

"I hate hospitals," Gordon said, looking toward where his pickup was parked.

"Beats the cemetery."

"Yeah. Hard to get a Navajo into one, huh?"

"If they're still alive."

"There's a lot of evil in burial grounds, right?"

"According to the more traditional *Diné,* yeah. Actually, it's more dangerous around where they died, not where they're buried," Charlie said.

"I remember. The evil in every man stays behind when

they die," Gordon said, pushing the key to open the pickup doors as they approached. "The *chindi*."

"After spending three days with me hiding out in that basement with the bodies of the Taliban, how could you forget?"

"Nine men, all gone to meet Allah. Was it worse for you because we were the ones who killed them?" Gordon asked, climbing behind the wheel.

Charlie entered on the passenger side. "Not something I'd care to ask my *hataalii*. If he knew all the dead I'd been around, I'd need a seven-day Sing before he'd come near me."

"Why don't you just get the ceremony already? I know you think about it—we all do, even those of us who don't go to church."

"Maybe I'm beyond help," Charlie said, opening the glove compartment and bringing out their handguns.

"Or just burned out. Still having nightmares?" Gordon said, taking his pistol and placing into the holster at his waist.

"Every once in a while. But they're so familiar, it's like TV reruns. I wish I could just switch dream channels."

"Me too. All I dream about are women, pizza, fishing, women, chile burgers, football games on TV, and women."

"We're going to have to trade dreams."

"Can Navajos do that?"

"Don't really know. Must be a ruling on that somewhere. Lots of Navajo taboos, though."

"Hope that doesn't include eating after hospital hours. I'm starved," Gordon said.

"There are rules about food, but I've always ignored them. Sit down or takeout?"

"Let's switch to your rental car, so we'll blend in, then get a bucket of chicken at the colonel's. Then, maybe we can cruise that neighborhood where Jake says Ruth lived."

Charlie nodded. "Okay. I think we can recognize the building from the partial in the photo. We'll circle the area for a half hour and if we don't get a probable, we'll call it a day."

"That looks like the place, all right," Gordon said as Charlie drove by the brown stucco apartment building a second time. It was nine at night but there was a streetlight at each corner of the block and a nearly full moon overhead. The main entrance to the building had overhead lighting beside a unit of mailboxes. They were the aluminum kind that residents opened with their own keys.

"I'll park along the street and we can walk past the mailboxes and check out the names. Maybe we'll get lucky," Charlie said.

"Okay. You think the Denver fan or his buds will be cruising this neighborhood tonight, looking for us?"

"Well, I'm betting we weren't followed this time. Whoever has us on their radar might have our places staked out, or maybe Three Balls. We'll have to stay alert when we go home."

Charlie parked the Ford sedan by the curb in the economically mixed neighborhood, which contained a few newer apartments along with inexpensive pueblo-style single homes probably built in the sixties and seventies. In Shiprock, back on the Rez, if you lived on a street like this you'd have it made. Here, there were even sidewalks on both sides of the street.

"How do you want to play this to get the least amount of attention?" Gordon asked, stepping out onto the sidewalk.

Charlie locked the car, then joined him by the curb. "Let's be two guys trying to remember Rosie and her roommate's address. You know, the ladies we met last night at the Appaloosa Bar. We're well behaved, not drunk, and just a little horny."

"Typecasting, for sure. I'll be Brad, and you're George, or maybe Gilles."

Charlie couldn't help but laugh. "We'll walk this side of the street, then cross at the end of the block. When we get to the apartments, we'll stop to read the mailbox names, and write them down, maybe."

The porch lights of the houses they passed were mostly lit this time of the evening, but nobody was outside except some youngsters looking for lost keys with flashlights, based upon their overheard comments. The two boys didn't even look over when Charlie and Gordon walked past.

Four minutes later they approached the cone of light around the entrance to the apartment building. The mailbox unit was set off the sidewalk on the building lawn, so all they had to do was stop and read.

"Eight mailboxes," Gordon said, bringing out his smart phone and pushing the record button. He read the printed names aloud, along with the apartment numbers, A-1 to A-4 on the ground level, and B-1 to B-4 on the second floor of the two-story building.

"Hmmm, no Ruth Adams," Charlie confirmed. "But there's an R. Cumiford in B-2, and that name is darker than the others. The paper is also little whiter than the others, which are yellowed."

"This label is for the newest tenant," Gordon put his phone away, reached over, and slid the thin strip of paper out. He turned it over. On the yellowed backside was R. Adams.

"Okay," Charlie whispered. "Put it back, carefully, then let's walk on."

They were fifty feet from the mailboxes when Gordon spoke, softly. "You think Rose changed her last name, at least with the landlord, when she found out Baza was dead? That ink was fresh."

"Or she moved out and somebody moved in with the same first initial. I'm not buying that," Charlie said.

"So we may have a hit, but we'll need to get visual confirmation."

"Yeah. There's not much more we can do tonight without attracting way too much attention. Let's go home and start fresh tomorrow morning."

They crossed the street at midblock, then got into the car. There was no traffic, so Charlie pulled out and turned around in the street to drive out the same way they'd come in.

"Whoa, do you see what I see in the apartment's parking area?" Gordon said, pointing. "Underneath the carport in the back row."

"A blue Lincoln Town Car. Suppose that's Ruth's ride now?"

"Looks new, at least the finish. Maybe Baza had it repainted, then kept it here. Part of his laying-low strategy?"

"Yeah," Charlie said. "Tomorrow we need to get a look at the place. I'd go back there now, but we don't want to scare her off—if that is her ride. Assuming she knows what happened to Baza, she's probably on edge. We need to catch up to her, not drive her into hiding."

"I hear you. If she's already changed her name, the next step for her is to load up her kid and drive off into the desert."

Chapter Eleven

Nancy walked into the pawnshop around 8:15 the next morning wearing jeans; a soft, sleeveless top; and a colorful long-sleeved shirt that she'd left unbuttoned.

Charlie looked up as she approached the counter. He was standing behind it, looking over yesterday's business transactions on the computer. "Good morning, Nancy, you look very . . . nonthreatening in your civilian clothes. Have you done any undercover work on the force?"

"Lucky me, I got to play hooker nearly every shift my first two years working for the city. So you think Ruth Adams still lives in that apartment?"

"Jake thinks it's the place. That, plus what we saw last night with the name change and that Lincoln Town Car. It's a fifteen-minute walk from there to here, and almost that close to the apartment complex where Baza lived. It makes sense."

"Let's hope it's not just a coincidence. So far in this case we've got three dead men, an equal number of shooting incidents, Gina in the hospital, and several thousand dollars in cash that the lab techs turned up on a second search of Baza's apartment. But we still don't have a shooter for Baza, and we know neither of those guys in the van could have done it."

"What's this about cash?"

"Thought I'd told you. It was, like, nine thousand dollars. Enough to buy plane tickets for three to almost anywhere, one-way."

"My guess is that Baza had more than that stashed away."

"Maybe he gave some to his girlfriend, Ruth," Nancy said.

"That would make sense, if they were going to run away together. He was basically in hiding, fearing for his life, maybe. Why put all his stash in one place?"

"Yeah, that's what I'm thinking too. You ready to go?"

"Whenever you are. We still taking your personal car?"

Nancy nodded. "Where's Gordon?"

Gordon stuck his head around the far corner of the hall that led to their office and the storeroom. "I'm right here." He walked out into the front room, followed by Jake, who was carrying a plastic container full of stacked transaction sheets.

"Good morning, ma'am, er, Sergeant," Jake said, a wide smile on his craggy face.

"Call me Nancy, Mr. Salazar. You keeping these pawnshop rookies above water?"

"What can I say? They need me. You three just go out and catch the animals who shot your friend. I can handle anything that crosses this threshold."

"We'll either be back in an hour or two or we'll call in," Charlie said to Jake. "If any news about our computer files comes in from the computer guy, let one of us know."

"Will do. And if you do find Ruth, send her my best, okay?" Jake said.

"What's the news on the Mazda driver from the mall yesterday?" Charlie asked as Nancy pulled out onto the street.

"The car belongs to the girlfriend of Hal Calero, a nineteen-year-old kid with a long record, mostly connected with a gang calling themselves the WezDawgz," Nancy said. "There's an ATL out on him, but no luck so far. His mother says that he's been staying with an uncle down in Belen. Says it couldn't have been Hal."

"How about the girlfriend?" Gordon asked.

"Can't be found either," Nancy responded.

"Let me guess. The Dawgz tat is a black dog on the forearm," Charlie said.

"So I hear. That the same gang that the tall Indian and short Anglo had the rumble with?" Nancy asked, a hint of a grin on her face. "This sounds like another Eddie Henderson connection. You two certainly set him off. Why would he send someone to follow you?"

"Something to do with Baza," Charlie said.

"Gotta be," Gordo added.

•   •   •

"I'll check out the Lincoln," Gordon offered as Nancy pulled into one of four visitor's slots in the apartment parking lot.

They climbed out of her Jeep, and he noticed immediately that the covered tenant parking was assigned. "Guess what, folks," he whispered. "The Town Car is in slot B-4."

"Look, but don't break in, got that?" Nancy told him.

"That's a buzzkill," Gordon said. "How about I keep watch in case someone tries to bail out the back door?"

Charlie patted him on the shoulder. "And keep an eye on the street for the overly curious—like our Westside fan club."

Charlie and Nancy walked into the building lobby and discovered there was a metal gate and a small office with an attendant behind a high counter, like in a bank.

Nancy walked over to the counter as a young woman in her mid twenties in a white silk blouse and dressy slacks looked up from the desk. "Hi, I'm Mary. Welcome to Hamilton Place. Are you here to visit one of our residents?"

"Yes, I'm a police officer and I need to speak with Ruth Adams, or maybe Ruth Cumiford, in B-4. Unfortunately, I'm not certain of her last name, but I know she has a preschool-aged son." Nancy brought out her APD ID and badge to show the woman.

The woman looked at the ID and nodded. "Can I let her know you're here . . . Detective?"

"Molina, Sergeant Molina," she replied. "Yes, we're not here to arrest her. This is just about her car."

"Oh yes, it's wonderful, new finish and everything. It wasn't vandalized, was it?"

"I hope not. Go ahead and buzz her. Which way at the top of the stairs?" Nancy asked cheerfully.

"To the right, at the end of the hall."

Nancy led the way, now switching her holster and weapon from the middle of her back to her left front.

"Cross draw, huh?" Charlie whispered.

"My nickname at the academy was Nancy Drew," she said as they reached the top of the wide oak stairs.

The quality of the woodwork and construction was hidden from the outside, but this was clearly a higher-end place. Charlie found himself wondering where Ruth got the money to pay for this apartment.

Nancy stood to the outside of the door frame as she knocked and identified herself.

A woman's voice came from the inside. "Are you here about Diego?"

"Yes, Diego Baza. Ruth, can we come inside to talk?" Nancy moved over so she could be seen more clearly from the inside though the peephole. "I hate putting myself in the bulls-eye like this," she whispered to Charlie.

"At least you're smart enough to wear some protection," he said, reaching over and touching the hem of her ballistic T-shirt. "I'll never wear body armor again."

There was the click of a lock, then another lock, and the door opened a few inches. Charlie knew those eyes as soon as he saw them—this was the Ruth in Baza's photo for sure. The image didn't do her justice; the woman had a subtle beauty that a man would remember long after she was gone.

"Come in, Officer Molina," Ruth said, opening the door and standing back. "Who's this?" she added, suddenly looking worried.

"This is Charlie Henry, a friend of the woman who was wounded, *and* a witness to the shooting of Diego Baza. I understand you and Mr. Baza were friends, and I'm sorry for your loss," Nancy said, then shot Charlie a dirty look as she handed Ruth her ID.

He realized he'd been staring. "Hello, Ms. Adams," he finally managed. "I'm also very sorry about what happened."

There was a noise from another room, and he and Nancy placed their hands down to their weapons.

Ruth jumped. "It's my son, Rene. He's playing with his Nintendo game. Rene, come out, we have company," she called softly, turning her head toward a half-opened door as she handed Nancy back her APD ID.

"Can I save first?" His voice was low, almost a whisper they could barely hear.

"Yes. Then come out," Ruth answered back, her voice almost as low.

Twenty seconds later, a boy of about five with longish brown hair poked his head out the door, looking toward his mother.

"It's okay, Rene. This woman is a police officer." Ruth waved her hand toward Nancy.

"I'm Sergeant Molina, and this is Mr. Henry," Nancy said, extending her hand to shake.

The boy looked at his mother, who nodded. "Hi," he said, shaking Nancy's hand, then Charlie's. He looked toward his mother again, clearly used to her signals.

"You can go back and finish your game," Rene's mother said. "But you can close the door so we can talk without all the . . . noise."

"I can use my headphones," he said.

"Good idea. Now scoot, the adults have to talk."

"Please have a seat," Ruth said, motioning toward a big leather sofa.

Charlie accepted the offer, as did Nancy. With his professional face back on again after the momentary infatuation with Ruth Adams, he quickly took in the room. Everything looked expensive and tasteful, decorated by someone trained in . . . decorology or whatever. He'd have been happy with only an easy chair, a big TV, and a table for his salsa, chips, and beer.

Undoubtedly there was a TV here too, but it was probably hidden inside that big oriental cabinet with the birds and blossoms all over it.

"Nice apartment," Nancy commented.

"Thank you. Now how can I help you, Sergeant?"

"I'm investigating the shooting incident that resulted in the death of Diego Baza and the injuries to Gina Sinclair. Can you tell me what your relationship was with Mr. Baza? Besides having worked for him for two years, of course."

"We were seeing each other, having a relationship. He would come here and visit two or three times a week. We'd have dinner, talk, and watch TV. He and Rene would sometimes play video games."

"He'd spend the night, then?" Nancy asked.

Ruth's face reddened. "No, we hadn't gone that far, not yet. He wanted to, I know, but he was willing to wait."

"Wait for what?" Charlie asked. "Were you going to get married in Costa Rica next month?"

"How did you . . ." Ruth looked at him with narrowed eyes. "I thought you're just a witness, not a police officer."

"I'm a witness to the shooting, and one of the new owners of the pawnshop. The woman who was nearly killed in that shooting was meeting with Mr. Baza on my behalf. I'm taking a personal interest in this tragedy. More than anything else, I want the person or people who did this brought to justice. I'm sure you want the same, Ms. Adams."

She nodded. "Of course I do."

"Did you change your name because you're afraid that whoever killed Diego might now be coming for you?" Nancy asked.

"Yes. I told Mary, at the desk, that I'd met someone at the library and he started to creep me out, watching me. I said I was afraid he'd try to follow me home, that he knows my last name now and might see it on the apartment mailboxes. She said she'd change it for me for a few days. It was a lie on my part, of course. I'm afraid of whoever shot Diego, especially for my son," Ruth said, lowing her voice to a whisper. "I'm afraid because I don't know who killed him or why. I wish I did."

"You must have some idea. How long was Diego involved in the illegal sales of guns, guns he bought or took in at the shop and failed to report to the authorities?" Charlie asked.

Ruth tried not to react, then thought about it a moment before speaking. "While I worked in the store, I never saw him fail to carry out the paperwork for the police on any newly acquired items—jewelry, electronics, or guns. I did a lot of the paperwork on that myself, though he or Jake signed the tags. Once in a while, the serial number of a gun we took in as pawn ended up on a stolen-property list, but Diego was very careful. He didn't want to lose the business."

"Later, after you no longer worked at the shop, he quit paying his bills, then defaulted on his mortgage and lost the business. You know why, don't you?" Nancy said.

Ruth nodded. "He started to keep every dollar he was bringing in, except for Jake's salary, trying to raise cash until the bank foreclosed. He sold a lot of stuff from the shop at real bargain prices, except for the guns."

She lowered her gaze, not making eye contact, then continued. "He sold those mainly to one or two local gangs through a middleman, someone with gang contacts. He didn't mention any names, though. He said he didn't want to burden me with having to keep secrets."

"And that money was going to make it possible for you three to run off to the tropics. Am I right?" Charlie concluded.

"We were so close to making it happen. In a few weeks we

were going to drive to Juarez, then to Mexico City, and from there to Costa Rica," Ruth said, her expression grim.

"In his repainted Town Car outside?" Charlie said.

"How do you . . ."

"We know a lot. Is there anyone you can think of that might have wanted Diego dead? A client, someone he met in the community, an old enemy perhaps, or his middleman with the gangs? We know Mr. Baza was hiding out, using a fake name," Nancy said, "Doug Tyler."

"Are you one of the officers who was involved in that shooting over by his apartment? When I heard the location and that the two men killed were gang members . . ."

"You think that was who killed him, members of a gang? Why would they come after him?" Charlie asked.

"Except for the guns, I have no idea."

"But he was afraid of someone," he said.

"Yes. Diego only came here on foot, at night. And he kept his car here, except for last week, when he had it repainted."

"We know he carried a gun. Do you have one as well?" Nancy asked.

She hesitated. "A revolver. It's legal, he said. It's out of Rene's reach." Ruth looked up at the top of the oriental cabinet.

"A thirty-eight?" Charlie asked.

"Yes, he taught me how to load and unload it, and we did what he called dry firing. But I've never shot it. Do you need to see it?"

"Could we, just for a moment?" Nancy asked. "I can double check the serial number and make sure it wasn't stolen."

She didn't seem concerned. "Go ahead, it's on the left side, out of sight behind the pediment."

Charlie reached up and moved his hand across the top. He felt the weapon, found the barrel, and brought it down, holding it by the front sight like it was a dead rat.

"My fingerprints are probably all over it," Ruth said. "Diego said I should wipe it with a soft cloth sprayed with silicon to protect the finish, but I only did that once. When I heard on that news that he'd been shot, I started carrying it in my jacket pocket every time Rene and I went outside. If someone threatened us, I'm sure I would shoot them."

Nancy put on a pair of latex gloves, took the pistol, opened the cylinder, and wrote down the model and serial number of the four-inch Smith and Wesson revolver on a page of her pocket notebook. "Six cartridges, all live. Looks like the weapon hasn't been fired since the last cleaning."

"I've never fired it, and it was clean when he gave it to me."

"When was that?" Charlie asked.

"Last summer."

"So he's been worried about your safety for a long time?" Charlie said.

"I suppose," she said, not making eye contact.

Nancy stood, then placed the revolver back up, out of sight.

"I'm not the lead detective on this case, actually. The officer is Detective DuPree, and he's going to want to interview you," Nancy said.

"Do I have to go downtown? I really can't leave my son here alone, and I certainly don't want to take him with me."

"I can't speak for the detective, but I'm sure he'll come here initially."

"That'll work better for me. When do you think he'll be here?"

"When we leave, I'll give him a call. He'll probably come over immediately, or maybe call first if he's involved with something else. No later than this afternoon, I'd expect," Nancy said.

"Do you have any more questions?" Ruth said, then stood and walked over to a closet. "Let me show you my driver's license, in case you need it to prove who I am."

She brought out a big leather handbag. Nancy's hand went down automatically to the butt of her gun, but Ruth didn't appear to notice as she brought out a big wallet, then removed a New Mexico driver's license. She handed it to Nancy, who gave it a cursory glance, then handed it back.

"I picked up a faint accent. Where are you from originally, Ruth?" Nancy asked.

"Philadelphia. Actually, I grew up in the burbs. I moved away when Rene was born. My parents were very judgmental—I wasn't married. But enough of my history. My son and I will have to rethink our future now and not dwell on the past."

"Well, I'm sure Detective DuPree will want a lot more details, we're actually running point on this, Ruth. Thanks so much for your help," Nancy said, shaking her hand briefly. Charlie did the same, and they left.

Charlie spoke as soon as they were outside the building. "Not all of what she said was a lie."

"Glad you saw that. I was afraid for a moment you'd been completely sucked in by her looks."

"Yeah, and she's got more than looks. It's some kind of natural charisma."

"It must be hard for a woman like that to avoid attention," Nancy said. "Especially when she's obviously on the run. The driver's license is a fake, but would probably pass a low-light inspection. I wonder who she really is."

"But now you've got her fingerprints on your ID card, which you stuck into your pocket instead of back in your wallet so you wouldn't smear anything."

"You noticed," Nancy said, smiling just a little as they approached her vehicle. "Where's . . . never mind," she added, seeing Gordon walking down the sidewalk toward them.

"You think she's going to run?" Charlie asked. "She's one cool customer, but there's no doubt she's afraid of someone. Eddie Henderson, maybe? She's from Pennsylvania, and so is he—supposedly."

"Could be, but I thought she was telling the truth about not knowing the middleman. Either way, with Baza gone, there's no reason to stick around and get hauled in for possessing fake documents, concealing your identity from the police, and God knows what else," Nancy said.

"How'd it go?" Gordon said, walking up to them.

"Let's talk about it in the car," Nancy said, unlocking the doors with a double press of her key fob.

"Where we going to park to stake out the place?" Gordon asked. "She's probably going to make a run for it."

"You read minds too?" Nancy asked.

"Something like that. She has two suitcases in that car, a five day supply of water and freeze-dried camping food, like what the military calls MREs—meals ready to eat. She also has TP, paper towels, two sleeping bags, maps, a burn phone, and a loaded thirty-eight revolver under the seat. All she has to do is walk out the apartment and drive away. Did I mention a full tank of gas?"

"I didn't hear any of that," Nancy said, rolling her eyes.

"Hey, I was bored."

"You don't suppose there's another vehicle in the area that's her real escape car?" Charlie asked as they cruised up the block. "It's what I'd do."

Nancy shook her head. "She's not that well trained. Smart, but we're smarter. I'm circling the block, then we'll park to the east and watch via the rearview and side mirrors."

Three minutes later they were in position, staring out the mirrors.

"Bad angle for me," Gordon said after a minute.

"You're short, what can I say?" Charlie said.

"Leave it up to us, Gordon, you've already done more than your part. Too much, as a matter of fact," Nancy said. "Just relax."

"Tell me what you two found out. Charlie, is she as good-looking as her photo?"

"God. You men are all . . . ," Nancy said.

"Wonderful. She was going to say wonderful," Gordon joked.

"Hold on, here she comes."

Chapter Twelve

Charlie watched as Ruth walked down the stairs, casually opened her mailbox, then took a long look up and down the street, not even looking inside. "Don't anyone move a muscle," he said.

She closed the mailbox, turned, empty-handed, and walked back up the stairs into the building.

"She'll be coming out the back, with her kid, within a minute or two," Gordon predicted.

"Get ready to move. Don't scare her too much, just don't let her get to the car. I don't want a high-speed pursuit in a residential neighborhood," Nancy said.

"No prob. Her car won't start. I think a fuse or two may be missing." Gordon patted his shirt pocket.

Nancy sighed.

"Hey, I haven't always been a half-owner of a pawnshop."

"Aren't you glad he's on our side?" Charlie said.

"You're having way too much fun with this," Nancy responded, starting the engine. "I'm moving a little closer so we can see the parking area a little better."

She had just eased into a shaded spot beside the curb when Ruth appeared at the side of the house wearing a jacket, with a big purse over her shoulder and Rene by her side. He was wearing a backpack and carrying his Nintendo.

Less than ten seconds later, Nancy had pulled up behind the Town Car, blocking her exit. Both Gordon and Charlie climbed out, hands empty and visible.

"Ruth, we're not here to create any problems and cause a disturbance. I'll keep you and your son safe, but I can't let you and Rene out of my sight until we get the truth—all the truth."

The woman panicked, turning around wide-eyed, looking for a way to run. Her son was watching her face, frightened half to death.

"It's okay, Ruth," Nancy said. "You and Rene can ride with me, and my companions will bring your car, or leave it here, whatever you want."

Ruth lowered her purse, setting it on the ground. "One of you can drive my car. Here's the key," she added, handing it to Nancy, who'd come up beside her.

"You'd better take my tote," she added to Nancy.

Charlie had approached from a different angle, trying to smile and look nonthreatening the entire distance. He knew Ruth was talking about the pistol. "I promise to keep it safe for you, ma'am."

"Gordon, you drive the Town Car," Nancy said with a smirk, tossing him the keys. "Mr. Henry—Charlie—will ride with us."

Charlie led the way, carrying the bag by the long straps like there was a bomb inside, not wanting to create the impression that he was comfortable doing this. He was followed by Ruth and Rene, then Nancy, close behind.

"I might be a minute or two, but go on ahead without me. Where we going, by the way?" Gordon yelled back.

"To your workplace," Nancy said. "For now."

They parked in the alley at the back of Three Balls. Charlie unlocked the back door and entered the shop first. "Jake, it's Charlie and friends," he announced as he led the others into their office, off the small hallway that split left into the pawn storage room, and right into the customer area.

"Have a seat," Nancy said, following Ruth and Rene into the room.

Rene looked over at his mother, who pointed toward Gordon's desk. "Sit there, Rene, there's space for your game. Just keep the sound off, okay?"

Gordon's desk was uncluttered, unlike Charlie's, which contained several stacks of folders containing transaction paperwork, still unsorted. Ruth chose that desk, turning around in the swivel chair toward Nancy, who remained standing beside a wooden chair that held two big cardboard boxes.

"Let me get those," Charlie offered, taking the boxes

and stacking them against the wall. "We're still fighting a paperwork battle here."

"Would you check out front?" Nancy asked, slipping him her ID card by the edges. "Detective DuPree should be here in a few minutes." She'd made the call during the drive.

Charlie stepped out into the main room, noting that there were three customers in the shop—two women looking at sale items, and the other, a man in his sixties, showing Jake a watch. Jake looked over at Charlie, nodded, then focused back on the customer.

Charlie picked up a paper bag from behind the counter, dropped the ID inside, then folded the top of the bag over. Then he walked to the front entrance and stepped outside onto the sidewalk. Gordon was approaching from the south in the Town Car.

A few minutes later, Charlie escorted Detective DuPree, who'd arrived right after Gordon, into the office. Another officer who'd arrived with DuPree was now on his way to the APD station with the ID card for fingerprinting. Gordon stayed out front with Jake, standing guard and helping with customers.

For a half hour DuPree questioned Ruth, gathering little more information than Nancy and Charlie had already learned. When Eddie Henderson's name came up, all they got was a shake of her head. Ruth claimed to have never heard of the man. Then Nancy showed her Eddie's driver's license photo.

Ruth took a long look, then, finally shook her head. The guy looked vaguely familiar, but she couldn't be sure who he was, his name, or where she may have seen him. It might have been at the pawnshop, but she'd seen so many people working there that the faces had all run together in her memory. Then DuPree received a phone call.

The moment it rang, Charlie glanced over at Nancy, who was now watching the detective. Both were waiting on news about the fingerprints.

"Excuse me for a moment," DuPree said, walking out of the office and into the short hall, phone to his ear. He was gone for nearly five minutes, then returned, still reading something from the display.

The detective handed the phone to Nancy. "For what it's worth, Sergeant, you've landed a big one."

Charlie saw Ruth's expression change from hope to defeat in an instant, then she looked up at DuPree. "Please, not in front of my son."

Nancy looked up from the display. "Charlie, can you show Rene the rest of the pawnshop?"

"I'll be glad to," Charlie said, not really wanting to leave right now, but seeing no alternative. After all, he wasn't a cop, and this was cop business.

"Rene. We've got a bunch of Xboxes, Wii consoles, and plenty of games in the storeroom. Would you like to hook one up and try it out?"

"Yeah—uh, yes sir. Okay, Mom?"

Ruth looked at Charlie closely.

"And don't worry, Mom, we'll find something that's G-Rated," Charlie said.

"Do you have Super Mario?" Rene asked, now on his feet.

"I think so. Let's check it out," Charlie said. He'd played video games of all kinds overseas while off duty out of sheer boredom, like most of the troopers in his unit. Time passed quickly and they always competed. It was a lot cheaper and healthier than partying or extreme drinking, and most of the games didn't create bad dreams or hangovers.

After five minutes Rene was familiar with the controller, and a natural. When his mother came to the door and called him, they didn't hear until she repeated his name.

As they walked back to the office, Rene noticed something was wrong. "Mom, are you crying?"

"Yes. We're going to have to move somewhere new, and I'm afraid we're not going to be able to go outside so much anymore for our walks."

"That's okay. I can play inside. When are we going?"

"Right away. You're going to be staying at me and my friend's house, Rene," Nancy said.

"For how long?"

"We have to catch a bad guy first because he's hurt several people. Then we'll know it's safe."

"Is it the same man who shot Mr. Baza and that woman?"

"Rene!" Ruth said.

"Mom. I heard it on TV. Is the man going to hurt us too?"

"No. We just want to make sure we're safe, so Sergeant Medina has invited us to stay at her house. You'll get to sleep on her couch."

"Sweet."

"And one of my friends will be there to protect you when I'm gone, right Charlie?" Nancy said, nodding.

"Um, of course. My friend Gordon or I will be there night and day," Charlie said, wishing he knew the rest of the story.

"If you're not the police, why do you carry guns?" Rene said, looking at their pistols.

Ruth looked Charlie straight in the eyes, and it took a second to focus.

"We were both soldiers, and now we have special permits to carry these weapons—to protect ourselves and other innocent people. Right now, we're just helping out." He noticed Detective DuPree staring at the ceiling, and decided it was time to shut up.

Detective DuPree stood. "Looks like we're done here, so . . . Ruth and your son will ride with me in Sergeant Medina's car over to her house, and Mr. Henry and Mr. Sweeney can bring your belongings from the Lincoln in one of their vehicles," he said, handing Charlie the key. "We don't want it anywhere near where you're staying, so I'm placing it in the impound yard tonight."

"Let's get going. My shift begins in two hours," Nancy said. "Here's your phone back, Detective," she added, handing it to DuPree.

"Uh, thanks. Forgot you still had it."

"Looks like someone's already gone through the Adamses' luggage," Gordon said, removing a piece of luggage from the trunk. "The suitcases have been switched around."

"One of DuPree's men, probably. He couldn't risk leaving her with a weapon," Charlie said, grabbing two smaller bags.

"So what's the real story on Ruth and her kid?" Gordon asked.

"Don't know yet, but we should be getting the details tonight. We're taking turns bodyguarding the two of them."

"When was that decided?"

"Nancy volunteered us. It might be her way of keeping us as part of the investigation. DuPree certainly wouldn't have thought of it. I'm surprised he went along with the idea."

"He probably isn't that worried, and it'll save him a lot of paperwork and manpower. I'm not really that sure APD would have provided an officer anyway. Suppose she's somebody really important?" Gordon asked, shutting the trunk.

Five minutes later, en route to Nancy and Gina's townhouse in Albuquerque's Northeast Heights, Charlie checked his phone.

"Got a text from DuPree here, that's odd. Whoa, not just a text—it's a report on the prints lifted from Nancy's ID."

"Since when does the detective send us police reports?"

"He doesn't. But he gave Nancy his phone for a while to read this."

"And she forwarded it to us. Smart girl . . . woman. So what does it say?"

"Give me a minute, and I'll try to give you the short list," Charlie said, reading down the screen.

"Okay, here are the highlights. Ruth Adams, based upon her prints, is really Sarah Brooks, the twenty-eight-year-old wife of Lawrence L. Brooks, an investment firm multi-millionaire living in the Pittsburgh area. Besides playing with his money, the guy buys companies that are in financial trouble, then fires the employees, shuts them down, and liquidates the assets. He's apparently very low profile, a one-percenter with a herd of lawyers and private security. The guy donates hundreds of thousands of dollars to those Super PACs, so he has big political connections. Sarah and Lawrence have a son, five years old, named Lawrence Rene Brooks Jr."

"So, it's a kidnapping or child-custody issue, right? She split with the kid?"

"Interestingly enough, Lawrence hasn't reported a crime or filed a missing-person report. According to local society gossip and newspaper reports, Sarah is living in seclusion at the Brooks's country home, suffering from postpartum depression after the birth of their son, and under constant care. She hasn't been seen in public for three years, apparently."

"And we're sure Ruth is really Sarah?"

"The fingerprints are a perfect match."

"Then what about her family? Parents, brothers or sisters? What do they have to say about this?"

"Sarah Westerfield is an only child, and her parents died while she was in college. She earned an MBA, then worked for an accounting firm until she met Lawrence Brooks. Nobody has said a word about her being missing—at least not to law enforcement," Charlie said, looking at the last of the message. The last three words were "erase after reading."

"So if the wife took off with the kid, the husband should be uncovering every rock to find her. Why isn't he? Sounds like he has the money to hire an army, including Eddie Henderson?"

Charlie shrugged. "Could be he's got a bounty out on her. She's hiding out, that's clear, and yet her husband is pretending she's still around. Pride, bad publicity, his image? Until we know the answer to that . . ."

Chapter Thirteen

Ruth, Charlie, Detective DuPree, and Nancy sat at Nancy and Gina's kitchen table. Gordon was in the living room with Rene, watching TV and keeping him out of earshot.

"Yes, I took Rene and left home three years ago. We've been living pretty much in hiding ever since," Ruth explained.

"Was your husband abusive, or is there another reason for what you've been doing?" DuPree asked point-blank.

"Lawrence is an obsessive, abusive control freak. He gave me no other choice but to run for my life. He beat me, but never where it would leave a mark that showed in public. He'd spank me with a paddle he made precisely for that purpose, like I was some misbehaving child, or he'd hit me with a rubber hose in the shins." Tears formed in her eyes, and she wiped them away angrily.

"What else did he do?" Nancy asked, reaching over and taking her hand. "You're safe here."

"I tried to use sex to keep him from being angry, and it worked for a while, but then he started getting really rough. It was more like rape after that," she managed, ending in a whisper and refusing to look up.

"Why didn't you report him to the police?" DuPree asked.

"He told me if I told anyone, or any of the staff, or people we knew, he'd take Rene away from me, then throw me out. He'd make sure I could never work anywhere again. Or he said he'd have some of his crew take me somewhere, rape and torture me, then burn my body into ash."

"And how would he get away with that?" DuPree asked, sounding skeptical.

"He told me he'd set it up to look like a kidnapping. He's wealthy, it would be believable. Nobody would ever find me, and he'd benefit from the sympathy, maybe make even more money. He could find another wife in a week," Ruth said.

Charlie shook his head, wanting to believe her story. "Sooner or later, he'd get caught," he said.

"But I'd be dead. He's crazy, but he's not stupid. I believed—I believe him."

"If you've never documented what he did to you, why didn't he report you missing, or tell the authorities that you ran away with Rene?" Nancy asked.

"I don't know," Ruth said, looking down at her clenched hands on the tabletop.

It was an easy read, and disappointing to see. *You're lying,* Charlie almost said aloud, then looked over at Nancy, who was shaking her head slightly. She also knew Ruth was hiding something. But what?

"You suppose he's worried about the boy?" DuPree offered. "You maybe threatened to harm his son if he came after you?" he added, whispering and looking toward the doorway. "Not that you'd really do it," he added.

Ruth looked up, surprised. "I would never harm Rene, or even threaten to do so in any way. He's my life—I'd do anything to protect him."

"Rene knows you two are hiding, doesn't he? I've seen how he looks at you first for approval before he says anything to us," Charlie said.

Ruth nodded. "I've been so worried, though. He's been very healthy, but once he reaches school age, what can I do? I can't use his birth certificate—Lawrence has his men out looking for me, and with his money, he can buy the information he needs, legally or not. If it hadn't been for Diego, taking care of me these past months, I'd have been lost. I was almost ready to give up. Now I'm at the end of my rope."

"You're afraid that your husband knows where you are now and that he'll come after you?" Nancy asked.

"I don't know what he knows right now, but whatever he does, he'll send some of his private security first. They'll harass me, make threats, or maybe try and take Rene back to his father. He knows I'll never leave my son."

"Brooks is the legal birth father, correct?" DuPree asked.

"In states where rape is legal for a spouse," Ruth said. "If there are any. But that hasn't kept me from loving my son. Lawrence doesn't love anyone but himself—and his money."

"Well, Mrs. Brooks, you're still a material witness in the homicide investigation, so the district attorney will need you to be available, and you've not been charged with any crime—not yet. And for the moment, we'll maintain your identity as Ruth Adams. But I'm reluctant to just walk away, and I can't let you have the Town Car. The system will have to decide who gets the fifty thousand dollars in cash you had in your purse."

"Diego gave it to me, to use for my son and myself. I'd get a job, but I can't use my real identity. My husband has people who can find me. For all I know, they've already picked up the trail. Can you tell me for sure Lawrence wasn't responsible for Diego Baza's death?"

"Can you prove he was?"

"No."

"Then, until we have more information, evidence, and a suspect, you'll just have to sit tight," DuPree said. "You'll be protected—by Sergeant Medina when she's off duty, and by her associates when she's not. These two men are decorated soldiers with combat experience, so that means they have the skills needed to keep you safe."

Charlie noted that DuPree kept from making eye contact with anyone during that last statement. It probably left a foul taste in his mouth.

"I'd trust my safety to Charlie and Gordon, Ruth. You and your son can do the same," Nancy said.

Charlie left Nancy's townhouse around four-thirty in Gina's car, having lost (or won) the coin flip on who had tonight's shift with Ruth and Rene. The only surprises he'd picked up within the past few hours was that Ruth was lying about why her husband hadn't made her disappearance public. What did she have on him, anyway?

Charlie walked in through the front entrance to Three Balls about a half hour before posted closing time. No customers were visible, though he'd seen a man carrying a big cardboard box leaving as he approached the store.

Jake looked up from one of the displays, where he was arranging some computer monitors. "Welcome back, stranger. I assume your last mission has been accomplished."

"Wish you could have visited with our guest. We'll try to schedule in some time the next few days. You know we have to keep all this to ourselves?"

"Just glad to see it's all okay," Jake said, nodding toward the office. "Your computer guy, Rick, is here."

"Great. He's been working on our computer for about a week."

"He came in with a smile, so it's probably good news. Looks like you're on a roll today."

"It's about time. Speaking of on a roll, did the auto shop call about my Charger?" Charlie said, walking back toward the office

"Not yet."

Charlie looked at his watch. "Damn. Maybe tomorrow."

"Yo, Charlie," Rick said, stepping into the main room from the hall. The man was in his fifties and had worked for many years at one of the pioneering computer companies. He lived on his investments, but ran his own one-man IT company. He only took on jobs when he was bored. "I finally caught a break. Looks like you're getting almost everything back, including that last six-month gap in the records."

"I thought all the files had been erased."

"They were, but they hadn't been overwritten, so once I broke the user encryption I was able to run a restore program. We lost some image files, possibly including graphs and charts, but the data and numbers all appear to be there. Of course it's possible that Mr. Baza had another computer off the network and there's something still missing."

"If he did, it's not here anymore, and if there's anything on the laptop found in his apartment, it'll be a while before I'll find out. Just show me what you've got, then I'll get Jake in here. He worked for Baza and is better equipped to recognize the system and spot if anything's missing."

"Okay then," Rick looked up, a confident look in his pale blue eyes. "Come in and have a seat. I've got the software up on both monitors, and you can access the old data too—the files you found in the safe."

Ten minutes later, Rick sat back in his chair and looked up at Jake and Charlie. "There's a complete employee file for Jake, and Baza too, but all I can find in the system for Ruth Adams is her name, address, and phone number. This is all stuff from her original job application. No payroll schedule is here, no employee number, and no Social Security number. If it had been entered into the system, it would be here. Of course it may have been deleted and overwritten already."

Neither Ruth's address nor phone number were accurate,

which was no surprise. Charlie suspected that Baza had done an initial background check on Ruth, found nothing, and confronted her. She must have convinced him to pay in cash and keep it off the books, which suggested that her charisma factor had been even more effective with Baza. Eventually, he fell for her—hard.

"Find any mention of someone named Edward or Eddie Henderson?" Charlie asked.

"Let me do a search," Rick said, clicking the mouse a few times, then entering both names in a box on the screen.

Less than ten seconds went by before "a not found" message appeared on Rick's computer screen, followed by a list of near hits. "Nope," Rick said, looking up. "A couple of Hendersons, and four Eddies and two Edwards, but that's it."

"That's not unexpected, I guess. But least we have what we need to confirm our inventory, clients, and transactions," Charlie finally replied. "Look that way to you, Jake?"

"It's just like I remember. There was a lot of merchandise sold just before Mr. Baza walked away, though," Jake said. "If these records had been available at the time of the foreclosure, I'm sure the bank would have gone after him."

"One of the reasons Gordon and I got such a good price on the business was because of that situation. The bank didn't want to throw good money after bad. By then, Baza had gone underground and would have been hard to find," Charlie said.

"Well, at least now you don't have to sort those paper copies anymore to make sense of things," Rick said.

"You made backups of the restored data?"

"There is an automatic backup on a second hard drive, and another going to an online site in the cloud. I've also got all the old stuff on these flash drives." He pointed to three devices sitting on the desk beside a mouse.

"Those are going into a safe-deposit box," Charlie said.

"If you need anything else or have any problems, let me know," Rick said. "I've also noticed that you're missing a surveillance system. Did the former owner sell that too?"

"Yeah," Charlie said. "Do you handle that setup?"

"No, but I have a guy I can recommend. His card is here somewhere." Rick dug into a leather notebook containing his business forms and brought out a card. "Here's his number. If you mention I recommended him, he'll give you a good discount."

Charlie took the card and Rick took his leave. They'd already closed for the night, and Jake said goodbye at the same time.

Walking out into the display area, Charlie looked around, thinking about Rick's suggestion. With all that was going on now, and with the recent break-in, it was probably a good idea. He'd discuss it with Gordon later. Right now, he was going to set the alarm, lock up, and go join Gordon over at Nancy and Gina's. He might just be able to connect a few more dots if Ruth was willing to cooperate a little more. He now had something to use against Ruth, who had years of unreported income—not that he'd be bastard enough to actually report her to the IRS.

* * *

Charlie woke up about three in the morning, grabbed the grip of the handgun beneath his pillow, then remembered he was back in the States and in his own rental home.

He was sleeping on his back, too, something he'd never been able to do while deployed because he snored. Not a good habit for a Navajo warrior, or his buddies, who'd just get pissed and throw things. Snoring was annoying to everyone in the barracks during basic, and in every quarters he'd shared along the way. The only solution was sleeping on his side. He'd tried a special mouthpiece, but it came out sometimes, and sleeping on his stomach made him too vulnerable, especially while dozing in hostile territory.

Gordon had given him a T-shirt with a dummy M67 grenade sown into the pocket and told him to wear it backwards. Roll onto your back, and ouch.

Tonight it hadn't been his own snoring that woke him up. It was that damn recurring dream, in one variation or the other. He'd be on patrol, heading along a narrow street, just out of view of his section. He'd hear a noise, and turn to look. An insurgent would step out from a door and shoot him in the thigh. He'd pass out, then wake up with his head underwater, drowning, unable to breathe. Gasping, he'd come up, choking, with angry faces staring him down. Then he'd go under water again.

Sometimes, instead of the torture, he'd awake and find himself tied to a chair—hands, legs, and torso. A curved sword would be pressed to his throat, then brought back, ready to swing. Metal would flash—then he'd wake up in a sweat.

He'd wake up angry, shaking, or so sad he'd cry for a while before he could catch himself. The day following those dreams would be spent on edge, looking over his shoulder and not knowing why. The shrinks that came around to their unit before his enlistment ended said it was all normal for most of those who'd seen combat—nothing to be ashamed of. Everyone had a little PTSD, they said. If you needed help, someone to talk to, they were there.

Most of the men around him never talked about it, though, or made jokes. Showing that kind of fear was unmanly, they all knew that.

Gordon wasn't like the others, though. He seemed immune—joking that combat had been safer than the streets where he'd grown up, and that the team was the only family he cared about. The army provided him with plenty of weapons—body armor, and his unit buddies for backup. Back in the Denver barrio, all he had was a pocketknife until he taken up the martial arts class at one of the alternative schools—Freedom High.

A year later, he was 140 pounds of muscle, teaching the course. Or maybe that was just Gordon's cover story. Maybe he was lying, just like the rest of them who pretended they could handle it. If he sweated, though, his pal never let it show.

One thing Charlie knew about Gordon Sweeney, however, was that Gordon would never commit suicide. He was a carrier, not a victim. The thought made Charlie smile.

He lay there for a while and listened, hearing nothing

but the quiet hum of the refrigerator motor going through it's motions, and a car pulling into a driveway or up against the curb. In the distance, he heard a car door close and a dog bark for a few seconds.

Gordon had somehow heard about Navajo Sings meant for returning warriors, and advised Charlie to seek one out— excise the demons or whatever, he'd suggested.

Charlie had never been big on Navajo traditions, and had left home at eighteen, choosing college just to get away from the Rez. His father was a tribal judge, retired now after surviving a heart attack. Dad now worked in the garage all hours of the night, restoring old cars.

His mother, who'd taught sixth grade, had been diagnosed with cancer five years ago. She's gone downhill for months, given up on medical treatment, then got better. Now Mom was doing volunteer work at the schools, according to Alfred, his older brother and a tribal cop.

Charlie sometimes worried that after all this, his parents would die in a car wreck like his uncle Carl. Carl was a Vietnam vet who'd been awarded two Silver Stars and died with a bottle of Thunderbird wine in his hand.

Yet, Mom and Dad were still very much alive. Last year, when he'd left the service and returned home to pick up his car and empty out his storage unit, they'd rallied the community to give him a parade. He was labeled a war hero, and people he'd never met had shown very un-Navajo pride in him. He'd been embarrassed when they had him ride through Shiprock in a convertible, flanked by a band and an honor guard. He'd smiled, shaken a lot of hands, and been a guest speaker at his old high school. In his mind, killing all those people, enemy or not, was no reason to be called a hero. Now he knew why his uncle had taken up drinking.

Maybe someday he'd go back to Shiprock and spend a little time with the family—after the dreams stopped.

He climbed out of bed, walked to the refrigerator, and brought out a bottle of water. Strange, since the army, he never drank from the tap anymore. Bottled water was expensive, and now he was paying for it. Perhaps he needed a water filter for the tap.

When Charlie arrived at Three Balls the next morning, Jake was sitting on the loading dock, a cup of Dunkin' Donuts coffee in hand. At his side was one of those lunch coolers favored by construction workers. Cheap and practical, Charlie remembered. He had a cousin who carried his lunch in one for years.

"Am I late?" Charlie asked, looking down at his watch as he climbed out of the accursed rental car.

"Not at all, boss. I'm just an early riser. Wife's gone, kids are grown up, and I need something to keep busy."

Not knowing if Jake's wife was gone dead, gone on a trip or gone divorced, Charlie chose not to ask. "How about making yourself a backdoor key so you can let yourself in? And remind me to give you the alarm code," Charlie suggested.

"Glad to know you trust me," Jake answered as Charlie opened the door and waved him in.

Charlie walked over to the panel and turned off the alarm. "Good help is hard to find. Gordon picked well," he added.

"I do everything well," Gordon said, coming up the loading-dock steps.

"Where you parked?" Charlie asked. "Out front?"

"Yeah. We're going to go out looking for Eddie Henderson once we open up and can get hold of Rick's friend. We're going to install the security cameras, right?"

"It'll make it easier for whoever's behind the counter," Jake said. "And the mounts are still up, so that should save some money. If you want, give me the number and I'll make the calls and try to get the guy in here."

"Do that ASAP. Now who's making coffee?" Gordon asked.

"I'll do it," Charlie said. "Jake, before you make any calls, you wanna show Gordon what Rick got up and running yesterday afternoon?"

"Sure. Then maybe you guys in management can tell me where to store all those old paper transactions we won't have to sort through anymore."

Gordon drove past the Premier Apartments where Eddie Henderson had once lived. Charlie kept watch for the gang they'd encountered there.

"No gang, no gold Mustang, looks normal to me. Not even any vehicles that look gangish," Charlie said.

"Gangish?"

"You know, stereotypical vehicle associated with gang-bangers around here. Big boats with small tires for the old bangers, low-rider cars, flashy rims, tiny steering wheels. Or the Acura and sporty Subaru that carried the six-pack plus one of hoods the other day. You did notice the oversized rims and the skinny-ass tires?"

Gordon shrugged. "I think that's only for locals. Back in my 'hood, gangs stole cars, then trashed them. They never actually bought their rides. Besides, I see old grandpas driving around in pimped-out cars nowadays."

"Maybe 'cause they're pimps. But either way, I haven't seen any sign of those guys. APD hasn't been any help in finding Eddie, and if no gang types are around to squeeze for info, maybe we should see if the assistant manager remembers anything else about burglar slash gun-dealer Henderson. Maybe with you there, she'll be a little less hostile. I got the impression last time that she doesn't like me. And, FYI, I passed myself off as a guy hoping to do some work on Eddie's Mustang—the seat covers and stuff."

"You, an interior decorator?"

"Never mind. Just get what you can about Eddie."

Like before, Ruby was cold as ice with Charlie from the moment they walked into the office. She opened up immediately to Gordon, however, and took a long look at the photo of Eddie provided via Nancy and the MVD.

"For sure that's Eddie. We didn't talk that much, you know, only when he picked up a package left by FedEx and stuff. I remember when he moved out. Most of the tenants load everything into a rental truck or a U-Haul, you know, but he had a service, Keri-It, do all the work. You've seen their ads on TV."

Charlie nodded, not knowing who the hell she was talking about, but it didn't matter. It was like he wasn't in the room anyway.

She continued, smiling at Gordon, who was eyeing her substantial cleavage. "He said something about a fifth-floor apartment—five was his lucky number, you know—and there aren't that many around that I know of, at least on the west side. The only tall apartment buildings I know about in Albuquerque are in the downtown area and uptown, over by the Coronado Mall. If I hear anything, should I give you a call?" She winked at Gordon, who produced a business card out of thin air faster than David Blaine.

For a second, Charlie thought she was going to hide the card in her bosom, but instead, she looked at it very carefully. "Thought you guys worked on cars. Guess there's a little moonlighting on the side. Three Balls, huh? That's something I haven't seen—yet. Maybe I'll drop by."

"You do that, Ruby," Gordon said. "You won't be disappointed."

Charlie avoided gagging, but not by much. "Let's check out these places, partner," he said, nodding toward the door.

"Bye now," Ruby said as they left.

"Where to first—downtown, or the Heights?" Gordon said as they climbed into the pickup.

"I was thinking for a moment you'd prefer staying here with Ruby," Charlie said, fastening his seatbelt.

"Hey, it's been a while since I shared coffee with a woman, much less the top of a desk. Give me a break. At least this bundle of potential delight isn't married. I saw how you were looking at Ruth Adams yesterday. Though I can't really fault you on that," Gordon said.

"But maybe she's still bad news. Ruth's holding back on something," Charlie said. "Let's check the east side apartment buildings. There can't be more than a half dozen that are five stories or higher. Downtown this time of the morning is going to be a traffic nightmare."

Just as Gordon got onto I-25, heading south for the Big I and the I-40 exit, his cell phone rang. It was Jake, and Gordon put it on speaker. "Hey, Gordon, I just got a call from some lady with a seductive voice named Ruby. She has some information on this Eddie Henderson guy you're looking for. She left me her number."

Gordon couldn't help but smile as he handed his phone to Charlie. "Take this, will you, and dial for me. No sense in getting pulled over by a state cop."

Charlie took the phone and dialed the number of the Premier Apartments.

She answered right away. "Gordon, hi, this is Ruby. Glad you called back." Charlie put the phone on speaker and placed it on the center console.

"Hi, Ruby with the sexy voice," Gordo said, a big grin on his face. "What's up?"

"You, I hope."

"You'll have to see for yourself. For the moment, though, I guess I'll have to settle for some news on Eddie. Our senior office manager said you had something for me."

"That's not all I have for you, cutie. Until then, though, you might be interested in something I just remembered."

"Go on."

"When Eddie turned in his key, the day he moved out, you know, he said something about being able to see the hippos at the zoo from his balcony," Ruby said. "Does that help?"

"Sure does, Ruby. I'm really grateful you're helping out."

"How grateful are you, Gordon? I get off work at five."

Charlie started to laugh.

"Quiet, bro, I'm on the phone," Gordon ordered.

"You put me on speaker?" Ruby asked. "Not cool."

"Umm, sorry, doll. I'm driving—on the freeway, trying to keep from rear-ending someone," Gordon said, shrugging.

"Well, that's not going to happen now, for sure," Ruby said loudly.

"Ruby?"

"She hung up," Charlie announced.

"Yeah. Thanks a lot, bro," Gordon said.

"Hey, if I have to be celibate, why not you too?"

"Yeah, well. I don't have the time anyway. I hate having to admit this, but I have more important things to do."

"That's the spirit, Gordo."

"Go to hell."

"Maybe later. For now, let's try and find that apartment. If he lives near the zoo, that places him south of Central Avenue, and a few blocks west of downtown," Charlie said.

"Yeah." Gordon checked the rearview mirror, then moved into a right-hand lane. "I seem to recall there's a pretty tall apartment building in that area. Last time I went out on a date, it was there just beyond the zoo. Girl and I had fun, lunch at the snack bar, and that was it."

"So where is this mystery date now?"

"Her name is Naomi. She's a flight attendant for Southwest and lives in Dallas. We e-mail, but they changed her schedule so she seldom has a layover in Albuquerque long enough to get together. Thought I'd mentioned her."

"Back in the day, we were the ones who couldn't stick around for long."

"True, true," Gordon said, taking the off-ramp. "And now, as businessmen, we're going to be settling down."

"Really?"

"No, but it's easier living a dream than having no dream at all."

Dreams, Charlie thought. That's all he needed right now.

Five minutes later, just east of the zoo by a couple of blocks, they saw a ten-or-so-story white building with brown balcony rails. "That's gotta be it, it's the only building in the area with more than four stories," Gordon said, pulling into the turning lane.

"Thirteenth Street. Is that good or bad?" Charlie asked.

"Luck favors the prepared mind. Didn't some old Chinese philosopher say that?" Gordon said, grinning as he made the turn across traffic.

"You mean Sun Tzu, the guy who wrote about the art of war?"

"Yeah. Or was that a line from a Steven Seagal movie?"

"Naw, I was thinking maybe Yoda," Charlie responded. "Slow down and let's do a drive-through."

"The parking lot is mostly on the east side. I'll circle."

"We still looking for a gold Mustang?"

Charlie shrugged. "He may have switched cars by now, but it's a start."

A few minutes later, slowed by traffic, they turned into the parking lot. After circling and seeing a dozen cars but no gold Mustang, Gordon finally parked in a visitor's slot at the north side of the building, which faced Central Avenue.

"So, we go see if we can charm the management into telling us where Eddie lives, if he lives here at all?" Gordon asked. "It worked on Ruby."

"They might be paranoid about security in a building like this. I was thinking maybe we should start at a lower level on the chain of command." Charlie glanced toward a linen supply company vehicle pulling up beside a loading dock.

"Maintenance and operations. The cleaning ladies?"

"Or the super's crew. A twenty for a yes or no is better than an hour's pay," Charlie said.

"And if we get a yes, we can work on the apartment number next."

Charlie and Gordon stepped out from the row of diagonally parked vehicles just as a black Acura turned into the lot. It headed down the first lane of cars, then turned at the end and drove right for them.

"I've seen that car before," Gordon said, stopping to give it room to pass.

"Gun!" Charlie shouted, grabbing Gordon and throwing him to the asphalt as pistols appeared in the front and rear passenger-side windows.

He dove across the hood of the closest car as a barrage of gunfire erupted from the slow-moving Acura. As he slid across the sheet metal he felt the thud of bullets striking around him.

Chapter Fourteen

Charlie flew headfirst off the far side of the car, ducked his left shoulder and head, and rolled onto his haunches, ignoring the hard impact and scrape of the asphalt. His back to the driver's-side door of the car, Charlie grabbed his .380 and inched over to the next car's engine compartment, hoping for an opportunity. If Gordon had taken a hit, it was time to even the score—then double it.

There was a sudden burst of gunfire just in front of him, and he ducked down instinctively. It was Gordon, shooting back. Charlie breathed a sigh of relief, seeing that his pal still had a few of his nine lives left.

Charlie raised up, pistol out, and saw the Acura picking up speed. The driver's head was barely visible, and the passenger-side doors had holes from by at least five rounds.

He aimed three shots just above floorboard level of the low-riding Acura, two through the front door, and one through the back. Someone yelled an obscenity and the car raced forward, leaving the lot so quickly that it bottomed out at the curb, throwing sparks as it entered the street.

"Gordo!" Charlie yelled, standing up and hurrying out from between the cars. Gordon was on one knee, his pistol on the asphalt beside him, rubbing his pant leg. "You hit?"

"No, dammit, but I skinned the hell out of my knee when you bounced me off the parking lot," he said. "Next time, just duck in front of me, will you?"

Charlie looked back toward the street, but the car was already hidden by a half-dozen buildings this side of Central. He holstered his pistol, then brought out his phone. In the direction of the high-rise, a security guard and a woman in a business suit were walking reluctantly in their direction. The guard had a yellow Taser out, but he didn't look all that eager to use it, considering the recent gunfire.

"Better put the weapon away," Charlie said to Gordon, then yelled toward the approaching pair. "We were just attacked by some hoods in a black Acura, license-plate number DXL something. There's a parking-lot sticker on the rear bumper with a big P."

"The plate was DXL-357," Gordon added loudly. "Call the police. The shooters are heading east and have several bullet holes in the passenger-side doors. Those inside are armed and may be wounded."

"Wanna go after them?" Charlie said, looking toward the street again. He knew chances were slim, and he wasn't very familiar with this part of the city anyway.

"No, but you better notify Detective DuPree that the red-headed bitch at the Premier Apartments just set us up. Those were her friends in that car, and nobody else had any idea where we were going but her."

Charlie nodded. "Ruby ratted us out, and there's no way Henderson wasn't involved in Baza's murder. We've got to nail his ass."

At least a dozen locals and apartment tenants watched from a distance and took cell-phone photos while Charlie and Gordon described the incident to the APD patrol officer first on the scene. The slender young officer was small, probably just tall enough to make the minimum height, and couldn't have weighed over 110 pounds, but she was confident and well trained.

The first thing she did was take their weapons and place them inside her white cruiser.

"You two have to be the luckiest people in the city right now. Eight shots fired at you, close range, and you only suffered a bruised shoulder and a rip in your jeans," she said.

"Well, my knee is really scraped up, and I think Charlie has skinned knuckles," Gordon said solemnly.

Charlie shook his head. "We spent four tours in Iraq and Afghanistan being shot at, bombed, and otherwise abused. Our instincts are working overtime, and in this case, we were able to see our attackers' weapons before they opened up. It also helped that these shooters were more interested in style than accuracy. Otherwise we'd probably be dead."

"What do you mean?"

Gordon jumped in. "The shooters were gang members, probably from a group calling themselves the WezDawgz. I've seen them around the Premier Apartments on the Westside, and the vehicle owner probably lives there. The punks jumped us the other day."

Charlie continued. "We've been searching for a lead regarding the recent murder of a man named Diego Baza. We're looking for a connection between him and a man named Eddie Henderson—Edward J. Henderson on his NM operator's license. Henderson has gang connections, maybe on the east and west sides of the city. He used to live at the Premier Apartments."

"Hold on. You the ex-Special Ops guy who backed up Sergeant Medina at that apartment complex shooting in the north valley?"

"That would be me."

"Then you're the good guys. I know Nancy—Sergeant Medina. She was my training officer a couple of years ago." She turned and looked at the car Charlie had ducked behind when the shooting started. "Damn, I still think you're one pair of lucky-ass troopers. I counted eight bullet strikes, three on the pavement, and five into this Chevy. Somebody's insurance company is going to be really pissed."

"Our luck just ran out," Gordon said, nodding toward an approaching unmarked cop car.

"Detective DuPree," Charlie said. "That didn't take long."

The APD detective was shaking his head even before he

got out of his car. He walked toward them, hitching up his trousers and adjusting his tie as if primping for the young woman officer now looking in his direction.

DuPree stopped, waved her over, and they spoke for about thirty seconds. Another squad car pulled up, and two uniformed officers jumped out and began to cordon off the area with yellow tape.

DuPree, meanwhile, was now on his cell phone, still watching them, but coming no closer.

Finally he approached. "Looks like somebody has seriously got it in for you two. If you were on my team, you'd be in a safe house, hunkered down beneath the covers or under the bed. Fortunately, I'm not responsible for either one of you, so you're gonna walk this time. My boss thinks you should be allowed to keep your weapons—for now. But if those gangbangers turn up dead or in an emergency room somewhere, an officer will come by to take your guns for the forensics team."

"If the three in that car—there were at least three—didn't take a hit or two, I'd be surprised," Gordon said.

"Neither of *you* were hit," DuPree pointed out.

"Training was on our side—and luck. We spent a combined twelve years deployed in combat zones, Detective, doing Special-Ops shit. Nobody ever got away from us untouched. We were that good," Gordon said without emphasis.

DuPree looked at Charlie, who nodded. Gordon was being modest.

"You're probably right," DuPree said. "One of the calls I

got reported a black '08 Acura full of holes about a mile east of here in a minimall lot. Lots of blood, no bodies."

"The shooters had a backup team waiting?" Gordon asked.

"Or they just carjacked somebody else," Charlie said.

"Officers on scene are checking with local business surveillance cameras. I'll know soon enough," DuPree said.

Charlie pointed toward the high-rise building. "They have more cameras here than at a Walmart. I'm sure they'll confirm our story."

DuPree looked at the cameras, then whistled over the young woman officer. "See if there's any video coverage," he said, waving toward the apartment building. The officer left at a quick pace.

"Detective DuPree, do you have any news to share concerning Baza, Sarah Brooks or her husband, or Eddie Henderson?" Charlie asked.

DuPree shook his head. "Only that Henderson is a fake identity, originating in Pennsylvania. If only states were more careful about issuing driver's licenses. New Mexico is the worst. First illegals, now zombies. The Social Security number belonged to an Edward J. Henderson in Pittsburgh, who's been dead since 1959. We don't know who the hell this guy really is."

"How about facial recognition? We still don't have prints."

"My captain is trying to convince the bureau to run the photo though their database. We're supposed to have access to a nationwide system next year, but for now, we're at their mercy. If we can get the feds involved, maybe through an interstate connection, it would speed things up."

"Hey, Detective," Gordon said. "We have a material witness—Sarah Brooks, who's connected to a murder victim who is apparently connected to two dead gang members. Another man involved has a stolen identity and partnered with the victim, selling guns to criminal types. Sarah's from out of state and has been on the run, playing fast and loose with her identity. I don't know if she's committed any real crimes, but there's evidence she was preparing to flee the country with the first victim. Sound like real Homeland Security intrigue?"

"Just might work," DuPree said. "Meanwhile, you give the patrol officer your statements and anything else she needs and be on your way. One of you needs to make sure Mrs. Brooks doesn't make a run for it. And try to avoid shooting at anyone else today."

A half hour later, Charlie and Gordon were on their way. They'd managed to get their weapons back, but weren't counting on having them for long.

"I know for sure we're going to be losing these pistols within a day or two. What do we have left in the shop that's not pawn?" Gordon asked.

"Bunch of revolvers, including a couple of big .44s and a Blackhawk 45 that must weigh eighty pounds," Charlie said, trying to remember what was in the for-sale inventory. "If we weren't so tight for money I'd say go by Ned's Sporting Goods and find something easier to hide than a cowboy gun."

"Hell, Ned's a good ol' boy, he 'trained' us for our concealed carry. He'd probably give us a great deal once he hears what we've been up against lately," Gordon said.

"Yeah, if I could, I'd find enough leather to hold an M4 right now," Charlie said, chuckling. Most of his sack time in Afghanistan was spent cuddled up to his rifle.

"How about Ma Deuce mounted on a Humvee? I've gotta have something with a magazine, eight rounds or more, and no smaller than a .380. Don't we have a pair of Walther PPKs?" Gordon asked.

"I think what we have are .32 ACPs. I'd almost rather carry a .22 than one of those peashooters. At least you'd have more rounds."

"Hitler offed himself with one of those babies, and I think the original James Bond carried one. Had to shoot the bad guys several times to do the job. But no, I think these are .380s," Gordon said, "with seven-round mags and a good fit in the jacket or pants pocket. Not as good as my Beretta, but still . . ."

"If so, they'll do until we get our M92s back. Nancy said she'd pick them up from the forensics people when they're released. Nobody was shot with those—that we know of," Charlie said. "Yet."

"So, we go by the shop to pick up some extra firepower, then over to see the ladies?" Gordon asked. "Call Nancy and see if we can bring by a pizza. Bet the boy could use a man's lunch."

It turned out Nancy and her two houseguests had already eaten, so they picked up some Five Guys burgers and ate on the way. The first questions Nancy had when they arrived were about the morning's drive-by. Their conversation was private by design—Ruth remained in the living room with Rene, mother and son reading together.

"So far nobody but me in the department knows the details of this little Westside story rumble you had with, what, seven guys?" Nancy said. "That alone could be motivation for today's drive-by."

Charlie shrugged. "There's more to it than that."

"It further confirms that two separate gangs were involved with Baza. We already know that the guys in the van were from a heights group, the ZanoPaks, not the WezDawgz," Nancy added. "And Eddie Henderson spoke to them while they were staking out Baza's place."

"We were set up by someone from this side of town—this Ruby chick. The shooters were WezDawgz for sure, we recognized the car," Charlie said. "Ruby must have told the gang or maybe Eddie that we were hot on his trail. He got the Dawgz to do the hit, and Ruby was told how to set us up. She all but led us to that high-rise—the only one in the area."

"Baza sold guns to two or more gangs, Ruth confirmed it. We know it was through Eddie, that came from one of the WezDawgz the other day. He must have either been tight with both crews or paid them well to do his dirty work," Gordon said. "And then there's Ruby."

"Eddie slipped her some cash, count on it. People will do a lot for guns and money. Didn't you hear that Eddie was well-funded? For a guy with no record of a job, that smacks of something illegal," Nancy responded.

"Maybe he's working for someone who's dirty and very rich," Gordon said. "Someone at the top of the food chain."

Charlie looked at him and nodded. Gordon, getting the message, nodded back. They looked at Nancy, and suddenly a light bulb came on for her.

"Ruth's husband, who has almost unlimited resources and is extremely bent—according to her," Nancy said, nodding. "Just how far would he go to find and snatch her and Rene back?"

"And get rid of anyone who gets in the way, like Baza, Gina . . . ," Gordon said.

"Or us," Charlie finished. "Ruth says she's never heard of Eddie Henderson, but she was still covering up her own situation when you showed her his photo. Let's show it to her again and see if her story changes this time around."

Nancy nodded. "Eddie was looking for someone named Ruth at that GA Foods warehouse, right? We need to press her on the issue. But let's not do this in front of the boy." She looked up at Gordon.

"Okay. I suppose I can be forced into hijacking Rene and playing a couple of levels of Super Mario in the kitchen."

Ruth—as she still insisted on being called as long as she was hiding out—stared at the photo of Eddie Henderson for just a few seconds, then nodded.

"I wasn't so sure before, it's been several years and people change. But yes, I saw this man with Lawrence a couple of times. It was never up close, and I didn't learn his name. We were never introduced—he was part of what one might refer to as my husband's entourage—the help. At the time, the man had longer hair and was a little heavier. Now that I think about it, Lawrence may have mentioned that he was part of his security detail," she finally said, handing back the picture.

"Did you see him at your residence or at your husband's place of work?" Charlie asked, trying to get a handle on Eddie.

"I saw him when my husband was driven home. He rode in the front passenger side, like he was security, and he got out of the limo first, then looked around before he opened the rear door for Lawrence. I don't know about work. I never went to my husband's office, or on business trips, especially after he started getting . . . abusive."

"How was the Eddie guy dressed? Did you ever see him with a weapon?" Nancy asked.

"I think he had something on his belt beneath his jacket—a pistol, maybe. He wasn't wearing a suit when I saw him. It was usually something like slacks and a casual jacket. No tie. He never looked like he was dressed for a business meeting, more like for the golf course or a sporting event," Ruth said. "And he never spoke."

"Was he still working for your husband when you . . . left?" Nancy asked.

"Can't say. By then, I was pretty much a prisoner in my own home, and the country home staff and security were always around me. I bet someone got fired, or worse, when I managed to get away," she said, shaking her head. "Too bad. Most of them were nice people. Unfortunately, Lawrence had convinced them I was unstable."

"Do you think your husband could resort to violence?" Charlie asked.

Ruth rolled her eyes. "If you're asking whether he'd do to others what he did to me, I'd have to say no, unless they were obviously a lot weaker—or a woman. Lawrence is a vicious man, but he's also a coward and a bully. He'd be too afraid of failure to do it himself. He'd hire it out."

"Even have someone murdered?" Nancy asked.

"Oh, he'd be careful so it couldn't be traced back to him, but yes, he'd order someone killed if they caused problems. I know him well enough to see the monster inside."

"We think he sent Eddie Henderson here to track you down and get rid of anyone who got in his way," Nancy said, glancing at Charlie.

"That sounds like something Lawrence would do. He could be incredibly patient at times, waiting for just the right moment. How long he knew or suspected I was here, I just don't know. But he had to act because Diego was going to take me and my son out of the country. We were going to have a new life where we'd be hard to find. I'm guessing that either this Eddie person killed Diego, or else hired someone to do it for him," Ruth concluded.

"Like a gang member?"

Ruth shrugged. "Maybe. It would be better for Lawrence if the link between him and the killer wasn't so direct. My husband would hire someone like Eddie, then let him handle it without mentioning Lawrence."

Charlie looked over and caught Nancy's attention. She nodded, and he knew they were both thinking maybe Baza's killer was someone in that black Acura today, or maybe one of the young men in the van.

"And if that person ended up dead at someone else's hand . . . ," Charlie said.

"Hard to make the connection when the shooter is out of the picture," Nancy finished.

Charlie stood. "With that thought in mind, I think that Gordon and I need to track down the woman who set us up. I got the idea that DuPree was going somewhere else first."

Ruth looked at him with narrowed eyes. "Set you up?"

"There was an incident earlier today," Nancy said quickly, I'll fill you in."

"We'll get going," Charlie said. "If Eddie is getting rid of loose ends, we could lose the connection."

"Be careful," Ruth said.

"Uh, sure," Charlie said.

"Be ready for anything," Nancy added. "One of these days, a gangbanger is going to get lucky and start getting hits on you two."

Twenty minutes later they were on their way to find Ruby, who supposedly lived at an apartment building in the city of Rio Rancho just northwest of Albuquerque. They'd called her office, but the manager answered the phone and said she'd left for an emergency dental visit.

"So, you think Ruby'll be at home?" Gordon asked, driving north on Coors Boulevard, approaching the same shopping center where'd they'd nearly been gunned down.

"I wouldn't be surprised. She'll want to maintain a low profile for a few days after setting us up," Charlie said.

"Yeah. And if she finds out we survived the drive-by and

can tell APD who led us into a trap, she might want to get out of town."

"On the other side of the coin, what if the guys who botched the job are thinking the same thing? If any of them are still in good enough shape, they might be waiting for us to show up at Ruby's," Charlie said. "Hoping to correct their aim."

"We've reloaded. Bring it on."

Gordon sped up, taking the bypass leading up onto the mesa and Rio Rancho proper. The GPS told him that Ruby Colón's apartment was in the oldest section of the city, just west of the second stoplight leading in from the south.

"It's the next left," Gordon said, pulling into the turning lane in the median of the six-lane street.

"Three-story place on the right, two blocks down—a puky green color," Charlie said, looking over at the GPS display on the dash to confirm the visual.

"We're finally well strapped—two-gun Charlies—if you'll pardon the expression. Here's hoping Ruby isn't packing an AK-47 and a RPG."

"I won't pardon the expression, but I'll let you off with a warning. And I thought you were convinced Ruby's a lover, not a fighter," Charlie said, checking his primary weapon, the Beretta .380. He'd topped off the magazine since this morning.

"There's the same VW Bug we saw where she works, parking sticker and all," Gordon said, pulling into the asphalt parking lot of the long, one-apartment-deep rental housing.

"No obvious gangbanger rides, so that's good news. Maybe she *is* alone."

"This place looks like a relocated Route 66 motel from the fifties," Charlie said. "Ever see any of the old ones with the pueblo look, flashy neon lights, and the fifty-foot arrow stuck into the ground in the parking lot?"

"Just in *National Geographic*. Hey, remember I grew up in the big city. Tall buildings, cold winters, bus exhaust, guys puking in the streets, rats," Gordon said, climbing down from his side of the truck.

"Yeah. I'll take sand, the smell of piñon resin, and clean air," Charlie said, walking toward the ground-floor apartment second from the end. On the sidewalk were skid marks in the layer of blown dust, like something had been dragged in or out of the apartment.

"I'll cover the back." Gordon circled the building to watch the alley in case Ruby tried to duck out a back door or window.

Charlie walked up to the door, then stopped, looked, and pulled out his pistol. The entrance had been kicked open. The jamb was splintered, the lock askew, and there was a boot print in the surface of the sheet metal door.

He stepped back and tried to look inside, but was unable to see much of anything because the venetian blinds darkened the room. His eyes in constant motion, Charlie brought out his phone with his left hand and touched the menu key. "Call Gordon," he said.

"What's up? Door's unlocked back here," Gordon said.

"Front's been kicked in. Step back, hold your position, and keep watch. I'll clear the living room, then let you know when to move inside. Stay connected."

"Copy," Gordon replied.

Charlie pushed open the door with his foot, keeping to his left and using the door frame for protection, remaining out of clear view from the window. "Hello, Ruby, are you okay?"

He took a quick look, saw something big and black on the carpet inside, then ducked back quickly. It was a trash bag.

"Shit," he said. "Either she's suddenly cleaning house, or there's a body bag on the floor."

Chapter Fifteen

Squatting low, he looked around the door frame into the open room, pistol out, arm half extended. There were two big trash bags on the rug, dirty and dusty, like they'd been dragged across the ground. One question answered.

He came in low, sweeping the room with his gun hand. It was furnished with low-end furniture and a third trash bag. There was a nearly black, reddish smear on the carpet next to one of the bags, where it had been torn open, probably from catching on something while being dragged. A bloody hand was sticking out up to the wrist. He could tell it wasn't Ruby since she'd been wearing nail polish.

"Three big trash bags hauled in from outside—smells like three bodies—at least one, for sure. There's also blood on the carpet. I'm moving through the apartment next," he said. Inching around to his right, he looked past a partition and counter that divided the kitchen area from the living room.

The kitchen was empty, and to his right on the back wall was a door leading out the back.

Charlie put away his phone, his actions on automatic. He'd searched hundreds of rooms in the past few years. "Come on in. We need to clear the bedroom and bath and check for survivors. Then we can call 911."

Gordon entered, weapon out. He leaned over the counter, covering the hall, and Charlie moved around the corner.

Charlie could see into the bathroom, but not through the dark blue shower curtain. Inching his way toward it, he noticed the bedroom door to his left was open. There was an open carry-on type suitcase on the bed, and women's clothes tossed inside.

Charlie signaled with two fingers for Gordon to watch the bedroom, then took a quick look in the bathroom. He shook his head. Empty.

Gordon inched up to cover him, and Charlie took a look through the gap between the open door and the jamb. Nobody behind it. He stepped into the bedroom, leading with his weapon, and noticed open drawers and clothes scattered everywhere. The closet was open—nothing but clothes, shoes, and a few plastic storage boxes inside.

"Clear," Gordon said, looking beneath the bed. "Where's Ruby? In one of those leaf bags?"

"You wanna look?"

"Not really. Let's think about this a minute before we call the cops," Gordon said. "Otherwise, we may have to wait for days to get any intel from this place. This is outside APD's jurisdiction."

"You're right. Okay, Ruby ratted us out to someone who wanted us dead, either Eddie or one of the gangs, or both. But she didn't stick around work after calling us. She came home, or at least her car did." Charlie looked around and saw a purse on the dresser. He stepped over and examined it. "VW keys on the top—and a wallet inside. No cell phone."

"So she didn't leave here in her car. Maybe she was snatched by whoever dumped the bodies," Gordon said, "or she managed to duck out the back with the phone. Door was unlocked."

"What's out there?"

"Rear of the apartment building and a high wall on the other side—the backyards of houses. It's just an alley with no place to hide unless she entered another apartment or climbed over the six-foot wall. There are two big Dumpsters . . . ," Gordon said.

"Maybe they didn't have a fourth bag. Let's take a look," Charlie suggested, still not eager to open the bags in the living room.

They stepped out into the back alley, then walked over toward the two green side-by-side trash bins. They were the size of cars with metal covers, the kind the trash collectors picked up with forklifts.

Charlie walked over and knocked on the metal side. "Ruby, this is Charlie Henry. I'm here with Gordon and you're safe now. Whoever kicked down your door is gone."

They waited for several seconds, heard a faint sound inside, but then it got quiet again. "Ruby, there are three body bags in your living room right now. Any idea who they are?" Charlie asked.

A minute went by, there was a faint sneeze from inside the bin, and Charlie looked over at Gordon. "I'm not too eager to go in after her, are you?" he whispered. "She likes you—or at least she did for a while."

Gordon shook his head, then held up his hand. Clearly, he had an idea.

"Ruby probably took off on foot. She could be halfway to Corrales by now," Gordon said. "I don't know about you, but I'm not going to wait around for the cops to arrive and end up in jail. Ruby left the keys to that shiny black VW in her purse, so I'm taking the Beetle. My girlfriend will love it."

"Better fucking leave my car alone," Ruby's voice came from inside the metal container. "Don't move. I'm coming out."

The side of the metal container thumped, the lid creaked open, and eight gun-metal gray fingernails appeared, then two painted thumbnails. Ruby's flaming red hair appeared next, and she peeked over. "You're shitting me about stealing my car, right?"

Gordon walked over, holding up his arms. "Climb out. I've got you, girl."

She scrambled up, leaned over, and gave both men a more-than-generous look at her chest as she inched out of the bin.

"Grab my girls and you're a eunuch," she grumbled as Gordon took hold of her sides just beneath her arms.

"Excuse *me*. Say the word and you're on your own. I'm just trying to help."

"Whatever. Just get me down from here."

As soon as her feet touched the ground, Ruby tried to duck away, but Charlie grabbed her arm. "You stay put, Ruby. Run from us and you get away. Not long after that, you get dead. Was it Eddie who showed up and dumped the bodies?"

Ruby looked around, anxiously. "Yeah, with some big guys I've never seen before. They were in a dark green van. What if they come back?"

Charlie and Gordon exchanged glances. "She's right," Charlie said, reaching for his phone. "Let me call 911."

The sound of a siren could be heard in the distance. "Too late. Someone must have seen our guns and called the Rio Rancho cops," Gordon said. "Let's split. Otherwise we could be tied up here for hours."

"Yeah," Charlie said, putting the phone away. "We don't want to lose Ruby before we have a chance to talk some more."

Keeping a tight grip on Ruby's hand, Charlie followed Gordon around the alley and to his pickup. Two apartments down, a door was open just a foot. He saw a woman's face for a few seconds before she ducked back inside. She must have been the one who called the cops.

A few minutes later, Ruby sitting between them, they were driving back down Highway 528 toward the river. They heard a second siren, but it was going in the opposite direction.

Charlie looked at his watch, almost gagging as he tried to ignore the not-insignificant stench coming from Ruby's garbage-enhanced jeans.

"Yeah, I stink. You try hiding in the trash bin for a half hour."

Charlie thought about the four-and-a-half hours he and Gordon had spent in hundred-degree heat, covered in flies and surrounded by mangled insurgents, with other hajjis roaming around outside. They were trying to look as dead as the men they'd killed, knowing that a gag or a sneeze or the brushing away of a single fly could cost them their lives, or worse. "Must be unpleasant."

"Damned straight," Ruby said. "Hey, you said there were bodies in my living room. You mean like animals? Cats, dogs?"

"Human. Thought you'd have guessed by now, considering what you'd been up to so far today. Setting us up to be killed over by the zoo didn't quite work out as planned, obviously. Who'd want to get rid of you *and* the shooters? Eddie?"

"Killed?" Ruby gasped, sat up straight, then started to sob. After a minute she looked over at Charlie, her eye makeup streaking down her face. "Three bags? Did you look inside?"

"Didn't have to. We both saw a hand. Smelled like a slaughterhouse. Can't forget the odor, lady, it gets into your clothes," Gordon said.

"I'm guessing you know who drives the black Acura?" Charlie asked.

Ruby started to cry, nodding, nearly losing control. Her head was down now, her hands over her face.

"Never send a boy to do a man's job. The Acura was found abandoned, full of holes. Somebody finished them off. You know who?" Charlie said. He wasn't too happy with the woman—she'd set them up as drive-by fodder—but right now she was their best connection to whoever was behind all this.

Ruby cried a little longer, then finally sat up, wiping away her tears with her fingers. "Eddie, that lying hypocrite bastard. I called and told Eddie you were messing with the Wez-Dawgz, looking for him. I thought he was just going to have some of the guys rough you up. He sold everyone out, not just me. It was Eddie and his new crew. They were the ones who killed Hal and Ernesto and Michael Oliver. The Acura belonged to the brothers. When they came looking for me, I could see they were carrying guns, so I ducked out the back door and hid."

Charlie brought out his phone and called Detective Du-Pree, describing what had just gone down. After a few minutes, he ended the call.

"Where we going?" Gordon asked.

"To meet DuPree, who's conveniently already at our place. He also wants to know more about what's going on. Up 'til now, we've been dealing with amateurs. Eddie's new crew must be the pros. DuPree insists on talking to us before he takes Ruby downtown and has to fence with the jurisdictional issues—mainly Rio Rancho and the Sandoval County

sheriff's office. Sorry, Ruby. You're probably going to be arrested." He almost felt sorry for her now.

She looked over at him and started crying again.

"He looks pissed, nothing's changed," Charlie said, leading
the way through the back door of Three Balls. Behind him
was Ruby, and Gordon took up the rear.

Detective DuPree was standing in the short hallway outside their office. Two uniformed officers flanked him. He took
Ruby aside and spoke to her for a few minutes, then sent her
to the station with the officers.

"Now, let's get to the details of your latest adventure,"
DuPree ordered, motioning them toward the office. "The Rio
Rancho police are freaking out after coming across the scene
at Ms. Colón's apartment. Their lead homicide detective is
on his way over. We've got about fifteen minutes, tops, to get
our stories straight before he arrives."

"What did they give you regarding the bodies in the trash
bags?" Charlie asked, taking a seat behind his desk. Gordon
motioned for the detective to take his chair, but DuPree shook
his head.

"They found three young men, gang members based
upon their tats. A black dog. Two of them had taken hits in
the leg or arms, that's still not clear. But all three were taken
out with gunshot wounds to the backs of their heads—
execution-style."

"The dead guys are the ones from our drive-by," Gordon
said.

"Most likely. They didn't have IDs, but their prints are being taken as we speak. Ruby said she never saw the bodies."

"She didn't, or she'd be dead too. But we asked her about it on the way here and she has a good idea who they are. She thinks the three are probably Hal Calero, who led us on the chase through the mall, and two brothers, Ernesto and Michael Oliver," Charlie said. "According to Ruby, they're the gang-bangers Eddie Henderson sent to work us over when we arrived at the apartment near the zoo. We were trying to track Eddie to his digs."

"The bangers took some hits from you two, then got polished off when they went to meet their backup. They'd failed, they were shot up, and that made them a liability. That what you're thinking?" Detective DuPree asked.

"You're the detective, but, yes, that's probably what went down," Charlie replied.

DuPree turned to look as a man in his early thirties, wearing a black Jägermeister cap, appeared in the office doorway. "Excuse me, Officer, but there's someone here to see you. All of you," he added, pointing up at the light fixture.

Charlie instinctively looked up, said nothing, then glanced over at Gordon, who shrugged. "You're Rick's friend, right?"

The man, pale and thin but with light blue, intelligent eyes, nodded. "Yeah, I'm Albert. He's waiting. Let's go." Again, he pointed at the light fixture, then put his finger to his mouth, warning them to remain silent.

"What the hell," DuPree mumbled, then followed the

man into the hall. Instead of going into the main room, Albert led them out the back door and onto the loading dock and shut the door behind them.

"Now, just what the hell is going on?" DuPree asked, looking anxiously up and down the empty alley. "Who's waiting?"

Albert shook his head, then turned to Charlie. "Jake said I needed to say something, right away, and out here. Do you know your shop is bugged?"

"Bugged?" DuPree asked.

Charlie looked over at Gordon. "Eddie!" they both said at the same instant.

"Eddie Henderson?" the detective said. "How the fuck did this happen?"

"Hang on, we'll fill you in," Charlie interrupted. "Where are these bugs, Al?"

"I was checking out your wiring, trying to find the best places to locate your security cameras and provide them with backup power. I found the device attached to the light above the main cash register, hooked up with an inductive connector that uses building electricity. Small, powerful, and never needs to be replaced. It's on constantly, day and night. I left it intact," Albert said.

"You think there might be one in our office as well?" Gordon said. "Up by the light fixture?"

"Yeah, in all likelihood. Want me to go in and take a look?" Albert said.

"Yes, but leave it alone if you find one," Charlie said.

Albert stepped back inside.

Charlie looked over at Gordon. "We're screwed. Almost everything we planned was discussed in that office, and broadcast to someone out there listening. No wonder it was so easy to follow us. Whoever's been eavesdropping knows pretty much everything we know."

"If they've been picking up our conversations in the office too . . . ," Charlie said, then grabbed for his phone and called Nancy.

"Shit. We talked about where the woman and her son are being kept," DuPree realized, the news settling in. "Let's get over there."

"Hell yeah," Gordon said, following Charlie, who was hurrying for the pickup, phone to his ear.

"Pick up, dammit, pick up," Charlie said, trying to fasten his seat belt with one hand as Gordon took the corner in a sliding turn.

There was the sudden blast of a siren, and Gordon eased over to the left just enough to let Detective DuPree whip by. "I'm on your ass, don't stop," Gordon mumbled, racing to keep up with the unmarked police unit.

"Come on, Nancy, come on," Charlie said, his heart in his throat. He'd been through dozens of operations, but never anything this personal, this close to home and family.

"Anything?" Gordon asked, his eyes on the road.

Charlie shook his head. "Crap, still getting her voice mail. Nancy, Eddie knows Ruth and Rene are with you. If he finds out where you live, he may be coming for you. He has men in a green van—pros. They're killers. Don't go outside, don't answer the door. We're on our way, ten minutes tops. Call back if you can."

It took nine minutes and they got no return call. Gordon turned the corner and raced up the block. Two police cars were in the street, emergency lights on. DuPree, ahead and just rolling in, screeched to a halt and jumped out. He was met at the curb by an officer standing across the street from Gina and Nancy's townhouse. As the pickup screeched to a halt, Charlie jumped out first. He ran past DuPree, who'd brought out his radio. The detective shook his head as Charlie raced by.

As he reached the sidewalk, Charlie saw Nancy, in uniform, standing just inside the open doorway, her hand near her holstered pistol. Somebody was standing behind her— Ruth. She was crying.

He slowed to a quick walk as Nancy stepped forward. "They grabbed Rene," she said, her voice shaky. "He was sitting on the back porch playing with his stupid Mario game. I was just inside, my back to the patio window, fixing coffee. I heard him yell when two men wearing masks came over the wall. I ran out but I was too late. One of them grabbed Rene. The other got in my way and cut me off."

An EMT unit raced up the street, sirens wailing.

Charlie looked over at Ruth. She had tears on her cheeks, but her fists were clenched and her eyes blazed with anger.

"I shot the perp who was blocking me from getting to

Rene," Nancy said. "Then the other one, holding Rene, Tasered me, and I dropped my weapon."

"Where's the guy you shot?"

"Gone. He must have been wearing a vest. I hit him twice in the center mass and the blows rocked him. Once the Taser darts hit, I couldn't stay on my feet. They ran off."

"Where's the boy?" Gordon asked, coming up and looking past Ruth.

"Kidnapped," Ruth said. "My bastard husband did this. The men who grabbed Rene left a phone and a note on the grass." She pointed to the coffee table. On it was a cheap throwaway phone and a piece of white computer paper. On the paper was a simple message. "No cops. Give me what I want and you get Rene back alive. Wait for instructions."

"Well, it's too late to worry about the cops. Did you call the FBI?" Charlie said.

"I asked Nancy not to, and she passed it along to the detective," Ruth said. "He's checking with his own supervisors on that."

"Okay, so what do we know so far?" Gordon asked.

Nancy looked down and brushed some leaves and grass clippings off her uniform as she spoke. "The man who took Rene and Tasered me was a big guy, six-three, 230—quick, like a pro linebacker. He carried the boy under his arm like he was nothing. The guy had on a ski mask and moved with confidence, like ex-military. The second perp was about six feet, 180. He screened the guy with Rene, then pulled a gun, semiauto, maybe a Glock. I already had my weapon out and fired two rounds before I got lit up. Wish I'd taken a head shot."

"Did you see anything else? A vehicle, a third kidnapper?" Charlie asked.

"I think they had a driver because it all happened so fast. By the time I was able to get to my feet, through the gate, and out to the street, all I could see was the back end of a dark green Dodge van. It had one of those auto-dealer paper tags on the rear window. I gave what I could read to DuPree and he's trying to trace it."

"Probably fake. All you need is a computer and printer to whip up a lookalike and tape it in place. Tear it off once you're out of sight and there's a legitimate plate underneath," Gordon said.

Nancy nodded. "Yeah, these guys carried this off like pros; they both wore latex gloves. No prints." She turned around to face Ruth. "Sit, calm down, and stay out of sight, Ruth. We'll find Rene. We already have a good idea who was behind this."

"We heard Eddie Henderson's got a new crew," Charlie said.

Nancy stepped up to within two feet of Charlie, so close he could smell the faint scent of rose perfume and mint breath freshener. Her green eyes were full of fire. "Who the hell gave up Ruth and Rene's location?"

"Guilty. We just found out that our office and shop are bugged, maybe even from Baza's time," Charlie said, his own gaze unwavering.

Gordon spoke next. "That explains how the man who killed Diego Baza and shot Gina knew when and where the meet about the safe was taking place. We discussed that with Gina in our office. He's known almost all of our plans in advance. All he needed to do was find out where you lived to find Ruth and Rene."

"With the Internet and some hacking skills, that wouldn't be so hard. Eddie placed the bugs. He got in tight with Baza for a while, selling guns for him and at the same time trying to track down Ruth for Brooks. During that time, he probably placed the first bug. He may have been adding a second bug the night we thought he was trying to rip us off," Charlie added, certain now that he knew the basic situation. "He must have gotten in before, when Baza was running the place. Eddie knew how to get in through the roof."

"And you just found this out, which is why you and DuPree showed up when you did," Nancy said. "Damn, if only you'd have gotten here ten minutes earlier."

"We called. It's on your voice mail. Now we know why you didn't pick up," Charlie said.

"Bro," Gordon said, "I was thinking that maybe we should leave the bugs. They don't need to know we know."

"Yeah, play them for a change," Charlie said. "Call Jake and tell Al to find every one of those suckers, but keep them in place. Hopefully neither of them have already given it away."

"Well, Al took us outside to tell us about it, and I think Jake's got it together too," Gordon said. "God's ears," he said, bringing out his phone.

Just then Detective DuPree walked up to the porch. "Everyone inside. We've got to get our shit together and find Rene, even if it means waiting for a phone call and playing it by ear. Also, Sergeant Medina, a detective is on the way along with the mobile crime lab." He looked at his watch. "And call your captain, Medina," he added. "You're going to be working with me for a while."

Chapter Sixteen

"I've got my captain trying to contact Lawrence Brooks, Ruth, but he's worried about blowback if your husband isn't actually involved. Extremely wealthy businessmen have very influential friends—even the shady ones," DuPree said.

They were all seated around the table in the dining alcove off the kitchen.

"He won't get through. My husband has all of his calls screened," Ruth replied. "He's paranoid."

"Gutless bastard. We're talking about a five-year-old boy here," Gordon said, looking down at the burn phone the kidnappers had left behind.

"I know," DuPree said. "My idea here is to first track down Brooks's current location. If Brooks does call back, I'm going to ask the chief to trace it. If he's nowhere near, at least we can rule out his physical involvement. Parental custody is a sticky legal issue."

"You're saying that Brooks might claim that this was just an attempt to recover his son and not really a kidnapping? That's damned low," Nancy said.

"Welcome to my world. Lawrence is as low as it gets," Ruth said. "We may never get a call on that phone now that they have him. They could just be stalling for time to get away. How can we find Rene before they hide him somewhere I can't get to him? My husband has the resources to take him anywhere in the world. In less than two hours they could be in Mexico."

"If I think this is going out of state, I'm going to have to bring in the FBI no matter what. But our chief has asked the other local agencies to set up roadblocks on all major roads, and all public transportation, from buses on up," Du-Pree said.

"Lawrence has his own airplane."

"Private flights are also being covered," DuPree said. "I'm trying to get help from everyone I can and still maintain control of the investigation. If they made it to I-25 or I-40, they'll still encounter state police roadblocks. They don't have enough lead to outrun the radio net."

"I get all this," Charlie said. "But I don't understand why the boy was taken and the ransom note and phone left behind. If this kidnapping was done for your husband, what does he want from you in exchange for Rene?"

"Yeah," Nancy said, "it doesn't add up. A police officer was assaulted and someone got shot. That makes this criminal, not civil. I have my doubts Lawrence Brooks would do something like this just to get his son back. He has too much to lose by not making this strictly something for the courts. And what would this exchange, this ransom, be?" Nancy asked.

Charlie spoke before she could answer. "Could this be one of your husband's enemies instead, Ruth? Someone out to harm Lawrence?"

"You mean that maybe the Eddie guy turned against Lawrence?" Ruth replied. "Oh no, he'd know better than that. Lawrence would make his life a living hell. And if it was someone out to get back at Lawrence, why come looking for me and Rene? How would he know where we are? Or that I'm not still back at the estate? No, it's got to be my husband doing this."

"But why would a father ransom his own son? What is it he wants from you?" Charlie insisted, staring her down. "It's not money."

Ruth could see all eyes were on her now. She thought about it a moment, then finally she spoke. "Okay, he wants the information I took—insurance—that has made him back off until now. I know it can't be anyone else but him."

"He hasn't made a move on you until now, because you've got something on him?" Nancy asked. "Leverage?"

"Lawrence was involved in dozens of insider-trading deals and he kept very careful records of dates, times, and even conversations with his sources. My guess is he did this to keep them from turning on him. But what I took would not only ruin him financially, it would send him and his corrupt partners to jail. I was also able to make a copy of some of his digital recordings of those conversations and put them onto a flash drive."

"So you copied his potential blackmail material and threatened to turn it around on him?" DuPree asked.

"Exactly," Ruth said, relief in her tone and expression. "When I took Rene and ran for it, I left a note and a small excerpt of the information I had. I told him that I'd put it all up on the Internet—everywhere—if he came after me, hurt me or Rene, or tried to force me to return. Leave me alone, and I'll leave you alone. That's what I told him."

"Apparently it worked, or at least until Eddie Henderson tracked you to Albuquerque. Lawrence hadn't backed off, he just couldn't find you until now. Any idea how they knew you and Rene had come here?" Charlie asked.

He already had an idea, but didn't think it wise to mention right now. Gordon caught his eye and mouthed the word "Baza." Nancy looked over, but not in time to get the message.

"I don't really know," Ruth said. "I've been extremely careful, not contacting anyone I knew from before, keeping my face out of every place he might be looking—newspapers, TV, social media, Facebook, anything else on the Internet."

"You worked for Three Balls. And I still hate that name," Nancy said. "So what did you do about your Social Security number and not carrying any real ID? How did you get hired?"

"When Diego agreed to hire me and needed my background information, I told him that I was fleeing from an

abusive husband. I couldn't afford to be found. He sympa-
thized and helped me out, not pressing for details. I had
enough money to keep us safe for quite a while already, but
Diego agreed to pay me in cash and keep my name off the
books. Along the way I guess he fell in love with me. He even
managed to help me get a New Mexico driver's license."

"And after he 'fired' you, he still paid your salary?" Gordon asked.

"Yes. I continued to do his bookkeeping from my apartment, then e-mailed it to the business computer. One night
he told me he was going to milk every penny he could out of
the shop, save up his cash, and the three of us would take off
to Costa Rica, via Mexico."

"And when Henderson found out Diego was about to
split with you and Rene, he had to stop you all," DuPree said,
nodding. At the sound of a big vehicle outside, he stood.
"That's the crime-scene unit."

Ruth asked, anxiety on her face. "What happens if we
never get contacted by the kidnapper and your chief decides
to get the FBI involved? We already know that all these
crimes are interconnected, but how long is it going to take to
convince the FBI?"

Detective DuPree cleared his throat. "If the FBI steps in,
we should just keep to the facts. A material witness in the
investigation of Diego Baza's murder just saw her son get kidnapped. Once we get Rene back, we can work out the rest.
Sergeant Medina will stick with Ruth, and when I can't be
here, I'll make sure another detective is present. I'll have a

tech set up a recording system for when the kidnappers contact Ruth. I'll also post a plainclothes officer in the area, but keep marked units away."

Charlie couldn't believe what he was hearing, and judging from Nancy's and Gordon's expressions, neither could they. Maybe DuPree wasn't a brainless asshole after all.

"Good idea, sir," Nancy said immediately.

Charlie nodded. "Now that's a strategy we can all work with."

Gordon stood. "There's one more thing I just remembered, and maybe it can help us find Rene a little bit sooner, if he's still in the area."

"Please, tell us," Ruth insisted. "Any idea right now that'll help."

"Did Rene leave his electronic game behind when he was taken?"

"I didn't see it anywhere," Nancy said. "He was still hanging on to it when he was grabbed. Maybe it's still with him. What's your point?"

"Well, I taught him how to get online with his game and play on the Internet, and prepaid for a few months to get him started. There's WiFi capability in his handheld console, and a built-in charger."

"I never let him go online," Ruth said. "He's too young."

"Then it's my bad, I showed him how," Gordon said sheepishly. "But if his kidnappers let him keep the game and play to keep him occupied, and they happen to have WiFi within range . . ."

"Then we can locate his signal, maybe, if he goes online," Nancy said. "Can we?"

Charlie nodded. "I think so. Eddie supposedly left his first apartment looking for better WiFi, remember? I'm guessing he's keeping Rene at a place where he can get a wireless hookup. But to find which signal is Rene's will require us to go through the game server, and even then, the WiFi range will be short, maybe a block or two tops here in the city. APD techs might be eager to try this."

"Anything that'll help," DuPree said. "I'll tell the crime scene leader when I go out there, and he can pass it to the techs and see if it can be done. Let's just hope Rene still has the game and that his kidnappers will let him log on."

"No better way to keep a frightened little boy occupied," Gordo said.

"Moving on, I've got another idea," Charlie said. "Let's see if we can have a quick conversation with Ruby. She may be able to give us a lead on Eddie Henderson now that she knows what he did to her friends," Charlie said.

"Who's Ruby?" Ruth asked.

"I'll fill you in," DuPree offered. "Go ahead, guys. I'll make a call and do what I can to get you access. I'll make sure they don't transfer her to lockup right away."

They were on the road again in three minutes. "So what angle do you want to take with Ruby?" Gordon asked as they drove south toward downtown.

"She has gang connections, and not everyone in the

WezDawgz was killed this morning. So whoever is left has to be looking over their shoulders. There are at least four of them who'll probably back anyone who can take Eddie and his new crew off the streets," Charlie said.

"How about their leader, the bleached-hair guy who talked about mutual respect after we kicked their asses?"

"If he wasn't Hal or one of the brothers killed. Ruby can fill us in, especially if we hint that any cooperation might cut down on her jail time. You know, if we don't press charges for her arranging for us to get shot."

"You mean roughed up."

"Whatever."

"So, let's do it," Gordon said, slowing as they entered heavy traffic moving into the downtown area.

They were sitting in a nearly bare office at the APD downtown headquarters when a barrel-chested Chicano cop with a shaved head appeared in the doorway. He nearly blocked the entire gap with his muscular build.

"You two the civilians who wanted to speak to Ruby Colón?" he said, his voice a deep rumble.

"Yes, Officer. We're hoping she might be able to provide us with some useful information about the shooting incident by the zoo this morning. I'm Charles Henry, and this is Gordon Sweeney, Sergeant Olivas," Charlie said, noting the stripes and name tag on the blue uniform.

"I understand you backed up our officers the other day in that confrontation with the ZanoPak crew. Any chance you're related to that Navajo war hero they held a parade for last year?"

Charlie was at a loss for words. For a moment he just stood there, feeling awkward.

"He's the guy," Gordon pitched in immediately, thumb pointed at Charlie. "Saved my ass more than once."

"Thanks for your service, both of you," Olivas replied, his voice softening to a growl. "Okay to shake your hand?" He held out an enormous grip to Charlie.

"Sure. We were just doing our jobs, like you, here," Charlie said, regaining his voice as he accepted the shake.

"Appreciate it. And you too, Mr. Sweeney," the officer said, nearly covering Gordon's hand in his. "The girl's in an interview room down this hall—with her attorney. You'll have ten minutes, then she gets processed. That enough?"

"Should be," Charlie said, noting the scent of disinfectant in the hall. It reminded him of the hospital, and he was still thinking of Gina when they were escorted into the interview room.

"I'll be outside," Olivas said, then left, closing the door behind him.

Ruby, still radiating a blend of perfume and ripe garbage, was sitting in a wooden chair beside a short-haired stern-looking woman in a gray suit wearing a stuck-on visitor's badge like theirs.

"Glad you're okay, Ruby," Gordon said immediately, remaining standing by the table.

"We both are," Charlie added, extending his hand to the woman attorney. Her shake was limp-wrist and reluctant, even to Gordon, who could usually charm the coldest soul with his smile.

"My client is willing to cooperate, but I have to agree with which questions she'll answer. Understand?"

Charlie nodded, taking a seat across the table from them, as did Gordon. "Then we'll get right to it. Rather than discuss what happened to us after we met with Ruby this morning, or how we rescued her from possible attack and took her to safety, we just need a little information."

"What kind of information?" the lawyer asked, holding her hand up, sensing Ruby was about to speak.

"We need to know everything Ruby can tell us about Eddie Henderson—especially where we might be able to find him. We believe Henderson is a dangerous criminal who's responsible, directly or indirectly, for the death of the three men whose bodies were placed in her apartment."

"These victims were friends of Ruby's. Weren't they?" Gordon added softly.

Ruby nodded. "I told you that already," she said, then spoke to her attorney. "I don't know where he is, really, and I don't know where he lives, if it's not over by the zoo. All I have is a phone number. It's 613-1315."

Charlie wrote the number down in a small notebook he brought out of his shirt pocket. Judging by her refusal to make eye contact with them, Ruby was probably lying, except maybe for the phone number. But perhaps there was another way.

The lawyer spoke. "You heard my client. She doesn't know Henderson's location or current residence. Any more questions?"

"Yes. We need to know the names of some of the Wez-Dawgz we encountered outside the apartments where Ruby works. We're not cops, so we can't arrest anyone, but if we can contact some of these young men, even over the phone, maybe they can lead us to Henderson."

"Ask that sergeant with the gang unit. He might know some names," the lawyer said.

"We'd rather hear it from Ruby. She knows these young men and has a bigger stake in keeping the rest of them alive. They're her friends. We're no danger to them, but clearly Eddie Henderson is."

"The bastard. The lying, shitty bastard," Ruby said, her voice raising with every syllable. "If anyone deserves to die . . ."

"It's Eddie," Charlie agreed. "Now, Ruby, who's the Wez-Dawgz leader, the guy with the light hair?"

"He's got a limp now," Gordon added solemnly.

"Oh, that's Güero," Ruby said. "That's what they call him."

"And his legal name?" Charlie prodded.

"Martin Bateson."

"Anyone else, in case we can't get in contact with Güero?" Charlie said.

Ruby looked at her attorney.

The woman shrugged. "Your call."

"Herman Maestas usually hangs with Güero. Herman's street name is Bluto," Ruby said, her voice low and controlled now.

Charlie looked at Gordon, who nodded. "The big guy, right?"

Ruby smiled weakly. "Duh."

"You don't have a phone number for either of these gentlemen, do you?" Charlie said, bringing out a small notebook and pen and sliding them across the table.

Ruby looked over at the lawyer again.

"Go ahead. It'll save some time," the lawyer said. "My client is cooperating, you can see that," she said to Charlie.

"Of course," Charlie said.

"I don't remember the numbers, but they're on my cell phone," Ruby said.

"They took it away from my client, but I have permission to return it to Ruby's mother. The detectives have already made a copy of the data card," the woman said, reaching into her purse for the phone. "Give me the names, Ruby, and I'll read out the numbers for you to write down for these men."

A minute or two later they were done.

"You might have a hard time finding them right now. They lost three of their friends today," Ruby said as she slid the notebook and pen back across the table.

Charlie picked up the notebook, looked at the numbers, and saw that she'd included the names as well. "Thanks so much, Ruby. Is there anything else you can tell us about Eddie that might help us find him?" He'd already assumed that

"Eddie's number" would be either fake or an untraceable burn phone. Why would Ruby remember it so easily, but not those of her friends? It didn't matter anyway, they needed his address.

"He's not from around here. He came from back east. His favorite football team is the Steelers. Once he bragged that he had season tickets before he moved to Albuquerque. And he had a bounty out for some woman named Ruth, if that means anything to you. Anyone who could find her for him got a new car."

"Sounds like a deal," Gordon said, nodding. "Who's this Ruth anyway? An ex-wife?"

"No idea. I'd hate to be her, though."

Charlie nodded. "I appreciate the info, maybe it'll help. Would it be okay if Ruby has you call us if she thinks of anything else?" he asked her lawyer.

"If you mention this to the detectives—and the county attorneys, as evidence of her continued cooperation?"

"Of course we will," Charlie said.

"Then we're done," the woman said, scooting her chair back slightly for emphasis.

Ruby's eyes began to fill with tears. "Um, guys, thanks for getting me out of there today. And I'm really . . ."

"Ruby. We're done. Not another word," cautioned the attorney.

"I know, sorry. Well, bye, Ruby. No hard feelings." Gordon stood, reached over, and gave her shoulder a gentle squeeze.

Charlie stood as well. "Thanks, ma'am," he said, handing the attorney his business card.

She looked at the card. "Ugh," she said. "Really?"

He tried not to smile, and failed. "Let's go," he said to Gordon, who was still looking at Ruby.

Ten minutes later, Charlie ended the call he'd just placed to Güero's cell phone. Gordon was driving, and they were heading west on I-40, the quickest route to Albuquerque's west side from downtown. Sergeant Olivas had given them Martin Bateson's current address, but warned them not to expect anyone to be at home.

"Think we'll get a callback?" Gordon asked.

"You heard Ruby. Güero has probably gone into hiding after losing three of his crew today. At least I was able to leave a message on his cell phone—if he's still carrying it around," Charlie said.

Gordo shrugged. "He's got to know by now that Eddie was the one who finished off his people. Ruby, apparently had already passed along the warning through that attorney of hers. The remaining WezDawgz are scurrying for cover."

"You think Ruby is really sorry she set us up?" Charlie said.

"Not so much. She's just come around to thinking that the enemy of her enemy is her friend. Lying bitch. Her alliances change with the wind," Gordo said.

"But you'd still like to hook up with her?" Charlie said, grinning.

"Yeah, sex maybe. But spend the night? No way I'd ever close my eyes around that girl."

Charlie's phone started to ring. "That didn't take long." He put the phone on speaker.

"You the Indian?"

Charlie recognized Güero's voice immediately. "Yeah. Nobody can trust Eddie Henderson anymore, so we're going to take him down. I need his address."

"I haven't got that information anymore, but Eddie had dealings with a crew in the Heights that we respect. The pecker got two of them killed, now three of us. I can give you the number of a person who might help. Kill Eddie, but leave us out of it."

"Done."

"His cell number is 505-2859."

"Got it. Thanks."

"Get the bastard," Güero said, ending the call.

Charlie started to dial again.

"The ZanoPaks, maybe?" Gordo asked.

"That would be my guess," Charlie responded. "Hang on." He put the phone on speaker, placing it on the console.

"If you know me, leave a message. If you don't, then fuck off." The young man's voice came through loud and strong.

Charlie looked over at Gordo, who was stifling a laugh.

"Someone said you might know where I can find Eddie Henderson. He's on my shit list and he's going down. Call back when you get this."

"Think you should be making that call? Even though the Zanos opened fire first, you and Nancy put them down," Gordon pointed out as soon as Charlie put away the phone.

"Yeah, but they were doing Eddie's dirty work, searching for Baza's place, and probably Ruth as well. And he put them on my tail."

"Why would the WezDawgz be on speaking terms with ZanoPak anyway?"

"I guess it helps that the gangs hang out probably ten miles away from each other and don't claim the same turf. There are Valley gangs between them that are bigger problems," Charlie said.

"So we're waiting for another return call—maybe. Wanna get an early dinner?"

Charlie nodded. "Let's pick up some takeout and eat at the shop. See how Jake and Al are doing. I'll give him a call and ask what he wants to eat."

They arrived at Three Balls a half hour later, not long before closing time. First, they'd cruised around the block, looking for anyone who might have them staked out.

They parked on the street, then walked in through the front door.

"Hey, it's the absentee owners. Thanks for bringing by dinner," Jake said, looking over from the counter, where he was conducting business with two customers, a man and woman in their early sixties.

"We'll put yours on the office desk," Charlie said, looking around the interior. There were two teenage boys at the counter with the video consoles, playing a shooter game that involved zombies, judging from the graphics. The sound was turned way down, but the boys didn't seem to mind.

Charlie looked up on the wall and noted one of the new video cameras, which was directed on that section of the interior. A green light atop the camera suggested it was on and operating.

"Al got the surveillance up and running," Gordon said, waving at Jake, who nodded back. "I wonder where the monitors are—our office?"

"Looks like," Charlie said, leading the way into the hall at the back of the shop. As he walked into the office and set down the food containers, he noted the wall-mounted flat-screen monitor split into four sections, one for each camera.

Gordon followed him in. "Hey, that's the big monitor from out front—good use for it. Didn't have to buy a new one. Always happy to save a few hundred."

"Yeah, and see how every spot is covered—the display area, the storeroom, even the office." Charlie stared into the camera positioned at the end of the hall. "Damn, I look tired. This day has been long. Too long. I thought being back in the States would make me less of a target."

"Me too," Gordon said, pointing up as a reminder someone was probably listening. "But we need to keep up our strength. Let's eat before these El Gallo's green-chile burritos get cold."

Five minutes later, Jake came into the office. "That bag mine?" He pointed toward the unopened bag on the counter beside the computer printer.

"Go for it," Gordon said, his mouth half full.

Jake opened the bag and looked inside. "So they had

chicken burritos? Great. How much do I owe you?" he said, looking from Charlie to Gordon.

"This one's on me. You've been pulling more than your weight around here, bro." Charlie said. "And it looks like Al did a great job. We'll have to thank Rick."

"There's the damages," Jake said, pointing to an invoice in a basket on Gordon's side of the desk. "And he included some extra instructions. You guys will want to read them."

Charlie looked over and saw photos of the three small devices hooked up next to the light fixtures, one of them just above his desk. He nodded. "We've got to pass his name along to our customers."

"He's got some good ideas on . . . ," Jake began, then stopped as they heard the sound of someone coming in the main entrance.

They all looked at the monitor. It was the two boys who'd been playing the video game earlier.

"Guess they rounded up enough money. Gotta go and make sixty bucks for Three Balls," Jake said with a smile, picking up his bag. "I'll eat out there and keep the shop covered."

"Thanks," Gordon said.

Charlie nodded, taking a bite of burrito. His phone rang and he picked it up. "Personal call, excuse me," he said, hurrying toward the back door. Gordon nodded.

By the fourth ring Charlie was outside and he took the call.

"You the guy looking for an address?" said the unfamiliar voice.

"Yes?"

"Room 705, the Richards Apartments, north of Lomas." The line went dead.

Charlie wrote the information down on his pocket notebook, next to the phone numbers Ruby had provided, then went back inside.

He held up the notebook as he came back into the office. "Beth wants me to help her brother move out of her grandfather's home. I told her to come up with a date and time, then call back." He showed Gordon the address the ZanoPak caller had given him.

"I can help."

"Good, I volunteered you," Charlie said, rolling his eyes.

"Let's finish dinner, then go see our sick friend first," Charlie said, shaking his head. "Jake can close up."

Gordon nodded, pointing to the notebook. "I'm with you."

Quietly confirming that they had their weapons ready, with spare magazines in their pockets, Charlie and Gordon went out into the display area. "We're going to visit our friend in the hospital, Jake. Great job today. See you in the morning."

They took Charlie's rental car, so he was driving as they passed by the large apartment complex. The site took up the entire city block, comprising nine separate four-story apartment buildings and several smaller offices and clubhouses.

"I don't remember ever coming by here," Charlie said. "For Albuquerque, this is pretty big."

"Yeah, I was wondering about a seventh-floor apartment anyway. From what I can see, we need to find building seven," Gordon said, looking at the units as they drove east up Lomas Avenue. "There's building 700." He pointed to a brick-facade building on the corner of the third row back. "Wanna circle the block, or come in from this direction?"

"If he's watching, he'll see us a lot sooner on the other side. Let's park down the street, cross Lomas, and come in past the other two rows," Charlie said.

"How about from the east? From the windows and balconies I think there are six apartments running lengthwise, so if he's in number five, he'll be on the ground floor facing south. No east-facing window," Gordon said.

"Good thinking. And we'll come in from the north lobby."

This was the Southwest, where few apartment buildings had security gates or systems where a tenant had to buzz someone in. Charlie thought they could probably get to Eddie's door without being noticed.

Charlie carried a six-pack of Coors beer and Gordon had a paper grocery bag from a local Smith's. It contained chips and beer nuts to put any casual observers at ease.

They entered the clean, well-maintained lobby of the building and came to the first of three hall junctions. Looking to the right, they saw a door with the number three on it. To the left was four.

They walked close to the wall now, side by side, and as they passed the first door, the apartment five door suddenly opened. Both reached down for the pistols concealed beneath their jackets.

Chapter Seventeen

A stainless-steel cart full of cleaning supplies appeared, pushed out into the hall by a pleasant looking black-haired woman in blue scrubs.

"Mr. Patterson isn't at home," the woman said. She looked to be around forty.

Charlie relaxed slightly, removing his hand from the butt of the pistol just inside his jacket. Just to be safe, he kept the interior of the apartment within his peripheral vision.

"Damn, we were hoping to get little poker game going. Where's he off to now, back to Pittsburgh?" Charlie said.

"He didn't say," the woman said, smiling at Gordon and fiddling with her loosely fitting top. "You just move in? . . ."

"Doug. I'm Doug, and I'm sure thinking about it, Vivian," he said, noting her name tag. "Are you available?"

"You mean as a housekeeper?" she said, smiling even wider.

"Of course," Gordon said, his face turning a little red.

"Oh, you're blushing, Doug. That's so cute," Vivian said. "I have a card here, call me. I can squeeze you in." She reached into her pocket, brought out a billfold, and handed him a business card. "Make sure you ask for me, Doug."

"Count on it, Vivian."

"Well, I've got work to do. Sorry Eddie—Mr. Patterson, wasn't here for your game."

Vivian shut the door to apartment five, checked the knob to see that it was locked, then smiled again and pushed the cleaning cart toward apartment six.

"Let's go, Pete, maybe we can get a game going over at Ollie's," Gordon said, motioning in the direction they'd come.

"Yeah, Doug, yeah."

Once outside, they cut across the center of the complex, heading directly for the car.

"What is it with you and women?" Charlie said, wishing he could open one of those lukewarm beers right now. "You're like a puppy. They all want to hug you and take you home. And how do you manage that embarrassed look? I've seen you play that a hundred times."

"I know you won't believe this, but every time, I've actually been embarrassed. I've always had a problem coping with a woman coming on to me."

"That hasn't stopped you from climbing into the sack with them nine times out of ten."

"Hey, sure I get embarrassed, but it's not like we're in high school anymore. Now I know what to do and I don't back down. But what about you? I don't recall ever seeing you turning red."

"Harder to spot on a Navajo," Charlie said as they reached the crosswalk at the end of the block. The light was red, and traffic was always heavy on this street.

"Ah, but you do get stupid. Nancy said your jaw dropped and you almost drooled when you first met Ruth."

"You ever see a woman and wish you were her type?"

"Yeah, I guess."

"Well, Ruth is one of them. But enough of that, let's cross the street and wait a little while."

"We're going back and breaking in, right?"

"How well you know me, bro."

Charlie was fast with locks and had the door open in twenty seconds. They stepped inside an immaculately clean, furnished apartment that still smelled faintly of lemon.

Gordon closed the door behind them, locked the knob and fastened the chain. They were used to these kind of entries and searches, though in 'stan they were more concerned about booby traps. Still, they remained as quiet as possible while they put on latex gloves. Here, unlike in their military missions, they had to worry about fingerprints, not staying alive.

Charlie went straight to a writing desk, noting the empty space where a laptop had probably sat. A small inkjet printer was beside the empty space, but there was no USB cable, which suggested a wireless connection. He opened the top drawer. Inside was a nail clipper, a manual on CD for the missing laptop, a few pens, and a pocket spiral notebook, unused.

There were two larger drawers, the top one locked, but this was a snap to open with his pocketknife. Inside was an almost-full opened package of photo-quality printer paper. Below it was an accordion-type folder and a half-full package of inkjet printer paper.

Carefully removing the folder, Charlie unfastened the string and brought out a combination of e-mail printouts and printer images.

He wasn't surprised to find printed-out images, taken with a telephoto lens, of himself, Gordon, and Nancy. There were also photos of their residences, and Three Balls, out front and down the alley, including his Charger.

Searching further, he saw two images of Ruth, obviously from several years ago. In one, she was holding a baby. Rene, probably. He noted that there were none of the apartment building where she'd been living most recently. Either Eddie hadn't found the place, or else had chosen not to print a copy.

Then he found a page containing images of Diego Baza, some of them in the doorway or the alley of Three Balls. There were also photos of the pawnshop interior, two of them focused on the light fixtures.

By the time he got to the e-mails, Charlie noticed Gordon had come up beside him. Gordon pointed toward the bedroom and kitchen area, shook his head, then stood beside him as Charlie skimmed the e-mail printouts.

Then he got to the meat of the matter. The next e-mail Charlie found listed the sender as L898BZm and was being sent to DNTCare. The subject was "HER."

Gordo read it in a whisper. "'*Eddy—check into this guy, Baza. He contacted me via my corporate address. I deleted the message, but here's a copy. Make sure nobody sees it but you.—L.*'"

"I was right. Baza approached Brooks. He's responsible for our Eddie being here," Charlie said.

Gordon continued reading. "'*Mr. Brooks. I know where your wife and son are. If you'd like to buy this information from me, please respond to this e-mail. I'm assuming you mean them no harm, or I wouldn't have sent this message.—DB.*' I'm guessing Ruth doesn't know this," Gordon added.

"No. She was played in the beginning, but it looks like Baza had a change of heart. Check this one out." He pointed to an e-mail dated a month later, which Baza had sent to "Eddie."

In the message Baza explained that he was playing Mrs. B, trying to find out where the "stolen documents" are. Once he did that, he'd turn them over for the final payout.

"Here's the last one. '*Baza is still stalling.*' That's just two days before he was killed," Charlie said.

Gordon nodded. "What's with the photos?"

Charlie slid them over. "There's a few more here," he said, looking at the remaining three. "Here's one of Gina getting into her car outside her office."

"Nothing on Baza's last apartment?"

"No, but here's something that confirms what we already knew." Charlie held up a specs sheet and installation instructions for hooking up electronic bugs.

"We still might be able to use that to our advantage," Gordon reminded him.

"If we'd have set up Gina and Baza's meet in our back alley she'd be at work right now, not in the hospital. None of those youngsters would be dead. At least part of this is our fault," Charlie said.

"Screw guilt and move on, bro. Gina was shot, and the gangs have already sold their souls to the highest bidder. Eddie was playing those boys and Baza, all the time trying to find Ruth. Let's work for payback—balance—as the Navajos say," Gordon replied. "How about we take photos of all this shit, put it back like it was, then get out of here? We don't know where Eddie is, and when or if he's coming back."

Five minutes later, they were clear of the building and walking across the complex grounds toward the rental car. Charlie's phone started to vibrate. He looked at the display. "Nancy," he told Gordon, putting the call on speaker.

"Still nothing from the kidnappers. We've relocated to a safe house," Nancy said. "Some off-duty volunteers on the force are cruising various neighborhoods, hoping to pick up the WiFi signal from Rene's game, but that's a real longshot. What's new with you?"

"We found Eddie's apartment, but no Eddie. He's going under the name of Eddie Patterson here. We've got images of some damning evidence that cinches who he's working for, and why. I'll send it to your phone, but don't let Ruth see it, okay?"

"Why not?"

"Baza hasn't always been her protector. He was the one who let Brooks know she was here. Then, later, he tried to undo the damage. You'll see."

"No shit?" A few seconds went by. "That sucks," Nancy added. "Just send me what you got, okay?"

"Okay. Can you be the one who tells her?" Charlie added.

"I knew that was coming. Yeah, but let me pick the time. Right now she's got enough on her plate."

"Yeah, she does. Thanks."

Nancy lowered her voice to a whisper. "You know we can't use any of this in court. I can't tell DuPree either. You guys just did a B and E."

"No trace, no fingerprints. We wiped the doorknob clean just in case. If this gets the kid back, it's worth it."

"Agreed. I can send Eddie's address to DuPree, though. You got your information through an unidentified informant. There may be enough there to get a warrant. And if the detective gets this damning evidence legally . . ."

"Exactly. Though if I was giving advice, I'd suggest that DuPree have the place staked out. Eddie took his laptop with him and is keeping a low profile somewhere, but who knows, he may be coming back, if only to pick up those papers. They link him to Brooks, Baza, *and* Ruth. And there's more. According to Ruby Colón, Eddie had a bounty out on Ruth. Anyone who could find her got a new car."

"What a bastard," Nancy replied, her voice cold. "I can't wait until we lift prints and DNA from his apartment. Who the hell is this guy?"

"We thought about bringing something back with his prints on it, but didn't want to tip our hand in case he missed whatever it was," Charlie replied.

"We couldn't have used it in court, not without a warrant, but I still wish we knew his real name. Good work anyway," she added. "You should consider joining the force. Where you going now?"

"I was thinking about visiting Gina. How's she doing?"

"Healing up, weak but getting stronger. She wants to come home."

"May not be the safest place for her right now. How's hospital security?"

"I thought about that—Eddie trying to get to Ruth via me, via Gina. There's a guard by her door now, and he's been given Eddie's photo."

"Good. Maybe I should just wait until visiting hours. I think we'll stop by the shop and check on Jake. He looks like he can take care of himself, but he's alone there now."

"I didn't say this, but maybe he should be strapped for a few days."

"Copy that. I'll send you those images in a minute. Stay in touch, and stay safe."

"You too—and Gordon."

Charlie ended the call as they came to the corner of the sidewalk, forced to wait for the light to cross Lomas. He handed Gordon the car key. "You drive, I need to send the stuff to Nancy."

Charlie spent the fifteen-minute travel time rereading and studying the images of the documents he'd photographed. He found himself staring at Ruth and the baby, then enlarged the image, checking out the background.

"If this is Brooks's home, it's a palace. Big lawn and grounds, garden, and a house that must have cost five million dollars easy."

Gordon took advantage of a stoplight to glance over at the enlarged image Charlie held up. "Reminds me of those big houses along Rio Grande Boulevard."

"Yeah. The guy is worth hundreds of millions."

"But not worth shit as a human being. When I was watching over her the other night—Rene was asleep—she told me Lawrence had come from a lower middle-class family. He'd gone to college on a scholarship and loans, toughing it out and even living in his car one summer. He was a whiz in business school and had made his first million in the stock market before he graduated. His roommate's father was a Wall Street trader, and apparently Lawrence got a bunch of insider tips."

"No moral compass. A gambler, eager to take short cuts, going for the big score?" Charlie said, remembering his father, the judge, who was always hard on defendants who'd abused their business position and cheated the little people. That was one of the few things where they'd always seen eye to eye.

"Yeah. But once he'd hit it big, he had to live large as well. Always the best of everything. Even when they traveled on vacation, early in the marriage, he rented the biggest place he could find. According to Ruth, no four-star hotel was good enough," Gordon said.

"So, if he came here, where would Lawrence Brooks stay?" Charlie wondered. "He's very private and likes his space. Big rooms, lots of space."

"He'd probably rent or lease the biggest house available— with an enormous yard, in a nice neighborhood. Like off Rio Grande?"

"Could be. Most of the big houses up in the Heights have much less property around them. It's worth a shot. Let me make a call to Claudia Espinosa," Charlie said, looking up the number of the Realtor who helped them buy the pawnshop.

"Nancy's right, you know. When all this is over, we've got to change our business name," Gordon said, grinning. "Maybe Claudia can make some suggestions."

"Yeah." Charlie brought out his phone. "Meanwhile, I'm hoping she can tell us if a place big enough for Brooks has been rented or leased recently."

"That still won't tell us if Lawrence Brooks is actually there. He'd have Eddie or someone else do it for him, using a corporate name for a rent or lease agreement," Gordo said. "What they call a shell company?"

"Maybe. But if Brooks's personality is anything like Ruth describes, once Eddie provided him the leverage, he'd probably want to be in on the score. Get his hands on her." Charlie felt a twinge of anger at the thought.

"What we can do is check any likely estates for that WiFi signal," he continued. "There can't be that many big homes—estates—available for rent or for sale. This is New Mexico, not California. Still, it's a longshot."

Gordon nodded. "God's ears. Make the call. Worse-case scenario, we can go house to house in those 'hoods and maybe trigger a reaction."

Charlie called, got Claudia's voice mail, and left a message. "Wait and see, I guess," he said, noting that they were within a few blocks of the shop. "Hey, four cars out front. Looks like business is picking up. Jake has been drawing them in."

His phone rang. "Speak of the devil," Charlie said. "Hey, Jake, need some help?"

"Probably, but that's not why I called. You need to get over here and check out an e-mail that came in through the business Web site," Jack said, his voice low.

"We'll be right there, coming in the back," Charlie said, ending the call.

"I know that look," Gordon said. "Something just hit the fan."

"Yeah. Looks like the kidnappers decided to use the Internet instead of a telephone. Disconnect the bug once we get in there, will you?" Charlie added.

Jake nodded to them when they came in the back, but shook his head when Gordon asked if he needed some help.

A half-dozen customers were in the shop, but only two were at the counter where he was serving them.

Gordon jumped up onto the desk and disconnected the bug from its power supply, then climbed down and dropped it into a drawer. Charlie, in the meantime, took a seat, then clicked the mouse to open the mail folder.

On screen was an e-mail sent to the contact feature on their business Web site. The first thing Rick the computer guy had done was create a Three Balls Web site. The only problem they'd had so far was showing up on porn Web site searches.

Gordon came around to read over his shoulder. The e-mail, which listed a likely untraceable ISP address, had the subject line "Ruth—deal."

"Crap, this is them, all right. *'If Ruth wants to trade, she'll have the original merchandise ready at eight* PM *tonight. We'll call the store number with the delivery details. Ruth can bring one friend to the exchange. This is a one-time offer.'* That's pretty clear," Gordon said.

Charlie was already calling Nancy. "I don't see how we can get this set up to cover the transfer. They'll probably give the location at the last minute."

"It's what I'd do," Gordon replied. "I'm betting it'll be in the middle of nowhere, in the wide open, maybe."

Charlie held up his hand. "Nancy, I've got some news. We need a plan in a hurry. Is DuPree handy? Okay, put him on the speaker. I'll do the same with Gordo."

●　　●　　●

Ruth insisted on listening in, and after a few moments of arguing back and forth, they came up with a plan they could all live with. If Rene was there at the transfer, they'd make the deal. First of all, however, they'd chose a place to meet, then they'd go together to pick up the stuff she'd hidden. Ruth needed to remain protected.

"Déjà vu all over again, huh?" Gordo said, watching from his pickup in the parking lot as Ruth and Nancy walked into the credit union.

"At least Ruth, unlike Gina, is with an armed cop. Hopefully, nobody inside will notice Nancy's carrying," Charlie said. "That tends to attract attention in a bank,"

"Ruth played it smart, using a safe-deposit box. Better than an old ammo box buried in the desert," Gordo replied.

Charlie glanced at his partner.

"How big a box?"

"Don't ask."

"Seriously?"

"Seriously," Gordon said, a hint of a smile on his face.

Charlie shook his head and looked in the side mirror again.

He had barely taken his eyes off the street and the drivers in passing cars since they'd pulled up. DuPree, with another plainclothes officer, was parked beside the curb fifty feet away, just in case.

As he watched, though, Charlie's mind wandered back to Gina, still in the hospital, and under twenty-four-hour guard.

They'd spoken briefly over the phone, and her voice was finally sounding stronger.

Maybe, by this time tomorrow, some of the debt he'd incurred putting her in harm's way would be repaid. The guilt, though, would remain. All he could hope for now was that the balance in her life would be restored, and that she'd be safe and happy for a while.

At least he'd never feel guilty killing his enemies; he knew that it had been necessary. There were others though, some who may not have been his enemies. How many ultimately innocent people had he brought before those who would do anything to extract information—useful or not? It was better not knowing; there was no way he could make up for that, except, maybe, by helping the innocent now. Like Rene and his mother—and Gina.

"Thinking too much isn't good for you, bro," Gordo whispered. "Concentrate on the here and now."

"Sorry, my mind was wandering." Charlie sat up in his seat just a little and took another look at the bank entrance. "Here they come."

Nancy and Ruth came out the door, both carrying big tote bags, but Charlie only noticed that out of the corner of his eye. Like feds guarding dignitaries, Charlie and Gordo kept eyes on passing strangers or nearby cars, doorways, or windows—not the people they were protecting.

DuPree pulled away from the curb, turned into the parking lot, and the women, who'd turned ninety degrees, climbed into the back seat of his cruiser.

Gordon pulled out first, leading the way. "Next stop, the police station," he mumbled.

Five minutes before eight that evening, Charlie, Ruth, Gordon, and Nancy were in Nancy's car, parked in the McDonald's parking lot closest to the shop. They'd made copies of the papers and thumb drive carried out by Nancy—Ruth's tote was a decoy—and had been at the station for most of the afternoon. They'd forwarded calls coming to the shop phone to Nancy's primary cell phone so they wouldn't be tied to one location. Only recently had they driven back to the neighborhood near Three Balls.

Exactly at eight o'clock, Nancy's phone rang. She put it on speaker.

"Drive to the parking lot on the west side of Isotopes Park. You've got fifteen minutes. When you arrive, you'll get a second call. Don't be late," the familiar voice instructed. "And tell Charlie and Gordon to stay out of this."

"Wait. We're in North Valley. It'll take us twenty minutes or more to get to the sports stadium," Nancy said.

"Hello?" she said. "He hung up. Was that Eddie?"

"Yeah," Charlie replied.

"Crap, I was hoping for some time to get into position. Hang on, everyone." She turned on her emergency lights and siren, then pulled out into the street and raced east toward I-25.

Detective DuPree, who was a block away in an unmarked car with another detective, got on the radio right away as he followed. "Where we going?"

Nancy explained the situation, and for a few moments their plan was adjusted to meet the not-entirely unexpected new situation. They already had a plan, and this didn't change it that much.

Suspecting that one of the kidnappers might be watching Cesar Chavez Avenue, which led east from the interstate directly to the baseball park, Nancy took the Gibson exit, farther south, then came north up University. To the east, on their right, was the football stadium, and west, directly across the street, The Pit—the Lobo basketball stadium. Nancy stopped for a second. Charlie and Gordon jumped out of the cruiser and ran west across two lanes of University to the sidewalk.

They entered The Pit's empty parking lot, the expanse interrupted only by curbs, light poles, and a line of small trees around the perimeter. Both men had powerful night-vision binoculars, courtesy of Detective DuPree. The cop had taken the Lead/Coal exit farther north, and was going to approach down University from that direction.

Gordon moved in a crouch toward the darkest spot he could find, away from the glow of streetlights and illuminated entrance to The Pit's eastern side. With no scheduled events tonight, the area was a vast wasteland. There was a string of hotels south of there, closer to the airport, but otherwise it was an old residential neighborhood of one-story houses. From here they could watch across Cesar Chavez to the north, where Nancy and Ruth were headed.

Charlie, ten feet away, stopped, down on one knee now.

Ahead, Nancy and Ruth were idling at the stoplight at the intersection of University and Cesar Chavez. Here, they intended to go straight another hundred yards, then turn into the empty lot to their left, across the street from the baseball stadium. Isotopes Park was just north of the football stadium, at the northeast corner of the intersection of University and Cesar Chavez. There was a research center farther west, across University and opposite Isotopes Park, but it had its own lot, with just a few cars present this time of the evening. That's where Nancy was headed.

"Think they're really going to bring the kid here?" Gordon said in a low voice.

"Why not? There's just enough light here to keep anyone from sneaking up except at a crawl, and four escape routes, two leading to I-25 north or south."

He surveyed the area on the west side of University, all the way around to The Pit. Gordon was responsible for watching to the northeast, toward the baseball park, and southeast, where the football stadium stood at their four o'clock. Whatever lay east of that structure was blocked by the tall bleachers and upper-level suites and press boxes on the west side of the stadium.

Nancy drove into the northwest lot, as directed, then parked fifty yards from either street and turned off her vehicle lights, waiting.

"DuPree has warned off university cops and APD patrols, right?" Gordon said, watching as he spoke.

"Yeah." Charlie's cell phone vibrated and he brought it to his ear. It was Nancy, on a second phone.

"No vehicles or people on foot, unless they're really prone or in a hole," Charlie reported. "Right, Gordo?"

"Right."

"All we can do now is wait for another call, I guess. Du-Pree is parked on University, north of my location. All I can see is his vehicle. He's just off the street in the shadow of a building. He can see me, he says," Nancy added.

"Charlie. You hear that?" Gordon called out, turning his head toward the south.

"Helicopter," Charlie said. "Could be a news copter, but more likely air force or army, coming from the airport."

"In our direction," Gordon said, turning and looking up into the clear night sky with his binoculars. "Not military, no TV logo."

"Nancy?" Charlie asked. He turned to Gordon. "She hung up."

"Maybe she's on the Eddie line."

A half minute went by, then Charlie's phone vibrated again.

"Get under cover, guys," Nancy said. "New instructions from Eddie. Believe it or not, he wants me to meet the helicopter in the northwest corner of The Pit parking. Your area."

"Copy." Charlie turned to Gordon. "Head for The Pit," he said. "We need to find some dark shadows. They're in the chopper, and they're going to land in this lot."

Gordon started running immediately, swerving to his right, hoping to keep out of sight of the copter approaching from the south.

Charlie stayed with him, careful not to trip while stepping

on and off curbs of the parking lanes. Fifteen seconds later they reached the north side of the arena walls, well away from the glass. Though much higher than the original design since the remodeling, the structure still wasn't as high as most sports stadiums because almost all the eighteen thousand-plus seating and the playing floor were below ground level.

Nevertheless, the walls at this spot were high enough to create plenty of shadow. They quickly found a vertical support beam that stood out from the wall, giving them a dark place to stand.

"Crap. Go here, go there. This is more like *Die Hard 3* than real life. I thought we'd left this behind," Gordon said. They looked up just as the helicopter, looming large even in the dark, hovered a few hundred yards away. It moved slowly, the pilot obviously wary of the regularly spaced light poles and the small trees.

Nancy's sedan came to a stop just inside the lot, headlights on and engine running.

"I count three adults, including the pilot. Where's Rene?" Gordon said, his binoculars on the cockpit of the noisy machine as it settled onto the parking lot. The pilot killed the engine, which whined quickly down to silence. The rotor blades slapped a while longer.

"Can you see Rene?" Charlie asked into the phone.

"Not yet," Nancy said. "Hold on, Ruth. Stay inside until we see your son," she ordered.

Charlie watched the helicopter, which was on the asphalt, resting at a forty-five degree angle to them. The cockpit was to their right, the tail to their left. "I see a big guy getting out. Looks like he's carrying the boy against his chest," he said.

The man, walking stooped over, finally stopped and stood just outside the sweep of the chopper blades. He was visible to the car but had his back to Charlie and Gordon. Another man got out and hurried over beside him, holding what looked like a phone, judging from the glow of the display.

Charlie heard a phone tone. Nancy answered it and put the call on speaker. "You see the boy," a man, not Eddie, said. "Bring out the blackmail material and walk toward the helicopter. When I tell you to stop, put the material down, then walk back halfway to the car."

"Let my son go first. I'll give you the damn papers, you son of a bitch," Ruth yelled.

"Sounds like he's the son, and you're the bitch, Mrs. Brooks. Just do as I say or we're leaving."

"Go ahead, Ruth. If you try anything, you bastard, you're the first one who'll die tonight," Nancy warned.

Charlie couldn't see Nancy—she was blocked by the two men at this angle—but he knew she had the M15s laser sight on phone-man's face. Unfortunately, there was nothing to do but wait and do nothing.

Ruth walked over quickly, set the thick portfolio down, then stepped back.

"Keep walking, lady, if you really want your son back," the guy with the phone said. Ruth walked away slowly, then stood beside Nancy, who was still aiming the assault rife.

The man walked over, crouched and picked up the port-folio, then stuck the phone in his pocket. He was far enough from the hot engine of the helicopter for his own heat signa-ture to stand out clearly, but Charlie still hadn't seen his face.

Charlie watched as the man opened the portfolio and aimed a penlight inside. After several seconds, he put away the flashlight, then stood, portfolio in hand.

"Let the boy go, now. Or I'll kill you where you stand," Nancy said clearly.

"Don't lose control now, lady, we're almost done. I'm go-ing to climb inside the helicopter, then my friend will set the boy down on the ground. Now don't worry, he's been drugged to keep him quiet, but he's just asleep. Start shooting or try and rush the helicopter and the kid will never wake up. Stay back."

Phone guy climbed into the helicopter and the pilot re-started the engine. As the noise level increased, the man holding Rene laid him gently on the ground. He hurried back to the helicopter, climbed inside, and the machine rose quickly, throwing dust and small debris everywhere despite the paved surface.

Charlie looked at the figure on the ground. "Nancy, keep Ruth back. Something's wrong."

"No frigging heat signature," Gordon muttered. "Either he's dead . . ."

"Or he's not real."

Ruth tried to slip around Nancy, who grabbed her arm. Ruth fought back, then suddenly gave up and collapsed, hysterical. Her scream was low and agonizing—the pain from a tortured heart, not ripped flesh.

Suddenly there was a bright spark and an almost instant explosion. "Flashbang!" Charlie yelled, too late to be heard or avoid the blinding light.

Chapter Eighteen

He couldn't see jack, but at least he could hear again, though faintly at first. Ruth was crying loudly and Nancy was shouting something.

"You guys okay?" she yelled.

"Yeah," Gordon said.

"Fine." Charlie looked at the ground, trying to shed the afterimage, like a giant flashbulb had gone on right in front of his face—which it had, actually.

"I think, hope, it was a dummy, not Rene," Gordon said, walking gingerly toward the shape on the ground, which was now dismembered.

"Keep Ruth back," Charlie ordered, stepping forward. His vision was improving, though the big blue and yellow spots hovered, like he was staring at the sun. His toe crunched on something solid, but not gooey. It didn't feel like a body part, and, unfortunately, he knew how that felt.

Bending down, he picked up the object and brought it up close to his face. "It's a dummy. One of those Halloween things. I just stepped on a rubber hand."

"It wasn't really Rene?" Ruth managed hopefully. Charlie could see her now, walking toward the shapes on the parking lots.

"Bastards," Nancy said, approaching and looking down at the child-sized articulated figure dressed in the clothes Rene had last worn. "They kept Rene after all."

They gathered around the figure, which was basically intact except for an arm and the missing hand, which had probably held the flashbang grenade and whatever timer was used.

"Lawrence thinks he's got me now. If I want my son, I'll have to come back. You were right, Charlie, keeping some leverage," Ruth said, her voice now cold and hard.

"Wish I'd been wrong. But you've still got the originals of everything, and he'll find that out once he discovers that little gotcha note on the flash drive. He'll have to deal again, and maybe this can buy us some time," Charlie said. "Hopefully it'll take a while before he discovers he's not the only one who's been double-crossed."

"Now what?" Gordon asked.

"We can't just sit still. Once we hear from Claudia, the Realtor, we can drive by any newly rented estates and see if we get a signal from Rene's game console," Charlie said. "It's a shot in the dark, but at least it's proactive."

He looked over at Nancy, who was on the phone to her

captain. From what he could hear, she was giving a description of the helicopter and its flight path. Maybe she'd seen where it had gone. His vision had been too trashed at the time to see anything at all except spots.

"Think it was a rental, or his own copter?" Gordon asked, also watching Nancy.

"I'm guessing it's leased or rented. It'll take a while to find out. The pilot will stay below the airport radar as much as possible, do some fancy maneuvering and changing of direction, then probably land behind a hill or ridge at some remote location where vehicles are waiting. It was on somebody's radar screen initially, but I don't know what protocol the feds require on flight plans. Our best bet is to find Rene, not these bozos," Charlie said.

"Right. And we need to get one of those black boxes that'll pick up his WiFi signal—assuming Rene was allowed to recharge and use the same game console. DuPree was supposed to get us a tracking unit," Gordon said. "What the hell happened to him?"

Nancy came over, interrupting. "DuPree held back, like we all did, and was far enough away not to be blinded by the flash. He and his partner tried to follow the copter and see where it was headed. It avoided the airport and went off to the west, toward the volcanos. Then it turned and disappeared south, flying just above the cottonwoods along the bosque. DuPree's already got the state police and feds looking for it down toward Belen and Los Lunas. Even Socorro."

"Here he comes," Charlie said, recognizing the vehicle

coming up the street toward the arena. "Let's get that black box."

An hour later, with a crime-scene unit and the bomb squad going over the Rene dummy and The Pit parking lot, Charlie and Gordon were heading west toward Rio Grande Boulevard in his rental Chevy, armed with information from Claudia.

"Good thing you thought to check your e-mail when the officer dropped us off at the shop," Gordon said. "Now we have some serious real estate to check out with DuPree's little gadget."

"He said they got the basic units from Sandia Labs, then the techs tweaked them a little," Charlie said. "Said the hardest part was tracking down the Nintendo people to get the codes or whatever for Rene's particular unit. Good thing you signed him up for online play."

"Even with the rest of the community ruled out, we'll still have to get close enough for a signal—and the boy will have to be online," Charlie said. "That'll take a lot of driving around—and luck. Who was it who said I'd rather be lucky than smart?"

"Every guy I knew who wanted to come back from their deployment with arms, legs, and head still attached," Gordon said.

"Amen to that. Okay, for the moment we've ruled out the fancy homes around the old country club—they're just too close to each other for Lawrence-level privacy. How about we start just north of the freeway, taking the east side of Rio Grande Boulevard? There are two houses on that side that are possibilities, including the newly sold one at the far end. We can catch the three on the west side on the way back south."

"Works for me," Gordon said. "I'm the tech genius. You drive, and I'll fire up the black box."

The speed limit was only twenty-five, so they didn't have to worry about attracting attention by moving too slowly. After fifteen minutes, they passed the last house and Charlie pulled over.

"Plenty of WiFi hits, but no traffic from Rene's game. Either he doesn't have the console anymore, isn't online, or just isn't around here anywhere," Gordon said. "I'm not sure how much range these WiFi sources have, and I'm sure we picked up some from the west side of the street too."

"Yeah, discouraging. But two of the houses we're targeting are on the street just west of Rio Grande Boulevard. When we get into that area, we'll get in as close as possible, just to be sure."

Charlie completed the three-point turn, then headed south, again at twenty-five mph. Traffic was mostly local because people in a hurry usually took Fourth Street, which had a higher posted speed limit and stoplights instead of four-way stop signs.

"We're approaching that $3.5 mil place," Gordon said after about five minutes. "According to Claudia, that used to be owned by a big Indy racing family."

"It's about a quarter mile down that private lane. If Brooks and Eddie are there with Rene, they'll have people out watching," Charlie said. "I'll creep along. Hopefully we'll be within range."

"Okay, we're getting some WiFi. But not gaming stuff, at least traffic from the right servers," Gordon said. "We can put this down as a maybe, then get more intelligence on the residents."

"Right." Charlie sped up to thirty, then slowed, looking at some old, probably two- or three-bedroom homes that had obviously been there long before the mansions. They were sturdy adobe, with pitched corrugated-metal roofs. "Cheapest house in the best neighborhood? That would be here."

"They've got WiFi. No Nintendo connection, however. Keep driving."

Finally, they made a sweeping turn, ninety degrees to the west, and came upon the road running parallel to Rio Grande Boulevard. Charlie slowed way down to make the curve and they headed north again.

"The two houses are straight ahead, diagonally across from each other. The biggest one, a modest $2.75 million, ten-acre place, had been on the market for two years until the owner decided to lease," Charlie recalled. "It backs up to conservancy land—the bosque."

"Coyotes, rabbits, ducks, and geese, and homeless people camping out next door to the one percent," Gordon replied.

"Hey, if Three Balls continues to pick up business, maybe someday we'll own houses like this," Charlie said.

"Or at least houses. Hey, I'm getting a hit on the one on the left—west."

They drove past slowly, Gordon watching the instrument.

"Well?" Charlie said as they reached the next intersection. The only turn was to the east, back toward Rio Grande.

"Keep going until we get halfway to Rio, then do a 180. I wanna drive past that house again."

Charlie's heart started beating just a little faster, like it always did when things picked up. Usually he was too busy to think about it, but at the moment all he was doing was driving through a dark, high-end neighborhood. Thinking too much was dangerous. He slowed, made a three-point turn in the basically empty street, then headed back.

"Lights out or on?" he asked Gordon as they cruised south again at about fifteen miles an hour.

"On. If they're watching, they might have thermal gear, and they'd get suspicious if we cut the lights. Burglars, casing the neighborhood?"

"You're right."

Thirty seconds went by, but Gordon remained silent. Finally he spoke. "Hot damn! Either somebody's got Rene's game, or he's somewhere close by."

"Which rental, east or west side?" Charlie asked, his heart now pounding. "No, wait. West side. It's bigger, and has more land."

"Well, one way to make sure. Just come up the bosque behind the house. If the signal is still as strong, we'll know," Gordon said. "That's when we move in."

"These people working for Brooks have to be ex-military. Maybe not Eddie himself, but certainly those from the copter. Or I guess they could be ex-cops who've worked in the field, maybe even SWAT. They'll be on high alert during the hours just before dawn. That's usually the best time for raids. They'll know that."

"So, we confirm the signal tonight, then make our move in broad daylight, right after a hearty breakfast? Theirs, not ours."

"Yeah, but we won't go in Special Ops mode. We're going to be transients, maybe trespassing," Charlie replied.

"Yeah, expect the unexpected. I like that. Who else we going to invite to this event?" Gordon said as they reached Rio Grande.

"Let's work out the details on the way back. I'm still up in the air about telling Ruth. Don't want to get her hopes up."

"She'll know, especially if we get Nancy involved."

"So, maybe we do this mostly by ourselves—with just a little diversion on the side."

"This shopping cart sucks," Gordon grumbled as he pushed it down the bike path that paralleled the bosque and the network of irrigation ditches. The metal cart contained dusty, dirty sleeping bags, a couple of rolled-up foam pads, coats and clothes, a large cooler, and everything else they could borrow from the homeless shelter to create the illusion. "The ground seemed a lot harder last night."

"Well, at least now you know why the transients try to

stick to the streets and sidewalks when they're hauling their stuff around. Wanna carry my backpack?" Charlie said, grinning.

"We're lucky the estate backs up to the bosque," he added. "I'm betting the residents along this stretch of the valley are used to seeing homeless campers."

"Well, we should blend in real well. These filthy clothes reek."

"Be grateful it's early November in New Mexico instead of the middle of summer. Or 'stan, with the temperature 105 outside, bodies in the street, and man-eating flies."

"I'll be grateful only when we get Rene back," Gordon responded.

Charlie nodded, feeling down into the pocket of his shabby, oversized denim jacket and touching his sidearm. One thing he liked about his partner was his attitude when the shit hit the fan. There were never any "ifs"—only "whens." They'd always come back from their missions with positive results. And now that it was personal, that made it all the more important to be a team again.

He'd also held back on the obvious opportunity to give Gordo a hard time. His partner was disguised as a pregnant Hispanic woman. His skin had been darkened slightly, his jeans enhanced with hips—not to mention his chest and belly. He wore a baseball cap fitted with bangs and a ponytail. Nancy had also added a trace of pale lipstick.

"Thanks for not mentioning my pink sneakers—or the rest of this, bro. I'm having a hard enough time trying to walk like I think a pregnant woman walks. And Nancy wasn't much help. She's got a nice ass, but she walks like a cop."

"Pushing the shopping cart probably helps cover any stride differences. I enjoy watching a Western woman's hips when they walk, but in 'stan, there are so many clothes you just can't see the action—if there is any. Remember the time we had to acquire the village Johnny Jihad for the spooks?" Charlie asked.

"First time I was a woman carrying an M4, but at least it was easy to hide in all that fabric. Got us into the compound and face-to-face with our target."

"The good ol' days, huh?"

"Yeah, but with just a pistol and a GPS tracker in my fake wristwatch, I feel underaccessorized." He looked down at the phony belly bump. "And with child."

"Better slow down, we're supposed to be tired from all this roaming around," Charlie warned. "Here comes the fence."

The estate had a large backyard with a five-foot-high chain-link fence and a narrow, padlocked center gate. Beyond was a pasture of tall grass. A loafing shed to one side contained four horse stalls, empty at the moment, and a few bales of sun-bleached hay. Clearly, whoever lived here now had no livestock.

A hundred meters farther east on the property was a four-foot-high solid wall, probably of stucco-coated cinder block, with a big, metal, double gate. Beyond was a flower garden, mostly roses, and a patio with outdoor furniture and a pool. Next was the rectangular six-bedroom house—according to the architect's plans they'd studied—courtesy of Claudia the Realtor.

"And there's the security," Gordon mumbled, looking out of the corner of his eyes at two men in dark pants and blue jackets standing beside the metal gate, halfway to the house.

"Ignore them. Here we go," Charlie said, veering left. He got in front of Gordon, helping him maneuver the shopping cart containing their faux worldly professions off the bike path. They continued down the sloped slide of an embankment to a dirt utility easement that ran parallel to the fence.

"Hard enough ground here to keep rolling. So far so good," Gordon commented.

Charlie made a point of not looking directly at the men in blue jackets, but noted that one of them was unlocking the big metal gate.

He stopped in front of the small gate in the outer chain-link fence, screening his partner from the men's view. Gordon reached into the shopping cart, brought out the bolt cutters, and reached under Charlie's arm to snip off the Master Lock with a dull thunk.

"If they saw that, I'd be surprised," Gordon said, stepping back and dropping the bolt cutters and lock into the shopping cart, covering them with an old jacket.

Charlie turned around and opened the gate as if he owned the place. "Come on in, Miss Sweeney."

"It's Mrs. Sweeney, smartass," Gordon replied, pushing the cart onto the grassy yard. It bogged down in the moist, thick turf almost immediately.

"Hey!" one of the guys yelled from across the pasture. "This is private property. Get the hell out of here before we call the cops."

Gordon stopped and turned to look at the two men jogging toward them. "Can I shoot them?"

"Mrs. Sweeney, we promised DuPree we'd keep the casualties to a minimum. If they get close enough, we'll just stick with Plan A."

"I still prefer Plan B."

"Maybe later," Charlie replied, reaching into the old cooler and bringing out a bottle of cheap wine.

"You assholes deaf?" The smaller of the two men called out, hurrying up with his companion. Smaller was a relative description, the short guy was probably six-two.

Charlie tried out the mellow, half-drunk tone he'd rehearsed more than once. "Dude, don't call my pregnant girlfriend an asshole. That'll bring our baby, well, her baby, bad luck. We're just taking a short cut over to Rio Grande. We've got to catch the bus to the free clinic behind Old Town," Charlie said, taking a swig of what was really warm water, then setting it back into the cooler. "You want her to have the kid right here on the lawn?"

The tall guy stepped around them and looked at the gate. "What the fuck did you do to the lock?" he demanded, stepping into Charlie's face.

Gordon groaned, grabbing his baby bump and wavering.

Both sets of eyes were on Gordon when Charlie made a two-handed draw and Tasered both of the goons in the chests.

In less than two minutes the men were unconscious, courtesy of knockout injections, then bound hand and foot with strong zip ties and dragged into some brush. Both had been carrying handguns.

These were unloaded, then thrown over the road into the irrigation canal beyond. The men had wallets and IDs identifying them as residents of Pennsylvania. No surprise. These, Charlie and Gordon kept. One had car keys, and Charlie threw them into the canal as well.

Charlie and Gordon had done this kind of thing before and they moved quickly and efficiently. Keeping low and screened from view, Charlie kept watch while Gordon shed his cross-dressing enhancements and they advanced to the wall with the double gate.

Gordon crouched at one side of the gate, Charlie at the other, and they waited. Charlie's cell phone vibrated, and he brought it out to look. A text message said *"Signal coming from SW corner bedroom—R?"*

One of DuPree's people—a tech—was east of the property, down the street, trying to narrow down Rene's game signal. They now had a location on the boy's likely location in the house. "Southwest corner," Charlie whispered to Gordon, who nodded.

Last night, Charlie had covered Gordon while he moved in close enough to watch the rear of the estate for about an hour. Both had stuck to cover and moved slowly, using their advanced training to advantage.

Gordon had observed a guard inside the rear of the home, watching toward the bosque with binoculars, probably with night-vision capability. He'd also reported that one of the bedroom windows facing the rear—the one in the southwest corner—was blocked off except at the very top. It was the logical place to keep a child prisoner, with the only escape route blocked. So far, last night's recon was paying off.

They waited another five minutes, then heard the patio door open and footsteps coming closer across the tile floor. "Darren! Jack! Where the hell are you?" the man called. He walked over to the gate, opened it, then stepped out onto the lawn.

"Hi," Charlie said softly.

The man jumped, startled, then turned toward him, grabbing for a pistol at his waist.

Gordon Tasered the guy in the back and he went down on the grass. Charlie thumped him on the head with a lead-filled sap. Gordo crossed from the other side of the gate, then turned off the juice.

"Hope he peed himself. Wish we could just shoot them and get it over with," Gordon whispered, pushing the knockout drug into the man's neck with a syringe. "Recognize the voice?"

"Guy who did the talking last night outside the helicopter," Charlie responded as he applied the zip ties. Then he took the gun and wallet from the semiconscious man, who was well on his way to dreamland.

"At least now we know for sure they're not security for a celebrity traveling incognito," Gordon said, dragging the inert figure next to the wall, out of view from the house.

"Yeah. If this had been Johnny Depp's hideaway, we'd be screwed for life," Charlie added.

"About time for that diversion?" Gordon looked at his watch.

"Yeah. I'll send the request." He thumbed his phone and sent the text message he'd prepared two hours before.

They waited just outside the wall, with their pistols directed toward the gate. There was the possibility that any diversion might panic those inside instead of merely distracting them. Impatient, he looked down at his watch, forgetting it was there to reveal his location to the SWAT people, not to help with timing the operation.

They heard a pop, then a distant shout Charlie knew came from the eastern side of the estate. The engine of a Realtor's car parked in the driveway of the other vacant house down the street had just caught fire.

Four minutes went by, then they heard the sound of a siren coming from the south. The fire department of the Village of Los Ranchos was only a few miles to the south, which had made this part of the plan very convenient.

Charlie took a quick glance into the patio area. No one was visible and he could see into a den and small kitchen alcove through the eight-foot-high windows facing the back. "Time to move," he said.

He went through the gate first, pistol out, with Gordon covering. Sprinting to the right, Charlie ran all the way up to the solid building wall just beyond the glass. Crouching, he watched the interior as Gordon came though the gate, closed it silently, then made his way quickly across the patio. Both were wearing rubber soles and neither made a sound crossing.

They waited, watching, then ducked back as Eddie came down a hall into the den, then crossed over into the second kitchen alcove. He walked to the cupboard and opened what turned out to be a classy half-height refrigerator. He took out two bottles of beer, judging from the shape and color, then disappeared back down the hall.

Charlie looked over at Gordon, who nodded and made a slicing motion across his throat with two fingers.

The sound of the fire engine came closer, then wound down to a stop. They could hear big engine sounds and more shouts.

Gordon just a few steps behind him, Charlie moved for the door, hoping it hadn't been locked by the guy now sleeping outside the gate. Otherwise, he'd have to stop and pick it. It was now or never.

Chapter Nineteen

The door, thankfully, was still unlocked and they both slipped in easily, taking positions on either side of the hall. Charlie had an image of the layout in his mind, and knew the hall was the center line of a sideways H, splitting left and right to back rooms on either side. There were two smaller rooms halfway down the hall, one an exercise room, the other a big bathroom, then the hall ended farther east, splitting again left and right. The hall on the left led to another bedroom and the four-car garage. The right hall led to more bedrooms farther south, splitting halfway south back to the east into an enormous front room running the entire length of the house.

According to intel via Nancy, Rene was probably in the southwesternmost bedroom, the first passage to the right. Charlie inched around the corner, pistol aimed down the hall, then hugged the wall. He ducked low and went around the corner. The hall was empty except for several generic southwestern landscapes along both walls. They reminded him of those at a bank or in a dentist's waiting room. Inoffensive and boring. He inched farther down, sensing that Gordon was right behind him.

With a hand signal, he told Gordon to cover their butts. Charlie continued down the hall alone, moving quickly now. He came across an open door and took a quick look inside. It was a bedroom, as expected. The bed was unmade, a suitcase sat on a chair beside a nice-looking dresser. He listened for a moment, then stepped inside. A quick search verified that the room and the small adjoining bathroom were empty.

Charlie came back out, looked over at Gordon and shook his head, then moved to the far southern end of the hall. This bedroom door was closed and padlocked from the outside. The installation was crude but effective, and would have really pissed off the landlord.

Gordon stayed at the opposite end of the hall, waiting in ambush for anyone venturing to the back of the house. Charlie picked the lock. He removed it, then turned the knob, crouching low and leading with his pistol.

Charlie stepped inside and smelled pizza. A box lay atop the dresser, containing two untouched slices and a third with several bites in it. There was a half-full bottle of Coke beside it.

"Rene? It's Charlie," he whispered. The bathroom door was open but he couldn't see anyone on the throne or in the shower. The room window had been blocked by a storage cabinet with louvered doors which reached almost to the ceiling.

He heard an electronic voice, the sound of a crash, and realized it was coming from down low. Charlie lowered himself to the hardwood floor and looked under the bed.

Rene was lying there, his game clutched to his chest, frozen in fear. Then he recognized Charlie. "You here to get me?" he said, his voice trembling.

"Yeah, to take you back to your mom," Charlie whispered. "But don't talk or make any noise. We're going to sneak out of here, if that's okay with you."

Rene didn't move except to nod.

Charlie set his weapon down, then reached out a hand. Rene took it, and Charlie pulled gently.

Rene slid out from under the bed, still hugging his game to his chest with his other arm.

"Shut the sound off for now, Rene," Charlie whispered.

Rene stood, with Charlie's help, then let go of his hand long enough to turn off the audio.

"Where's Gordon?" Rene whispered, looking toward the door.

"Down the hall, guarding us." Charlie looked at the boy's bare feet. He had no socks or shoes, probably to slow him down if he somehow got outside. At least he could move quietly.

"Take my hand and don't make a sound," Charlie said, leading Rene to the door. "Outside, I may want to carry you a ways. That okay?"

Rene nodded.

When they stepped out into the hall, Gordon looked over and smiled, giving a thumbs-up. Then he motioned for them to approach.

When they got to the center hall, Gordon held up his hand. They stopped and listened. They could hear a conversation in the front room. One person was Eddie, and the other, presumably, Lawrence Brooks. It was time to leave.

Charlie put away his cell phone, having sent a prearranged signal, then nodded to Gordon. Charlie picked up Rene, and moved past Gordon and quickly down the hall toward the back of the house. With the boy under his arm, he hurried through the combination den and kitchen. He kept going, opening the French doors, then stepped outside and turned to his left. Moving past the windows to the wall, he set Rene down behind him, out of sight from the inside, then crouched, watching through the glass into the den.

Gordon moved quickly, joining them.

"Take Rene and get behind the garden wall," Charlie whispered. "My turn to cover your back."

"Ready, bro?" Gordon whispered to Rene, who nodded.

"Make a move and the kid's dead," Eddie yelled. They turned toward the far side of the patio, where a door led to the garage. The door was wide open now. Eddie was standing there, aiming an assault rifle at them from the hip. Behind Eddie was Lawrence Brooks, judging from the Internet photos they'd previewed. He was holding a phone, but no weapon.

Charlie stood and Gordon turned to face Eddie, with Rene behind them both now.

"I can shoot through you and take out the boy," Eddie said. "Hand him back."

"You're too late, Eddie. A SWAT team is moving in right

now. I've already sent them the signal," Charlie replied. "Give up or get dead."

"No way I'm sticking around. Cover me," Brooks said, striding across the patio toward the garden gate.

"There goes your meal ticket," Gordon called out. "Better follow your master like a good puppy."

A loud crash in the house was followed by shouts in the front rooms.

"That would be SWAT. Lay down your weapon, Eddie," Charlie said. "It's not too late."

"Like hell," he said, sidestepping his way across the patio, trying to watch them and the house at the same time, waving the assault weapon back and forth.

"Lay down and close your eyes, Rene," Gordon whispered, pushing the boy to the tile. He stepped away from Charlie and the boy, then raised his pistol.

"Eddie, stop!" Gordon yelled.

Eddie raised the assault rifle up to his shoulder, swinging it toward Gordon. A shot rang out.

One side of Eddie's head exploded in a mass of blood, bone, and tissue. His forward motion carried him another step and he fell across his rifle as he hit the patio floor, face down.

Brooks, who'd already made it onto the lawn, stopped, finally noticed the prone sniper on the ditch bank, then threw his arms into the air.

"Don't move, Brooks," DuPree yelled from the fence gate at the far end as he ran into the grass, pistol out. Nancy was right behind him, armed with a shotgun. Two more officers were covering the creeps tied up out there. The sniper remained in position.

Gordon picked up Rene and turned him away from Eddie so he couldn't see the dead man. Four SWAT members came out through the kitchen. That helped to block the view of the carnage scattered across the tile like a thrown dish of pasta.

"Make sure you get the guy on the other side of the wall," Charlie yelled to the SWAT team, holstering his weapon. "He's probably asleep."

Charlie turned to Gordon. "Maybe you should have let Eddie get out into the grass. You could be dead right now if the sniper had been two seconds slower . . ."

"Then you'd inherit my half of Three Balls. You coulda had it all."

Charlie shook his head as a SWAT guy looked over with furrowed brows. "We've gotta change that name, Gordo. And sometime real soon, you'd better wipe off your lipstick."

Chapter Twenty

"Thanks for saving me all that paperwork," US Marshal Crowley said, taking the deputy badges back from Charlie and Gordon. "You didn't shoot anyone. Detective DuPree says it was a miracle."

"Well, now you have your fugitive, Lawrence Brooks, and the evidence Mrs. Brooks handed over that will put him in a federal lockup. How long had he been under house arrest when he took off?" Charlie asked.

"Just a day before he disappeared, which makes it a week ago. Good thing APD put his name up on a bulletin and called into his office. We'd have never thought to look here," Crowley replied. "If I hadn't deputized you two, we'd have had to send in strangers to get the boy and the child might have freaked out."

Charlie nodded. "We're used to this kind of work, and Rene has spent time with us. Mrs. Brooks has been hiding out with him for years, apparently, and the boy has learned not to trust strangers."

"The service thanks you."

"Glad to help out," Charlie said, looking over at Gordon, who clearly wasn't ready to leave yet.

"I've got a question, Marshal Crowley," Gordon asked. "Just what did you find out about the guy we knew as Eddie Henderson? Did you get anything from his prints?"

"Actually, we did. Henderson is actually Viktor Kozhara, twenty-eight. He was adopted from a orphanage in Ukraine at the age of eleven by an American couple in Arlington, Virginia. He had a measured IQ of 140, spoke perfect English, and aced all his classes at school. Unfortunately, he also had a lot of trouble with authority—lying, stealing, and a shitload of petty stuff. Street-smart, he was careful not to get more than a juvenile record. At the age of seventeen, he left for school one morning and just disappeared. Rode off on a bicycle, according to the report."

"Didn't the cops try to track him down?" Charlie asked, knowing his own parents would have never given up on him.

"There was no AMBER Alert back then, and law enforcement didn't work too hard on it, judging from the reports. It might have been different if he'd been an innocent five-year-old girl instead of a pain-in-the-ass hoodlum wannabe. Anyway, the adopted parents hired a private eye, and the search went on until they ran out of money and gave up. Looks like the kid was smart and covered his tracks," Crowley added.

"So when did he become Eddie Henderson?" Gordon asked.

"I believe the Henderson identity goes back at least seven years, at least that's when he got his first driver's license under that name," Crowley added.

Charlie nodded, and Gordon crossed his arms against his chest. "Guess the rest of the story will have to come from Lawrence Brooks or somebody back in Pennsylvania," Gordon surmised.

"If I get anything else, I'll fill in Detective DuPree and he can pass it along," Crowley said, standing and shaking their hands. "Thanks, again, guys."

Three minutes later they were in the parking garage, climbing into Charlie's rental Chevy. "We got lucky, finding a way to do what we did aboveboard," Charlie said to Gordon as he backed out of the parking slot.

"Yeah, but we'd have done it anyway," Gordon said, fastening his seat belt. "Makes shopkeeping seem kinda dull, doesn't it?"

Charlie followed the yellow arrows and reached the street exit, stopping for traffic. "Maybe we're not cut out for civilian life—but I don't think it'll hurt to slow down a little. I'm sticking with the pawnshop. You want out?"

"Naw. I'm just being nostalgic for the bad old days."

"Good. And speaking of the shop, I'm thinking we're going to need to add another full-time employee if business continues to pick up," Charlie said.

"Meanwhile, I guess it's back to work, after I go home and shower—a lot," Gordo said. "Drop me off?"

• • •

It was three PM the next day and Charlie and Gordo were climbing into the rental Chevy parked in the visitor section of the downtown police station.

"Well, that took forever. But maybe we're finally done with Detective Dupree and company—at least until the ADA comes calling," Charlie said. "I'm looking forward to a regular life for a while."

"Might be nice. Where to next? We going to Gina and Nancy's for that cookout now? We're still a little early."

"Why not? Jake's covering the shop and this is Gina's first day back from the hospital. She's gonna be moving around pretty slow, if at all. We'll help Nancy with the company," Charlie said.

"And you'll get to see Ruth," Gordon said.

"That too," Charlie said, then shrugged. "I'm hoping she and Rene will stick around a little longer. The feds like the idea of her staying away from Pittsburgh. It keeps the press focused on Brooks and the indictments regarding his business practices."

"Better for her and the boy."

"Yeah," Charlie said, finding an opening in traffic and pulling out onto the street. "Call though, and see if we can bring anything."

Twenty minutes later Charlie parked behind Nancy's department vehicle in the driveway of her and Gina's townhouse. He reached for the enormous apple pie they'd picked up at the

Smith's. Gordon already had the red wine and two six-packs of Coke.

They'd just stepped onto the porch when the door opened. It was Ruth, casually but elegantly dressed in a soft burgundy shirt and dark blue slacks. For the first time since they'd seen her, she was also wearing lipstick and a trace of makeup.

"You've got a smile on your face," Gordon said as she opened the door and waved them into the foyer.

"Thanks to you two, Nancy, and the others. We don't have to hide out anymore. Hi, Charlie," she added, reaching out and squeezing his forearm gently.

"Um, hi. You look really nice, Ruth."

"Thanks for noticing," she said, backing into the large open space that doubled as living room and kitchen in houses these days. "Let me take that delicious-looking pie off your hands."

Charlie handed it over, then looked around the room and saw Gina sitting in the big recliner chair, wearing silky pajamas and a fluffy robe. "Welcome home, Gina."

"Yeah. You've really perked up," Gordon added.

"Doing a lot better. Once I get the energy to stand up again, guys, I owe you both hugs. Okay?"

"Something to look forward to," Charlie said, winking.

"And if you want to stroll around a little, let me know. You have my shoulder to lean on," Gordon said.

"Sounds nice," she said. "But the doctors want me to do all I can on my own. Now, if I get tired . . ."

"Just flash me a smile," Gordon said. He turned and saw

Rene over in the corner, on the carpet, wearing earbuds and playing with his handheld video game.

"Hey, Rene," he called, waving.

"Hey, Gordon. Uh, Mr. Sweeney. Mom says I should thank you again for showing me how to play online. I'm still on the second level, but I'm getting better."

"Practice, practice," Gordon said.

"Who invited these strange men?" Nancy said, coming through the patio door just beyond the kitchen nook.

"We brought provisions, Sergeant," Charlie said. "Dessert—apple pie."

"And red wine," Gordon added. "From a foreign land," he said, holding up the bottle. "Some place called Callyfornya."

"What, no beer?" Nancy asked, coming over to take the wine and the Cokes. She placed the wine on the counter next to the pie.

"Sorry. The only women I know who like beer can also kick my ass," Charlie said, then grinned.

"Include me in both categories. I've got a six-pack of Sammy Adams in the fridge," Nancy said.

Charlie moved over and opened the refrigerator door so Nancy could store the Cokes. She brought out three beers and handed one to Charlie. "Gordon?" she asked, waving the third bottle.

"Thanks," he said, taking the brew.

"Need some help outside with the steaks?" Charlie offered, nodding toward the backyard. He'd smelled the grill when Nancy had come inside.

"No, but come and join me. We need to have a little information exchange," she said.

"I'll stay inside and keep the party going," Gordon said, smiling at Gina.

Charlie stood and watched as Nancy turned the steaks, keeping downwind to appreciate the aroma. Smoke, he was used to, only this time it was pleasant.

He looked back through the glass patio door, noting that Gordon had Gina and Ruth laughing already, probably from his vast repertoire of tall tales.

"So everything local except for the kidnapping is going to be low priority," Charlie said. "Bet DuPree is annoyed."

"A little, but he still comes out looking good within the department. With Eddie, well, Viktor gone and the local crimes all but solved, the pressure is on Brooks for the millions he's made ripping off financial institutions and investors. Outside of Albuquerque, nobody cares about the death of a half-dozen men. Priorities haven't changed. Gangbangers die every day, but when big money is involved . . . ," Nancy said.

"Not to mention kidnapping."

"My captain is tongue-tied over that particular problem, trying to explain everything that went down. Getting the marshals service involved instead of the FBI was unexpected, but that was the easiest path to take. It's all legal, just very nonlinear. And, of course, Brooks is trying to blame Eddie for all that illegal shit, including the killing of Baza. Brooks claims he was just trying to get his kid back, but his employees went rogue on him," Nancy added.

"And Eddie won't be contradicting him from the grave," Charlie said. "I'm glad this isn't my problem. Sounds like you were briefed on Eddie's real background?"

"Yeah, DuPree sent me an e-mail with a summary, including pretty convincing evidence that Eddie *was* the one who shot Baza and Gina. The thirty-eight used in the attack was found in his room at the estate and his prints were all over it. I wonder at what age Eddie was already beyond hope?" Nancy said, shaking her head.

"Kinda scares me when I think about becoming a parent one day," Charlie replied. The idea seemed so distant at the moment, it sounded almost like a fantasy.

"I got a feeling you'll do fine, Charlie. But you're going to have to settle down first."

"Not right away," Charlie said, looking away, thinking about all the chaos he'd already experienced. It was going to take time to get back to any kind of normal.

He stared at the coals for a moment, his mind wandering. Finally he spoke. "So, how's APD handling all this excitement, being in the national headlines?"

Nancy grinned. "The department is looking good on this, and I might even be up for a commendation. Meanwhile, Brooks's crew are stumbling over each other trying to cut deals of their own. Prosecution should be easy."

"So what about Ruth—or Sarah, I should say?"

"All of the Brooks money is frozen by the courts, so she

won't get any financial help until those legal issues are settled, which could take a year or two, depending on the lawyers. Ruth—she wants to keep that identity—is going to stay here in Albuquerque with her son. Of course she'll be scaling down her living quarters. She's also going to need a job," Nancy said, taking a long sip of beer. "Know of any openings?"

Charlie looked over at the window. Ruth turned just then, catching his eye and smiling. "Think I might," he said.